War, WV

Michael Abraham

War, WV

A fight for justice in the Appalachian coalfields

Pocahontas Press
Blacksburg, Virginia

Also by Michael Abraham

The Spine of the Virginias
Journeys along the border of Virginia and West
Virginia

Harmonic Highways
Exploring Virginia's Crooked Road

Union, WV
A novel of loss, healing, and redemption in
contemporary Appalachia

Providence, VA
A novel of inner strength through adversity

For updates and ordering information on the author's
books, excerpts, and sample chapters, please visit his
website at:
http://www.bikemike.name/

The author can be reached by email at:
<bikemike@nrvunwired.net>

War, WV

This is a work of fiction. Any resemblance to any living person is coincidental and unintentional.

Copyright © 2013 by Michael Abraham

ISBN 0-926487-67-1

Cover photograph by Fred Wolfe
Author cover photograph by Tracy Roberts
Maps by Bob Pearsall
Illustration by Rob Agnew
Book design by Michael Abraham

Printed in the United States of America

Pocahontas Press
www.pocahontaspress.com

To Jane and Whitney Abraham,
the two most important people in my life.

Acknowledgements

I am deeply indebted to many people who supported my effort. My editors worked countless hours to help me make my book readable, relevant, and grammatically correct.

Jane Abraham, Blacksburg, Virginia
Sally Shupe, Newport, Virginia
Ibby Greer, Rocky Mount, Virginia

I am also indebted to the people who helped me understand the technical aspects of the book and gave me encouragement, support, and ideas.

Jane Abraham, Blacksburg, Virginia
James Berger, Blacksburg, Virginia
Donna Branham, Lenore, West Virginia
Kathy Cole, Galax, Virginia
Fred First, Floyd, Virginia
Maria Gunnoe, Bob White, West Virginia
Wess Harris, Gay, West Virginia
Mary Ann Johnson, Blacksburg, Virginia
Tommy Loflin, Blacksburg, Virginia
Jerry Moles, Roanoke, Virginia
Bob and Barbara Pearsall, Christiansburg, Virginia
Anne Piedmont, Roanoke, Virginia
Dan Radmacher, Roanoke, Virginia
Phil Ross, Blacksburg, Virginia
Sally Shupe, Newport, Virginia
Erica Sipes, Blacksburg, Virginia
Paula Swearingen, Beckley, West Virginia
Benton Ward, Yukon, West Virginia

I give special thanks to Fred Wolfe who provided the cover photograph, Rob Agnew who provided the helmet illustration and Bob Pearsall who provided the maps.

Dedicated to the memory of
War Mayor Thomas Hatcher, PhD

Photo by Tracy Roberts

Tom Hatcher with War's drinking water, 2012

In July, 2012, Mayor Tom Hatcher, 72, was found dead in his home in War, West Virginia.

I met Tom in April, 2008 when I was working on my first book *The Spine of the Virginias*. Tom was informative and generous with his time, telling photographer Tracy Roberts and me about the history of his tiny city.

Tom was an energetic and supportive advocate for his community, although he was forthright about its enormous challenges. Shortly before his death, which was investigated as a murder, he was extensively quoted in a *Playboy Magazine* article entitled "Overdose County, USA" in which he spoke candidly about his area's epidemic of prescription drug abuse.

Tom earned a B.S. and an M.A. Degree from West Virginia University and a Ph.D. in Developmental Psychology and Education from the Ohio State University. He was a teacher and administrator during his career.

He will be sorely missed.

Southern West Virginia and the environs of War, WV

Proximity of War, WV

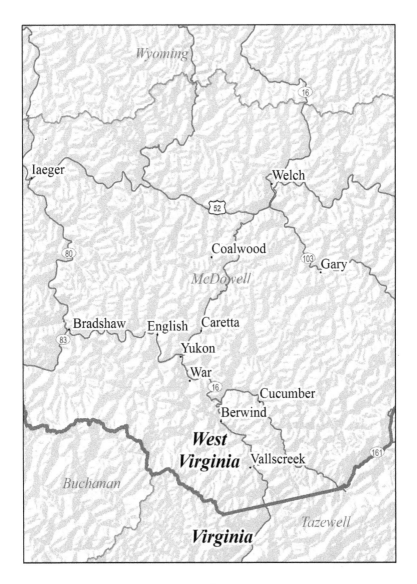

War, WV

Part 1

THE DAYS OF THE WINTER SOLSTICE are haltingly short in War, West Virginia, with ephemeral glimpses of sunlight peeking over the tight, deeply forested mountains above the tiny Appalachian coal town. This year was no exception, with a light dusting of snow covering the ground and stubborn remnants of the prior week's larger snowfall, six-inches in town and more on the mountaintops. Piles of snow mostly turned to dirty ice lay at the edges of the town's few parking lots. Snow flurries were hardly worthy of conversation amongst the 850 or so residents who ventured into public spaces like the War Room Café, the Hotel Fretwell, the FoodFair Grocery, or any of the few other businesses still operational in what the sign at the outskirts called, "West Virginia's Most Southern City."

Almost by the minute since the heyday of pick-and-shovel mining in the late 1940s and early 1950s, the central Appalachian coal fields surrounding War diminished in revenue, importance, and vitality. War's own population shrunk by two-thirds.

A century of unbridled industrialism and repeated unnerving swings of boom and bust culminated in the last great outmigration of former miners, primarily to the industrial cities of Cleveland, Detroit, and Pittsburgh beginning around 1950 and continuing in fits and starts to the present. It left scores of ghost towns and abandoned coal camps, sucking the vigor from the region and leaving behind a pervasive sense of despair, a despondency heightened by isolation provided by densely packed hills choked by overwhelming vegetation and the tentacles of dizzying, winding, dirty, potholed roads throughout the area.

The sense of gloom was deepest in McDowell County, by far West Virginia's poorest. It was a gloom accentuated by the physical confinement of the topography, the abundance of abandoned structures – residential, industrial, and commercial – and the encroachment of poverty, drug abuse primarily in the form of opiate based pain killers, and violence, a dreariness furtively brightened by the smattering of Christmas lights. A musty, moist, redolence drifted through the tiny community's frosty air.

Lucas "Pug" Graham helped his mother up the slick, makeshift wooden ramp to their Living Waters Full Gospel Church past a sign that said, "God's last name isn't 'damn'!" He felt a stinging drop of sleet strike his nose, reminding him of a happier childhood day. But the present mood was decidedly somber, reinforced by the story of tragedy he knew was just inside the white-framed church door. The wake began almost as soon as he'd gotten his mother situated. They were already late because of the care demands of his mother to her husband Emmett – Pug's father – in his infirmity.

"Dearly beloved," preacher David Karwoski said as Pug and his mother found places to sit on the hard wooden pews, "we are gathered here today to send to the bountiful hands of our Lord and Savior Jesus Christ in eternal salvation, Patricia Thompson Getgood, and her infant son Roscoe Dale Getgood."

The newly deceased were the wife and son of Donnie Getgood, an employee of Graham Coal, a company Pug ostensibly recently inherited. Pug's brother, Millard, was dead, or was likely dead, missing for seven weeks. Nobody knew. Regardless, he wasn't around and vanished without a trace. That's what brought Pug back to War, that and his father's condition.

As Pug's mother kindly patted him on his knee, he was

lost in thought, his personal demons swirling around the pall of the death he saw in front of him. He was deflated by his own situation, a life that started with so much promise.

As a child three years younger than Mill, he was eager to follow father and older brother into the mines. But in his first summer job at age fourteen, shuttling food and lightweight supplies to the face of the underground mine, he began to have doubts. His father loved mining, but soon understood how his son, at least this son, might not. Pug excelled in sports, was competitive, pugnacious according to his mother, earning his nickname. He got a baseball scholarship to West Virginia University where he played as a catcher on four consecutive losing teams. He got a degree in Industrial Engineering and gravitated to the textile industry in Southside Virginia. As plant production manager, he was the last employee, tasked with shutting off the lights, when Axton Industries in Martinsville shipped its 300 jobs to Cambodia. For sixteen months, divorced, unemployed, and alone, he lived in boredom and anguish before retreating home, disheartened and demoralized, to War.

Pug's father was in declining health for years, but his parents' increasingly less subtle pleas for him to return home to assist in their care fell on indifferent ears, at least until his brother's disappearance. He finally relented when his mother insisted that his father's pneumoconiosis, or black lung disease, was finally catching up with him and his days were numbered. What the hell? Pug was unemployed anyway.

Pug's mother's touch refocused him to the scene before him, the preacher's extortions still wafting through the chilly indoor air. Gay decorations of the Christmas season hung above the sanctuary, but failed to brighten the solemn mood. In the front row, three rows ahead, sat the entire Getgood family, with the back of the new widower and his twin, Ronnie, listing towards one another. Ronnie's wife Elsie sobbed uncontrollably over her dead sister-in-law and sister.

She and Trish were double-kin, married to twin brothers. Ronnie's and Elsie's five- and seven-year old girls, April and June, squirmed in the wooden pews, clearly uncomfortable. The dead young woman and her infant lay in parallel coffins of pine. Both faces were badly smashed, and at Donnie's insistence, were not retouched by the undertaker's artistic hand. Pug was always revolted by open-casket funerals, but this was particularly horrific, with such an obvious show of physical violence.

With Pug's return and at least the interim management of the mine, the twin brothers now worked for him. He was at the mine office when Vernon Dale Coles, Jr, a West Virginia State Trooper, arrived with the horrible news. "There's been an accident," he told Pug, who was working on some paperwork. "I need to see Donnie Getgood."

Pug and Coles, a huge, out of shape black man, rode one of the low-slung electric carts into a four-foot tall shaft in the cold, dark earth to the mine face where Donnie was assisting Lacey Reedy, the oldest miner, on the roof bolter. Seeing the sheriff appear before him, Pug instantly feared something horrible happened.

It occurred two day earlier, Friday, December 20th, in the morning. Coles was blunt, speaking in front of Donnie, Pug, and Lacey, the primary operator of the bolter machine, as they all crouched under the low ceiling of the mine, underground where Pug from childhood days always felt uneasy.

"Donnie, I'm sorry. Your wife is dead. So is your boy, your baby. I'm sorry."

Donnie's dirty hands moved to his dirty face.

Pug spoke next, "What happened?"

"A rock," the officer explained to Pug. "You know their pre-fab is just below the State Line Mine."

"What do you mean, 'below a mine'? Mines are underground." Pug insisted.

"Not below. Sorry. State Line is a strip-job, a strip mine.

Donnie's house is a half-mile away and at a lower elevation. They do a lot of blasting up there. Apparently an airborne rock smashed through the roof of their home and killed them as the baby was at her breast. Trish, I'm sure didn't feel much pain; it was too fast. Her skull was fractured. The rock was the size of a basketball. Went right through the floor. A neighbor found their broken and crumpled bodies. Trish's torso was halfway through the hole and the baby was lying dead on the ground."

"When?" Donnie asked, tears already streaming.

"I just left there. I'll investigate the mine records and see exactly when the blast was, but I'm guessing around 9:00 a.m."

Shaken from his reverie by Elsie Thompson Getgood's wails three rows ahead, Pug choked for a moment on phlegm and as he coughed to clear it. His grief overwhelmed him and he found tears streaming down his cheeks. Again, his mother patted his thigh, embarrassing him more than calming him. At 56, he didn't appreciate his mother's maternalism.

The last funeral he'd attended was three months earlier in a large church in Martinsville, for a former co-worker. That church was opulent by the standard of this tiny, minimally adorned church in War. The wake followed the preacher's remarks in the same sanctuary, where mourners immediately queued up to pay respects to the deceased's family. Pug inched with his mother slowly into line, she clasping a white handkerchief to her face.

He turned briefly and squinted at the diminutive woman behind him in line as a spark of recognition touched him as it also touched her. "I'm sorry. Are we acquainted?"

"You're Pug Graham, then, aren't you?" she replied.

"Yes, ma'am. And who would you be?"

"'Ma'am'? You treat me like an ol' lady. I should get you to guess," she said, showing a wan smile.

"You look familiar. But forgive me. Senior moment. I'm

sorry, I can't place you." Her eyebrows were black, permeated with grey streaks. She had a worn expression, but soft, green eyes, framed by crow's feet creases. She wore a silk scarf, tied tightly around her head. Her breath was of a frequent smoker.

"I'm Zola Wilkerson. You'd know me as Zola Elswick. We're second cousins."

"No shit! Oh, sorry," he shrugged with embarrassment at his spontaneous profanity. "It's been years."

"Decades," she corrected him. "What are you doing here?"

"Me? What are YOU doing here? I thought you left years ago."

They reached the first of the deceased's family, and Pug's attention was drawn away from Zola. His mom gently took the hand of Donnie and Ronnie's mother and expressed her condolences. Pug did the same. They made their way across the line of mourning family members before Pug turned back to Zola.

"Zola, you remember my mom, Dolores Graham."

"Hello, Zola," Delores said, "Nice to see you. It's been so many years."

"Yes, ma'am. Dad and I moved to Beckley, gosh, it must have been thirty-five years ago now. Ten years or so ago, he moved down here. I moved into his house a couple of years ago after he died."

Pug and Zola spoke only for a moment before Dolores said, "Pug, please, I need to get home."

"I'm on my way to the café," Zola told Pug. "Once you get your mother situated, why don't you join me for some coffee? It's awful but it's the best there is."

"I'm just back in town. Is it the War Room, where it's always been?"

"Yup. It's the only one in town."

Delores said goodbye to Zola and Pug took Delores home.

+ + + + +

Forty-five minutes elapsed before Pug opened the wood-framed, fogged-up glass door and let himself inside the War Room, where wooden chairs left scrape-marks across a vinyl-composition tile floor. Pods of fluorescent lights shone with an unnatural blue tint from above, with some lamps blackened at the edges and flickering distractingly. A woman sitting at a table looked up as Pug entered. She wore a dirty blue sweatshirt that said, "I got laid in War, West Virginia."

Zola sat at the third of three booths on the left row, but Pug almost didn't recognize her because she was as bald as Michael Jordan.

"Sit," she implored, as he approached. Seeing his astonishment, she said, "Sorry, I should have warned you."

"Cancer?" he queried, sympathetically.

"No, you fool; I had a chance encounter with a razor blade."

"'Scuse me?"

"I took part in a protest at the state capitol back in September. A bunch of us tree-huggers cut off all our hair. I looked like a Marine rat. So I took a razor to what stubble was left. I guess I haven't wanted it to grow back."

Zola explained the scene, where activists from several states staged a protest on the steps of the West Virginia State Capitol building in Charleston against mountaintop removal mining. She talked about the enormous destruction and how an organization she'd joined, Mountaineer Mountain Stewards, organized a publicity stunt to draw attention to the issue. Eight women, six of them West Virginians, volunteered to have their hair cut off, with the shorn locks left to litter the granite steps. They wore matching, pure white dresses. "The media came, took pictures and printed them in the newspapers. We got lots of attention."

"Was it effective?"

"Hell no. We got lots of publicity. But nothing has

changed. They're still strip mining."

Pug envisioned a line of female prisoners at a concentration camp interrupted by her next words, "Where do you stand?"

"Pardon me?"

"On strip mining?"

"I don't stand anywhere. I've had a lot on my mind lately," he sipped coffee from the Styrofoam cup just been placed before him. It had a strange, metallic taste. "This coffee's awful."

"I told you! It is made with municipal water. I'm sure it has heavy metals in it," she concluded. "All the water around here is polluted with selenium, cadmium, beryllium, arsenic, nickel. You name it. Our water is a damned periodic chart of the elements."

Pug put the cup down on the table. He ripped the top off a plastic cup of creamer and poured the contents into his cup, hoping it would soften the taste.

He spoke about his life in Martinsville and his wife leaving him seven years earlier for another man, her telling him that his ennui was too much for her to bear. His two kids were out of college and on their own, one in Texas and one in South Dakota. He seldom spoke with them.

"I could see the handwriting on the wall for years. The the decline in textiles mirrored the decline in the coal mines I'd witnessed when I was growing up."

Pug admitted he lacked the fortitude to be proactive, instead letting the mill owners chip away people, equipment, and work from his plant, until he and an empty building where the only things left.

"The operations manager from New York came down and talked with the last 30 of us last year. 'There isn't anything I can do,' he said. Jobs were moving to Asia. Peasants were flocking to the cities where they'd work for a dollar an hour or even less. We'd already lost work to a plant in Mexico where they paid what no American worker could live on."

He had trouble focusing on his story, staring at the image of a bald woman across his table. Zola seemed so familiar, with the high cheekbones so prevalent in his father's side of the family, but so unearthly with her shorn pate. She pulled a Chesterfield King 20-pack from her pocket, shook it to get a cigarette to protrude, then pointed it at him.

"Smoke?"

"No thanks," he replied, tapping his fingernails on the Formica tabletop.

Zola lit it with a clear yellow Bic disposable lighter which she dropped loudly on the table. She took a long drag and blew smoke from the side of her mouth. A heavy young woman at a nearby table glared at Zola for a moment, then returned her gaze to her own company.

Pug re-directed the conversation back to Zola.

Zola coughed and brushed her other hand over her baldness. "I think I mentioned I moved here shortly after daddy died. This is it, here in War. I mean, this is the last stand. Do or die. Now or never. We're at the shore of the Rubicon."

"What do you mean?" He stirred the cooling coffee with a short plastic straw.

"There's an application for a new strip mine just south of town, across the hollow from where that poor woman and her baby were killed. It will be the largest strip mine east of Wyoming, if it goes through. It is in clear violation of SMCRA. I'll die lying in front of a bulldozer before I let it happen."

"SMCRA?"

"Where have you been, cuz?" She wiped her mouth with the back of her hand. "SMCRA is the acronym for the Surface Mine Control and Reclamation Act. It regulates how strip mining is done and where. It was passed in 1977 and was one of the most comprehensive laws our nation has ever had. But you know, if it's gonna work, somebody's gotta enforce it. If it was enforced, you and I wouldn't have been at a funeral this afternoon."

She explained that SMCRA set standards for environmental performance, operating guidelines, inspection, and reclamation. It also set forth rules to reclaim already abandoned mines. Its 200 pages dictated virtually every activity and safeguard. But a few loopholes were included that the mining industry was squirming through. The current administration was increasingly lenient towards the industry. In fact, the Vice President of the United States, Dennis James Hughes, previously presided over an energy company with significant holdings in the coalfields.

Her eyes diverted towards the entry door. Pug turned to see a uniformed man step inside. He was short and stocky with a belly overwhelming his belt. The belt was laden with black patent leather gun and duty holsters. A "McDowell County Sheriff Department" patch was on the shoulder of his navy blue jacket. A small nametag said "Webber".

"Dammit," Zola murmured, lowering her eyes.

The officer took off his trooper hat and nodded at another table of diners. Then he walked towards their table. "Well, if it ain't Ms. Skinhead. How's the war going for y'all Nazis?"

"Why, Deputy Webber, good afternoon to you, too," she smirked, oozing sarcasm.

"Who's your friend here?" he insisted, sniffing his nose as he examined Pug.

"Deputy Doug Webber," she said, "This is Lucas Graham. Lucas, this is Deputy Webber of the McDowell County Sheriff's office."

"Charmed," Pug said.

"Likewise," Webber said, with equal disingenuousness. He had a wide, pock-marked face and a surprisingly high voice. He looked to Pug to be around 30.

"What kind of trouble are you getting yourself into these days, Ms. Q-ball?" he said, turning back to Zola.

"No murders, extortions, or rapes for me today," she claimed. "But tomorrow is another day. You'll be the first to know."

"You try anything fishy on my watch and I'll be on you like stink on excrement," he sneered.

"Like I said, you'll be the first to know. Perhaps you have something better to do than ruining the day of law abiding citizens. We were enjoying ourselves until you arrived." She blew smoke towards his face.

Clearly fishing for a retort but finding none, he smiled without showing any teeth and nodded his head. He touched the brim of his hat with his index finger, turned, and moved towards the waitress' counter.

"What was that all about?" Pug whispered.

"Who knows? I'm guessing the storm troopers in Charleston put out a notice after our protest on the state capitol steps to be on the lookout for wild, bald women. But that bastard had best leave me alone. If I go down, I'm taking him with me."

She took a sip of her coffee and said nothing for several moments, until she watched Webber retreat through the same door where he'd arrived. Beside the door, a neon "Open" sign flickered and buzzed noisily.

"Now then, where was I? Oh yeah, the mining industry. The fat-cat bastards come to town with their band of lawyers and their bulldozers and their drag-lines."

"Drag lines?"

"The excavators. They're huge pieces of equipment, basically a crane lifting a bucket. These are some of the biggest mobile land machines ever built. The scoops alone can be big enough to lift a house.

"Anyway, they fence off areas as large as mid-sized cities. Go to Google Earth sometime. You'll see mines as big as Beckley. They cut down all the trees. They sell the good ones and throw the rest into the ravines. Lord only knows what happens to the wildlife. Well, we all know, don't we? The wildlife is annihilated. Then the real demolition begins. They start blowing off the mountaintops. They use ammonium nitrate, the same explosive that terrorist used to destroy the Federal Building in Oklahoma City, except each blast is ten or twenty times as powerful and they do thousands of blasts every day across West Virginia."

Another customer came inside and a blast of cold air from the open door swept over Pug. He glanced outside where there were swirls of snow flurries.

Zola continued, "They unearth the coal and carry it off. But you've got to figure there are 50 to 100 tons of rock for every ton of coal. The industry calls it 'overburden.' Overburden! What kind of crap name is that? All that rock gets pushed into the valleys. The streams are destroyed."

"I thought all that was regulated," he said.

"Like I said, it's SMCRA. A law is only as good as the people at the top. It gets worse. With all the rock exposed and pulverized, the rainfall picks up the trace heavy metals faster, so the streams become polluted. The groundwater is often either polluted or the aquifer is emptied. Few of the towns around here have municipal water. So if the wells are polluted, people have nothing to drink. That's why this coffee has heavy metals in it." She took a deep sip, appearing to savor it. "Mmmm. Good to the last sip!"

She brushed her hand over her head, reflexively, as if there was still some hair to straighten. "Anyway, this is the line in the sand, as far as I'm concerned. There's a bill in Congress that will essentially eviscerate SMCRA and they won't have to bother ignoring it any more. It's deadlocked. The Vice President will cast the deciding vote, I assume, right after the first of the year."

"Which way do you think it will go?" Pug asked.

"It'll pass. That lying bastard is in the pocket of the energy industry. Hell, he used to be president of an energy resources company. If they bulldoze that mountain, it'll be over my dead body."

DEC 23 Monday

The next morning was a clear, crisp day to begin a week interrupted by Christmas on Wednesday. Pug bought a turkey for each of the eleven employees and he asked them to report to work even though he was sure nobody would be doing much of anything so close to the holidays. He took nine of the birds, expecting that the grieving twin brothers Donnie and Ronnie, wouldn't be there. He would visit them at home on Christmas Eve.

He arrived to find Gloeda Spangler already at the desk in the mobile home they'd converted into a mine office. She was principal owner of Spangler Business Services, and she was a contract bookkeeper to several of the few family-owned mining companies left in the War area. She kept a small office in a former elementary school in Caretta, the next town to the north. She was of average build, paunchy with her age he guessed at sixty, with peroxide-blond hair and half-cut reading glasses that she kept hanging from a string around her neck more often than in front of her eyes.

"I'm so sorry to hear what happened to Donnie's family," she said sadly. "His momma and I used to work together years ago at the Piggly-Wiggly, but I never knew him very well. Every time I came here to the mine with the paychecks, he was underground."

"I think he likes it there the best," Pug sighed, taking off his heavy coat and woolen stocking cap and hanging them on the bare metal bar hanging over the fax machine. "He's not here today, is he?"

"I don't think so, unless he went into the mine before I got here," she said. "If he's not here, I can't imagine what he's doing. He lives in a pre-fab home, I'm told. There's a hole in the roof, a hole in the floor, and I'm sure a lot of blood everywhere. It's damn cold outside, so it won't be livable until he gets it fixed."

"Or gets another one," Pug suggested.

"I doubt he can afford another one," she said.

"I suspect he'll get some sort of compensation from the company, won't he?"

"You know how it is," the older woman said. "No, maybe you don't. If he gets a dime, it'll be years from now. Nobody holds the corporate players' feet to the fire around here. The legislature and the courts are all wings of the industry."

"Are you telling me that a man can lose his wife and child and then his house in an industrial accident and not be compensated? At all?"

She looked at him like he was as naïve as a kindergartner, then shrugged her shoulders. She held her hands to her side, palms up.

"Listen," Pug said, changing the subject, "I'm going inside and see how everybody is doing," he grabbed a miner's coverall and a hardhat, affixing the battery-powered headlamp.

"We need to talk when you come out. There are some things you need to know about the books," she said.

He nodded and opened the lightweight door into the cold air. It was a stunning winter day, with clear skies looming over the tight hillsides, thick with leafless hardwood trees. He walked to one of the golf-cart like buggies and twisted the key, engaging the electric motor. Then he pointed it towards the mine shaft entry and drove in.

The air inside the mine came blasting at him, cool at an even 53F, but still much warmer than the outside air. Although the flow of air was reassuring to him, giving him the knowledge that the massive fan was working to expel the gasses that might accumulate and create a flammable mixture, he was always uneasy underground, forever unable to shake his claustrophobia.

When Pug arrived three weeks earlier, the foreman, Lacey Reedy, showed him the three entrances into the mine. Their permit allowed them access to the 4-foot tall Pocahontas 6 horizontal seam. Their site plan, drawn by a licensed engineer, dictated the mining process. They were digging three parallel, horizontal shafts simultaneously into the horizontal seam, connecting them inside by perpendicular corridors. One shaft was for access for personnel and mining equipment. The second had the conveyer that delivers the coal to the outside. The third was an air-flow shaft, continuously blowing air into the mine which was directed where necessary and then diverted to the other shafts where it exhausts, carrying potentially flammable gasses with it into the atmosphere.

Pug bumped along the uneven floor of the shaft, driving through puddle after puddle, often deep enough to cover the floorboard of the cart, wetting his boots. The walls and ceiling were covered in white powder, the rock dust purposefully sprayed to prevent the flammable coal from igniting. The only light was from his helmet lamp and the cart's headlights. Lost in thought about the prior day's grief, Pug's helmet repeatedly bumped against the roof of rock.

He found Lacey Reedy talking to several of the men, all hunched over with their hard-hats resting against the mine roof. There was no mechanical activity, although two guys were working on the motor of the transfer cart. Pug thought about the explanation he'd gotten from Lacey the prior week about the operation of the mine.

Generally speaking, there were two phases in the operation of this type of "room and pillar" mine: moving inward and moving outward. During the inward phase, the three parallel corridors were continually lengthened until they reached the furthest extent of the planned mine. At regular intervals, perpendicular cuts were made to link them to allow access from one to the other and to allow for proper air circulation, in a checkerboard fashion. The unmined coal left in place between the corridors acted as pillars to support the roof.

"Think of a coal seam as a layer of icing inside a layer cake," the grizzled older man explained to Pug a few days after his arrival. "What we're doing is removing the icing without damaging the cake."

The most critical and expensive piece of machinery used is the continuous miner. It is a stout, low-slung, worm-like earth-eating machine. The business end has three contiguous drums about 30-inches in diameter with rows of carbide-tipped teeth, each 8 inches or so long with the teeth rotated to get the maximum bite as the drums spin away and over the top. The entire drum apparatus is movable vertically by hydraulic lifters to allow for clawing of seams of various heights. Below that is a motorized scooping system which collects and funnels backwards along a conveyor the length of the machine the coal that the scraper deposited below the machine. The operator's chair is in a near reclining position behind one of the drive wheels, necessitating nearly blind operation. The operator senses variations in the rock by feel, much the same as someone driving a car can sense the textures of highway surfaces.

Machines like this revolutionized mining and spawned a massive productivity improvement beginning in the West Virginia coal fields in the 1950s and 1960s, as one machine could do the work of forty or more human miners. The great influx of miners who came from around the nation and the world to work in coal mining beginning in the late 1800s became a great exodus by 1950. McDowell County's population had grown from 3000 in 1880 to 99,000 in 1950, and then plummeted to 22,000 by 2010, with a corresponding fluctuation in coal mining employment. The deeply corrugated topography, along with the corporate coal mining companies' active efforts, discouraged any employment diversity. People either worked in coal, worked for the people who worked in coal, lived "on the check," some other form of government assistance, or simply scavenged through resale of used items or hawked drugs.

Closely behind the continuous miner in importance and cost is the roof bolter. This machine drills vertical holes into the roof of the rock above the coal seam to allow for the manual insertion of a re-bar like rod with a metal plate at the bottom to secure the roof and prevent rocks from flaking and falling. Thousands of these bolts are affixed at regular intervals throughout the mine.

The third piece of essential equipment is the shuttle car, used to transfer the coal from the continuous miner to the conveyer, which then transfers it outside. From there, it is carried by tractor-trailer to one or more of the area's tipples, the huge industrial facilities where coal is cleaned, sorted, and prepared for shipment via rail, mostly to Norfolk, Virginia, the world's largest coal port.

Each piece of equipment is powered by sparkless electric motors. No combustion motors of any type are allowed in the mine, nor are any cigarettes, lest a fire be sparked in the intensely volatile environment. Several of the guys chew tobacco in lieu of smoke.

The men spoke to one another briefly, but it was clear to Pug that they were in no mood to work, given the grieving of a co-worker and the proximity to the Christmas holiday. He told everyone about the turkeys he'd brought for them and then offered that they could go home whenever they wished. Lacey caught a ride with him back outside.

"It's a shame, a cryin' shame," the older miner offered.

Pug had no answer and gave an imperceptible nod to his foreman.

"Miners are like brothers," Lacey said, clearly in a talkative mood. He had close-cropped, wavy hair, fully gray. His nose was framed in black dust where he'd evidently brushed it with his hand.

"Yes sir," Pug agreed respectfully, envisioning the parallel open caskets he'd seen the day before.

Lacey continued, "I was in the Marines, back in Vietnam. It was hell, fighting and dying in the jungle. We called ourselves the 'Band of Brothers' in the Marines, but it's filled with tension and racial strife. It's nothing like the brotherhood of miners."

Pug managed a sardonic smile. He parked the cart in front of the office and turned it over to Lacey. Pug entered the office and grabbed a metal chair to sit with Gloeda.

"I don't sugarcoat any shit," she said, bluntly. "Things aren't good."

"Why? What's up?"

She explained that the financial condition of the mine was dire. The price of their prized low-smoke metallurgical coal was down. They sold all their coal to a corporate tipple in Raysal, over near Bradshaw, about ten miles away. Deliveries had been consistent over the past few months, but what they were paying dropped off. "You may need to speak with them. I'm seeing some discrepancies."

She also explained that there were increases in fines from the federal regulator who called on them every few weeks. Lacey had told Pug about him. He was a snarling, humorless man named Merritt Lee Lawson who Mill had tangled with often. Pug resigned himself to the fact that he'd need to deal with him as well.

Everyone emerged from the mine by early afternoon and Pug handed out the turkeys as they left for home.

+ + + + +

As Meredith Goldschmidt sat on a toilet seat and cried, a tear fell from her cheek onto her bare thigh. She didn't really have to pee when she entered the stall in the women's room outside the Cabinet office of the President of the United Stats. But she sought refuge in this unlikely, private place to wallow in fleeting minutes of self-pity.

She took a few moments to overcome her despair over her humiliation, suffered moments earlier inside President Andrew Cooper's Cabinet Room, a disgrace almost joyfully metered out at her by Vice President Dennis Hughes. She was Secretary of the Interior of the United States of America, a position for which when she was first nominated was the proudest moment in her life. As the three years of the presidential term unfolded, it became abundantly clear that she was the token of the President's cabinet, one of two women and the only member to be vaguely moderate in a swarm of conservatives.

The topic was Israel and the Middle East. She had some experience and expertise, having lived in Israel and studied at Tel Aviv University for a year. As Interior secretary, foreign affairs were not her official purview but she felt empowered by her personal experience to lend her opinion. When she offered what she thought was a reasoned assessment of the current situation, Hughes chose to cut her off at the knees, not only marginalizing her suggestions but belittling her as if she was a child.

She lingered in the stall, knowing the President's brief recess would end soon and she would return to his lair with as much composure and determination as she could gather.

What began as the most impressive career position on her resume was quickly coming apart. But her worries weren't confined to the difficulties she'd faced vis-à-vis the Vice. Her department faced continuing obstructions from the administration in her efforts to do the work she understood the job to entail, to protect America's outdoors and its natural resources. This administration was overseeing the most rapacious and insatiable resource grab in a generation, and she felt powerless to stop it.

To make matters worse, her marriage was strained. Troy, her son from her first marriage, was grown and living in

Thailand. The empty nest life she'd envisioned with Arnie wasn't playing out as she hoped. Their life in Arizona before her appointment was good. She worked in private practice as a lawyer in Phoenix before her election as State Attorney General. Arnie was President of the Maricopa Community College system. When President Cooper tapped her for his Secretary of the Interior, Arnie got a job as dean of students at the University of the District of Columbia. Life was supposed to be good. But he worked long hours and she traveled extensively, and the spark in their marriage dimmed. She suspected him of having affairs, but had no proof, and she was ashamed at her unproven intuition.

One thing she knew for sure. She would have no patience with Arnie if he was cheating. Her first husband, Troy's father, was a serial adulterer. When she finally divorced him, she swore she'd never deal with infidelity again. He died a few years later from cirrhosis of the liver.

Sound from the opening of the door to the ladies room shook her from her sorrowful introspection. She wiped herself, stood, repositioned her underpants and skirt, and left the stall. She washed her hands at the mirror where she lingered for a moment, staring at her own visage. The graying of her hair, resting stylishly shoulder length, was now complete as she aged. But she was still pretty; at least she thought so herself. She was tall, with an elegant gait and a pleasant smile, accentuated by deep blue eyes. She had a fond flashback of being selected Homecoming Queen during her senior year at the University of Montana where she got her bachelors and masters degrees in geology, followed by her JD from Georgetown University. She took a folded brush from her pocketbook and straightened her hair. She took a cloth towel engraved with the Presidential Seal from the vanity counter and wiped her hands, and then wiped the channels her tears made through the rouge on her cheeks. She dabbed on some new makeup.

Then she returned to the Cabinet Room, determined not to utter a word unless specifically called upon by the president. Blissfully, she was not. At the meeting's conclusion, she left the room quickly, and retrieved her cell phone that wasn't allowed inside.

Turning to depart, her eyes met a Secret Service agent with a flash of recognition. "Ma'am," he nodded at her. His name badge said, "Eisley."

"Russell? Is that you, Russell?"

"Yes, ma'am. Nice to see you."

During her term as Arizona's State Attorney General, she met Russell Eisley through a fellow Rotary International member and recommended him to their Congressman for a service academy nomination. He was thirty years her junior, but she remembered that he'd gone to West Point.

"You, too. Are you in the Secret Service?" she inquired.

"Yes, I'm senior staff, assigned to the Vice President."

Her eyes rolled and she was chagrined to think he saw her involuntary act of defiance and displeasure. They continued to exchange pleasantries, as she asked him about his family. Her questions about his life and family were met with taciturnity, which she took to be an expression of his estimation of appropriate behavior for his position. He didn't ask about her whatsoever.

Then she continued down the hallway from the Cabinet room with her head low.

She rejoined Jenni Wilson Wilkins, her personal assistant, in the White House foyer. Wilkins was dressed professionally, with a grey striped skirt and white blouse. Her hazel eyes were framed by stylish blonde locks and she wore a perpetually cheerful expression. "How'd it go?" she asked hopefully. The icy stare which Meredith fired back stifled any further entreaties from her subordinate.

They walked together back to Meredith's car, parked in the official White House lot. She glanced towards the three-car, twelve-people entourage which she knew to be of the Secretary of State. Meredith was eighth in line for succession to the presidency, yet she had no Secret Service protection – in fact, no protection of any kind – and drove her own personal car, her red Lexus around Washington. Her department, responsible for management and conservation of natural resources and all federally owned land, was one of the oldest in the nation's history, the fourth to be established after State, Treasury, and War. And yet it was seemingly a mere afterthought in the modern era, unless disaster struck somewhere. Election season was already underway although the election itself was another eleven months off. She already decided she would be one of the Secretaries who wouldn't return, even if Cooper and Hughes were re-elected, a prospect for which her feelings were increasingly mixed.

It was a mere four blocks from her office southwest of the White House, a distance Meredith would easily walk, were it not for the heels she wore. A chilly December wind blew in a swirl from the buildings in Foggy Bottom to the Northwest. She felt a smug pride in knowing that if nothing else, her complex was closer to the White House than the Secretary's of State.

As she pulled into her designated space, her cell rang. She put her Lexus in park and looked at the caller ID. It said, "Sibley Mem Hosp". She turned to Jenni and said, "Go on in. I'll be in momentarily." Then to the phone, "Hello, this is Meredith."

"Madam Secretary, I am Kenneth Tingley, head of Sibley Memorial Hospital. We admitted your husband this morning. We tried to call you earlier, but your staff said you were in meetings and I didn't want to leave a message."

"What's wrong?" she gasped, her heart racing.

"Your husband has been in an accident."

Her heart pounded her chest cavity. Tingley described Arnie's situation further, saying that Arnie caused a serious accident by driving his Lincoln SUV through a red light. He sustained multiple injuries, including a broken pelvis, four broken ribs, a collapsed lung, and a broken left leg and ankle. "Madam Secretary, there's one more thing you should know. He had a young lady in the car with him. She has a fractured skull. We don't expect her to survive the night."

Meredith's skin prickled and her eyes fell shut. A shiver shot from her upper arms into her spine.

Tingley continued, "The police are working on an accident report. But from the preliminary findings, it would appear that her head was in his lap at the time."

The phone grew quiet on both ends.

"Madam Secretary?"

"I'll be right over."

Without leaving her car, she called upstairs to her office. Jenni was not yet back to her desk yet, so she left a message for Jenni with Todd, telling him she'd be gone the rest of the day. Then she raced to Sibley.

She found Arnie under sedation, being prepared for surgery on his lung, pelvis and leg. She was given several consent forms to sign, but then encouraged to leave, pending any further information on his condition.

She thought to ask to see the woman who had been in Arnie's car. But as she envisioned the fractured skull of her husband's paramour, she changed her mind and returned to her car.

She drove to their home in northwest DC and called Jenni again. "I won't be in the rest of the day. Please take my calls." She tried to do some correspondence on her laptop but was too distracted by her heartrending kismet. The Christmas tree lights he hung the week before around their living room were soporific, and she fell into a fitful sleep.

DEC 24 Tuesday

Pug woke in a buoyant mood in the bedroom of his childhood on Christmas Eve, trying to convince himself that he was 7 years old again, eagerly awaiting the arrival of Santa. He fixed oatmeal for his parents and helped his mother get his father situated on his leather recliner in the living room. His mother sat in front of her desk and typed away on an antiquated Smith-Corona. He walked outside towards his Toyota Sienna minivan, sliding briefly on a frozen puddle.

He carried two turkeys, one each for the Getgood twins, fully knowing that Donnie, bereaved and homeless, would have no ability to cook it.

He drove south towards the Virginia State Line to Vallscreek, to Donnie's place. He knocked, but nobody answered the door. The rock that killed his wife had been removed from below the trailer, but the skirting was still out of place and the roof had a sheet of blue plastic draped over it where the rock penetrated.

Ronnie's place was next door, an identical pre-fab home. Pug knocked on the door and was greeted by Ronnie's wife, Elsie, and two blond girls he'd seen at the church. Pug re-introduced himself, and she let him inside where Ronnie was at the Formica-topped kitchen table cleaning some guns. Pug gave the turkey to Elsie and wished her a Merry Christmas, acknowledging the somber mood. A pot-bellied woodstove churned out heat to the small house. There was a small, fake Christmas tree in a corner near the woodstove and several wrapped gifts underneath. A framed photo of Jesus Christ hung nearby as did a photo of Dale Earnheart and Dale Earnheart, Jr., NASCAR racers. Several rifles hung parallel on hooks on the wall and two others rested vertically against each other in a corner of the room.

"Listen, Ronnie, I'm really sorry about what happened."

"Donnie's taking it real hard. Bein' twins, you know, we talk about everything. But he hasn't really said a word to me since, you know, since he found out. He and I, we been through some tough times together, but nothing like this. Our parents died young and the only way we made it was with each other." He was a young man; Pug estimated him to be in his late twenties. He wore a pair of torn jeans and a navy blue West Virginia University sweatshirt.

"Do you know where Donnie is?"

"We have a cabin we built togther. It's up on a ridgeline west of town in the Shop Hollow area. It's more his than mine. We're into guns and we can shoot up there all we want without nobody bothering us."

Pug decided to leave both turkeys with Elsie and try to find Donnie, getting good directions from Ronnie. He and Ronnie continued to talk before he left.

"Donnie – he and me was in Afghanistan together. When we enlisted, we told the recruiter we'd only join if we could fight the A-rabs together. So we were assigned to the same unit. What a crock of shit that war was! It was a rich man's war. I guess all of them are. The longer we stayed the more pissed and disillusioned we got. Donnie got into demolition. I got good at driving and working on the trucks. Donnie still loves blowing things up. Both of us are good shooters. I can shoot out the eye of a gnat at 100 yards."

Pug let himself out, saying goodbye and wishing Merry Christmas to Elsie and the girls. He drove back through War, noticing the Christmas lights on the few commercial buildings still occupied in the nearly vacant downtown. Several two-story brick buildings had broken windows in them where pigeons flew in and out.

He drove upwards on a paved side-street up a hollow. The road became increasingly steep and turned to gravel. He drove another few hundred yards where he parked alongside some detritus of prior mining operations. A continuous mining machine had been cannibalized for parts and was rusting in the open air. Various conveyor pulleys and belts were strewn about. He walked steeply up the drive which became a narrow path with two ruts, too small for a passenger car. He found Donnie sitting outside on a white plastic chair with a broken arm rest, smoking a cigarette, seemingly oblivious to the day's chill. He didn't move an inch to acknowledge Pug's arrival. He was a slim man with disheveled auburn hair that seemingly hadn't seen a comb in years.

"Hi, Donnie."

"Pug."

"Listen, man, I just wanted to tell you..."

"I know. You're sorry. Everybody's fukkin' sorry."

"Hey, I didn't mean..." Pug sneezed, and then holding one nostril shut blew some snot from the other onto the ground. "Do you mind if I sit down?"

"Suit yourself. Grab a chair from inside."

The cabin was little more than a plank-board frame with spray foam insulation covering the joints. The door was wide open. As Pug entered, he could see that it was filled with an amazing assortment of survival gear, as if its interior decorator had only known camouflage. There was an army cot with a green blanket folded neatly at the foot. The shelves were crammed with tin cans of food and cardboard boxes on the floor with more. A string of handcuffs and carabiners hung on a peg on the wall. There were multiple weapons, including a variety of rifles, handguns, knives, and grenades. There were several pairs of night vision goggles. There were military helmets, scarves, and what appeared to be blindfolds. There was a propane heater on the floor and a camp-style stove on a counter-top. There were several small boxes containing electrical devices, one he thought was a Geiger counter. He saw an army surplus folding chair leaning against a wall, which he grabbed.

Pug carried the chair outside and positioned it beside Donnie's, so eye contact wouldn't be necessary. He watched some birds flit into some nearby bushes. He tightened the collar of his jacket against the cold.

Donnie took another drag from his cigarette and set it down on a wooden picnic table, it still sending up a tiny stream of smoke into the still, cold air. He looked astonishingly like his brother, save a nasty scar down the side of his cheek from his earlobe to his chin.

Without a word of urging from Pug, Donnie yelped, "I'm 'bout to explode. I'm madder 'n hell. I don't mean takin' it out on you. I like your brother, I mean liked, if'n he's still alive. He's the only honest man I ever met in my life. My wife and my child were the only things I ever cared about, 'cept Ronnie. Then they're both killed by a goddamn rock."

Pug thought to speak over and over, but there were no words. A crow flew to a nearby tree and cawed loudly and repeatedly, eviscerating the silence. Donnie reached over to the end of the table and grabbed a .22 rifle, took a quick sighting on it, and blew it into a black feather-splatter oblivion with one shot. The silence returned.

The two men sat in awkward silence for a time. Pug shuffled in his chair, a move Donnie apparently took to be him preparing to leave.

"Hey," Donnie began.

"No need to say anything. Come back to work when you feel you can."

"You don' wanna to be around me right now. I'm gonna hurt somebody. I don't want it to be you."

Pug lumbered down the mountain, trying to shake the notion in his head that Donnie could put a bullet cleanly through his head at any moment if he chose to.

Back in War, Pug stopped at the coffee shop to collect his thoughts. He was delighted to find Zola sitting in the same booth as before, quietly sipping coffee and reading a thick novel.

"May I?" he motioned to his erstwhile seat.

"Please," she nodded. "Nice to see you. Merry Christmas."

"Not much to be merry about these days. I suppose that's

what Christmas is about, though, sorting through our lives to see if there are any blessings."

He ordered coffee and a cinnamon bun for himself. The coffee had the same metallic taste as before and it left a subtle but uncomfortable aftertaste in his mouth. The bun came still wrapped in puffy cellophane as it had apparently been heated in a microwave oven. On the plate was a tiny, plastic tub of margarine and a dirty knife which he wiped on his sleeve before he used it. Florescent lights still crackled overhead. They talked for a while, he telling her about his visit on the mountainside with Donnie and at the trailer with Ronnie and his family. He asked her about her living arrangements, and she told him about her father's place where she now lived. She asked him about his parents.

"Oh, dad is nearing the end. His breathing is labored with his black lung. I'm sure he'll pass soon. We're just not sure whether soon is a few days, a few weeks, or a few months. He doesn't talk much; it takes too much breath. He doesn't move much, either. It's sad. But I guess we're all headed that way."

She expressed condolences. Then she changed the subject, "I hate to ask you, but I need a favor. My car is in the garage over on Vine Street. They're waiting on a new fuel pump that has to come from Beckley and they don't think it will arrive until Monday or Tuesday. My mother is long dead, but this Thursday woulda been her 65th birthday and I want to visit the graveyard. Would you mind if I borrowed your car? I'll return it with a full tank of gas, I promise."

"Where is it?" he said, meaning the graveyard.

"She's buried in Amherstdale. It's north of here in Logan County. It's about 65 miles."

"Sure. Listen, why don't I drive you there? We've got the mine closed until the weekend, so I have some time off. Would you want the company? I don't mind driving and it might help me clear my head."

"Yes, that would be nice. I'll walk over here; would you mind picking me up?"

"Not at all. Say 9:00 a.m.?"

"Sure."

+ + + + +

Meredith Goldschmidt left her northwest DC home and drove again to Sibley Hospital. Getting preferential treatment due to her lofty position, she was met again immediately by Kenneth Tingley, the hospital president. Briefly exchanging pleasantries, he got right to the point. "Orthopedically, your husband went through surgery well enough. But there are more problems."

"What kind of problems?"

"We think he has a concussion. Brain injury is moderate to severe. We're keeping him sedated and are feeding him intravenously. He may or may not regain consciousness; he hasn't yet."

A surgeon with a nametag that said "Susila Subramanyan, MD" joined the conversation. Subramanyan told Goldschmidt that she was a brain injury specialist and had evaluated Arnie. With a deep Indian accent, she said, "He has some swelling on his brain. He has some bruising around his eyes and some cerebrospinal fluid leaking from his ears and nose."

Subramanyan continued with her diagnosis, but it fell on deaf ears, as Goldschmidt's concentration wavered. Finally, Subramanyan excused herself and departed.

Tingley said to Goldschmidt, "Madam Secretary, the woman in your husband's car with him died early this morning. Her name was Erin Morgan Bowles. She was 26 years old. From what we can gather, she was a graduate student at your husband's college."

Meredith processed this information, having it confirm her most horrible suspicion. Then Tingley continued, "Madam

Secretary, Ms. Bowles was about five weeks pregnant."

Meredith was surprised... but she wasn't.

"I suspect Ms. Bowles' family will request a paternity evaluation."

"Yes," Meredith answered through her tears. "I suppose they will. Please let me know."

Meredith sat by Arnie's bedside for a half-hour or so, watching the machines that were monitoring him, with his heartbeat regularly and slowly spiking the electrocardiogram. His eyes never opened. She envisioned happier times with him, teaching him how to sail the way she'd learned as a teenager on trips to Lake Havasu on the lower Colorado. They bought a 42-foot Island Packet yacht and kept it docked in a small marina beyond Saluda, Virginia, where the Rappahannock River meets the Chesapeake Bay. They named it "Hopeful." She and Arnie spent many weekends sailing the Bay from there. He was still a handsome man, at 54, four years her junior, but youthful and energetic. She could see why he was attractive to younger women. But that youthfulness that she'd always appreciated now disgusted her.

She finally left and went home again. She called Troy in Thailand but he didn't answer his phone and she didn't want to leave a message.

DEC 25 Wednesday

Pug awoke on Christmas day as freezing rain fell outside. His mother fixed him some breakfast of Bisquick pancakes, topped with Aunt Jemima syrup and Blue Bonnet margarine spread. The coffee reminded him of his meeting with Zola and he wondered about their planned trip the following day. He thought about Zola's mother, unable to remember what caused her death.

His mother went to church, but he stayed home, trying to discern from some paperwork Gloeda had given him how serious the company's financial problems were. He felt that somehow they were being cheated by the company that ran the tipple. Another obvious problem was a dramatic increase in fines for safety violations.

+ + + + +

After checking her watch to determine the time of day there, Meredith Goldschmidt called Troy in Thailand again.

"Hello?"

"Troy, it's me."

"Hi Mom. Merry Christmas."

"Where have you been?" she asked, maternally.

"I've been out doing field work. Is everything okay?"

"No." Meredith said, bluntly. "There's been an accident involving Arnie." She told him about his step-father, albeit only about his condition and not about the woman's death.

"Do you want me to come home?"

"No. Arnie's not conscious anyway. I'll be all right."

"Are you sure, mom? Somebody should be with you."

"Don't worry about me. Arnie has some really good wine in the cellar. There's one bottle he's been saving for our 20th anniversary in February. I'm going to drink it myself tonight."

"Take care, mom. Why don't you call an old friend, maybe Cathie, or do something special for yourself. It is Christmas."

"Thanks, Troy. I will."

"Keep me posted. Love you, mom. Bye!"

"Bye. Love you, too."

She went to the hospital around 11:00 a.m., finding Arnie in the exact position she'd left him the day before. She wanted desperately to be caring and empathic, but found herself furious with him. So she left, driving aimlessly northwest on Clara Barton Parkway. She parked at a picnic area in Great Falls Park and walked towards an observation platform overlooking the falls of the Potomac. She punched the speed dial setting for Cathie Silverman. Cathie's deep, cheery voice rang out on the other end, "Hello, Meredith. Merry Christmas."

"Cathie."

"How's it going?"

"Not so well."

Meredith told her about Arnie and the accident. This time, she was blunt about the death of the passenger and her pregnancy, sparing no details.

"What's Arnie's condition now?" Cathie asked respectfully.

"Possible brain injuries. We're not sure. The doctors have no idea of his prognosis."

They chatted more about his condition and the plausible outcomes of his recovery. Neither woman uttered the word "adultery" but Meredith sensed it was on her friend's mind, having counseled her through her prior episode and divorce.

"Listen, sweetie," Cathie volunteered, "I suspect you might want to stay near the hospital for awhile, but if you do want to take a break, you know I have a spare bedroom here. The weather is amazing this time of year."

Meredith pictured her friend's home in Barbados from frequent visits.

"Actually, I think a break might be good. When can I come?"

"Whenever you want."

They settled on January 7th, two weeks away.

Part 2

DEC 26 Thursday

UNDER A COLD, OVERCAST SKY, Pug parked his minivan in front of the War Room. Zola reached for the passenger door handle and let herself in before he even realized she was there. "Thanks again," she noted, removing the scarf from her shaved head.

"Where to?"

"North."

He did a U-turn and drove out of town on SR-16, making a left, westward, at Yukon and taking SR-89 towards Bradshaw. The scenery was typical of the area, with steep, modestly sized mountains tightly framing the highway corridor. Barren, black-trunked trees clung to the steep, brown leaf-littered slopes. The ground beneath the trees was brown on the south-facing slopes to the right and frosty-white on the left. All along, small houses, some occupied but most not, clung to the slopes.

Unoccupied homes were in every state of decay and shabbiness. Some had concrete walls and steep stairways leading down to the road. Most had broken or collapsed porches and caved-in or burned-out roofs, with skeletons of framing, long stripped of the copper plumbing but still with the worthless porcelain. Some had trees literally growing through where the living room had been. Some were stripped clean, holding only the ghosts of long-departed people who carved hard lives for themselves with the hills pressed against their backs.

The occupied homes were often festooned with colorful but fading kitsch figurines, plastic Jesuses and Santas, toy plastic cars, and spinning whirligigs, and had wafts of smoke drifting from their chimneys. Porches held white plastic chairs and upholstered bench seats removed from scrapped automobiles. House trailers stood beside many ruined houses, most with small yards littered with all manner of abandoned rubbish. Smoke drifted lazily from several chimneys, lit in colors by the Christmas lights.

Abandoned, often disemboweled vehicles, both personal and commercial, spilled from yards into the creek. Piles of amorphous scrap metal rusted under the light coating of frost.

There were a number of tiny churches along the way, most constructed of wood and in various states of maintenance. All had signs in front, welcoming parishoners and guests. One said, "Read the Bible - it will scare the hell out of you." Another said, "Concealed weapons class, Jan 6."

All along, a creek ran beside them, their road crossing it over and over again. The creek was garlanded with tires, washers, rusted trucks, and rags. Occasional bridges spanned the creeks, some drivable and some only for pedestrians. And all along, a railroad paralleled the road. A train locomotive trailing fifty coal-cars rumbled along noisily in the other direction, shattering the peacefulness of the valley. Just past Bradshaw, they passed the huge, sparkling new brick River View High School, one of two of McDowell County's high schools, closed for the holiday. He thought of his graduation decades earlier from Big Creek High School – recently demolished – in War, and how happy he was then to be leaving the area, seemingly forever. Now he was back again, looking for a way to find something to like, some peace and satisfaction.

Zola spoke very little, occasionally giving directions as they approached intersections. In Iaeger, at Pug's insistence, they left a short bypass and drove the main street through the tiny downtown, where Pug's first girlfriend from high school had lived. There was a modern, suburban-style bank in operation along with a tattoo parlor, a clinic, a bookkeeping business, and a tanning salon with colorful lights glowing, but most of the twenty-five or so storefronts were empty. Several had broken windows with pigeons flying in and out. It was a scene of utter decrepitude, appalling to strangers and debilitating – consciously or not – to locals.

On they continued, now on SR-80, north. They passed what appeared to be a family compound, pieced together from the salvaged wreckage of other abodes, with a main house surrounded by sloping shipping containers, old school buses, scrap metal roofing material, and plastic sheeting. A pen of angry, anxious, emaciated hound dogs yelped noisily and darted frantically across the cage-like enclosure.

They crossed into Wyoming County over a small pass, then into Mingo County, and then into the towns of Justice and Gilbert, which were seemingly more prosperous, if only marginally so. Never for more than a mile or two was the road straight. There were signs of industrial and mining activity everywhere, with shuttered repair shops, heavy trucks, and bulldozers scattered about, along with long-abandoned tipples and conveyers.

They crossed another small mountain pass and entered their destination county, Logan. At Man, they left the highway and drove northeastward on Buffalo Creek Road. Like so many hollows in coal country, the Buffalo Creek basin was developed in a string of micro-towns. Pug noticed signs saying "Kistler unincorporated," "Accoville unincorporated," and "Amherstdale unincorporated." A small, cheerful billboard had a photo of a fish and said, "Nasty people litter; Keep Buffalo Creek clean."

Amherstdale was a smattering of houses, some occupied and many not, positioned closely together wherever the narrow hollows gave enough flat ground to build on. The homes were wooden clapboard, many with waist-high chain-link fences surrounding them. Many were nicely kept, but more had rubbish thrown about and a myriad of brightly-colored plastic toys around the yards.

Zola directed Pug to leave the highway where they drove a flat, narrow neighborhood street called "Picture Perfect Drive" of broken pavement and mud-puddles past a destroyed school that had the letters "HER TD LE CHOO" in green metal block letters still attached to a brick wall. Pug deduced the missing letters and concluded this was the AMHERSTDALE SCHOOL." The architecture led him to believe that it was constructed in the 1960s. They turned onto an even smaller street where Zola wordlessly motioned Pug to park. She emerged from the van and walked away towards what Pug discerned was a small cemetery. He watched as she walked to the metal gate, which she opened.

Moments later, Pug joined Zola as she stood in front of a single, multi-person headstone. It had four inscriptions:

Elswick

Mother	April R.
Born	December 26, 1941
Died	February 26, 1972
Father	Odia P.
Born	March 11, 1939
Died	October 31, 2009
Son	Stuart T.
Born	May 26, 1961
Died	February 26, 1972
Daughter	Zola E.
Born	February 26, 1963
Died	

Pug always thought it was creepy, having a headstone already chiseled for a living person. He put his arm around her waist, in familial affection. He noticed that her mother and brother died the same day, but nothing more registered with him.

Zola had forgotten to bring her scarf and heavy coat from the minivan. But she seemed unmindful of the cold. He turned and walked back to the van where he retrieved her wraps and gently placed the coat over her shoulders and the scarf over her head. She nodded almost imperceptibly in thanks.

"I think I'll take a walk around," he said. "I'll be back in a few minutes."

She nodded again acquiescing as he turned to depart. Walking towards the gate, he noticed that several other tombstones had the date of death as February 26, 1972.

He walked back past the van and down the residential street. The poverty was extreme, but in his view was no worse than most of McDowell County. An older woman watched him warily from her front window inside a house that badly needed to be painted. He waved but she never reciprocated; she never reacted at all.

He walked back past the school, wondering how and why it had been so abandoned, and why it had never been demolished after abandonment. He ambled towards the nearby railroad tracks where he saw a white-faced black cat ramble slowly across the ties. He walked the ties himself, reminding himself of his childhood days when it was a game to skip one or two ties as he and his boyhood friends played on the tracks. Rubbish was everywhere, both the detritus of railroad operations – ties, spikes, rail-bolts – and of the more prosaic type, mostly plastic grocery store bags flapping from spiky entanglements on the leaf-shorn brambles.

His mind flew into introspection, thinking about the older woman behind the window. She was clearly West Virginian pure. He didn't know what he was any more. West Virginians can be among the largest-hearted, generous and warmest on the planet, but in equal or greater measure suspicious, chary, and distrustful, especially of strangers.

Nobody ever comes to the hollows of West Virginia by accident. Everybody has a reason. Mostly they come home, because so many have left. Others come from curiosity, the burning desire to see and experience the poverty, inexorable crawl of natural reclamation, the deterioration of manmade structures and of the souls of the people themselves. Anybody else who came inevitably brought more misery: the land speculator, the coal baron, the gas driller.

A buzzard flew lazily overhead, its silvery underwings shining in the sunlight, drawing Pug's attention upwards. To the north, up a hollow, was a staircased earthen embankment, denoting the lower end of a mountaintop removal mine. It was eerily lime-green with newly seeded non-native grass. Pug spun around to take in the panorama of mountains enveloping the narrow valley and understood the impediments they provided to the transfer of people, materials, and ideas from inside out but more perniciously from outside in.

He remembered early forays elsewhere, back in his twenties, as he had made two cross-country trips and one to England to meet a girlfriend's family. He remembered feeling strangely alien, as if he wanted to feel like everyone else but knowing that as a West Virginian, he wasn't. Somebody he met in Idaho wasn't even aware that West Virginia existed as a state, rather than as a region of Virginia, even though its statehood was decades earlier than Idaho's, and had little idea of its whereabouts, even though it was surrounded by America's most populous and affluent states.

To people like this, he'd extend his right hand, palm towards them, with the thumb and middle finger hyper-extended. He'd say, "Here's what my state looks like," relishing in the perceived vulgar brush-off. "And I'm from the very bottom," he'd point with his left index finger at the base of his right palm, laughing to himself that no truer likeness could ever be drawn of any other state by any body part.

West Virginia was image-addled, and he understood why. The town of Matewan and the epicenter of the Hatfield and McCoy feud, our nation's most notorious and infamous, was only fifty miles to the west. Television had a field-day with *Buckwild*, a show that feasted on the stereotypes of young, reckless West Virginians in a sensationalized derogatory manner. But the escapades in *Buckwild* paled in comparison with the tap-dancing outlaw Jessco White and the inane, coltish, self-defeating antics of his family, portrayed in the documentary, *The Wild and Wonderful Whites of West Virginia*, set in Bandytown, just east of Amherstdale, over a couple of mountains. Most quixotic of all were the snake handlers, at several Pentecostal churches throughout the area, where parishioners and preachers often died from bites.

The only time he'd seen West Virginia on the front pages of the nation's newspapers was for ecological abuses and coincident protests, mine disasters and the inevitable mournfulness and acrimony, weeping children, and sorrowful wives, corruption scandals, meth lab explosions, and abysmally high smoking, illiteracy, and obesity scores. Find any index of economic well-being and West Virginia was anchored near the bottom.

Pug knew every stereotype had some basis in reality, but was infuriated that outsider perceptions were fueled by such unflattering images. He grew tired of the eye-rolls and the constant deprecating jokes he heard when he announced the state of his birth. He often gave Welch as his hometown, it sounding more distinguished, less confrontational than War. No, as a West Virginian, he wasn't like everybody else. And West Virginia wasn't like any other state. And War wasn't like any other city. Now as an adult, he didn't care, and he relished the novelty.

As with the dichotomy of both warmth and suspicion, West Virginians were both proud and lowly. As residents of one of the nation's poorest, most maligned, least understood states, habitually dominated by extractive resource exploitation and domination by outside interests, how could anybody feel better than dissatisfied and somehow dishonorable? West Virginia's parent, Virginia, produced eight presidents, more than any other state. West Virginia produced a goose-egg, zero! Virginia boasted founding superheroes Jefferson, Madison, Washington and Monroe. Most Americans have no idea of any famous or noteworthy West Virginians. One of Pug's friends in Martinsville could only name comedian Don Knotts, Andy Griffith's bumbling sidekick, as a native son.

Yet the pride was omnipresent, as was the solidarity, even though maintenance of it was often by the exiled. The psychic compass of most native West Virginians swung violently backwards, and the longing view was from the rear-view mirror. The state looked better from behind, fleeing away to better jobs and opportunities elsewhere than through the windshield, where the harsh realities emerged in clearer visions. West Virginia suffered the largest non-disaster related diaspora of any state, and many exiles spoke longingly of "home" better conceptually than through reality.

Pug heard the word "solastalgia," a neologism coined by an Australian to describe a longing for a home that no longer exists, and knew it to be the way many Mountaineers feel when they return to the coal camps of their youth that now exist only in decayed ruins if at all. Many mountains vanished, too, having literally been blown to dusty oblivions. Homesickness among those who left is endemic.

Pug met a man in Martinsville from a coal camp in Wyoming County who said, "I've only been back twice since I left for the Navy 35 years ago. There were only two buildings still standing, both in ruins, and all my memories have been choked away. I'll never go back again. It's just too depressing. I feel like a man without a homeland or history." Pug understood the scourge of fatalism so ubiquitous among his brethren.

Pug remembered reading a story about an Irish man and woman who moved from Ireland to Virginia to escape the ravages of the potato famine. All their lives, they longed for Ireland, never to return. But at least Ireland was still there. For those who left West Virginia, much of what they remembered was simply nonexistent.

His mind flew back to the woman in the window, aching to know her, what moved her, what she thought when she saw him walking her street. She was surely poor; everybody was, or almost. West Virginia was like a banana republic with a third-world-like level of income disparity. West Virginia was among the nation's poorest states, and while "blessed" with unfathomable mineral wealth, Southern West Virginia was habitually the poorest region. The state's wealthiest county, Jefferson, was at the extreme eastern end, furthest away from the state capitol and everybody else, a place where de-secession straw-poll votes to re-join Virginia were often held and won.

Feeling chilled, he returned to his minivan. He saw that Zola had moved to a nearby bench, but was still inside the enclosure. He opened the driver's side door to his minivan and sat inside. He turned on the radio, but a country-and-western song seemed strangely incongruous, so he turned it back off again. He closed his eyes, rubbed them, and pushed his head against the headrest.

He must have nodded off, because when she opened her door it startled him. She took off her coat, sat inside, and said simply, "Okay, I'm ready to go."

+ + + + +

The ride back to War was even quieter than the outbound trip until they'd passed just beyond Gilbert when Zola suddenly spoke, unprompted, as if already in the middle of a story she'd long rehearsed in her head.

"It was my birthday. It was a Saturday. I was turning nine. It was the day my life was destroyed.

"Daddy took me with him in our pickup truck to the store to buy candles for the cake that Momma was baking. I always loved riding in the pickup truck with daddy. The seat was so high and I felt tiny in it. I had to crane my neck to see over the dashboard. Daddy had left his wallet the day before at the mine. We drove up the hollow so he could get it. Mom and Stu stayed at home. Stuart wanted to watch cartoons on TV. He was my older brother; he was eleven.

"It had been raining for several days, really hard. There was thunder and lightning the night before; it was scary. There were several giant retention ponds at the head of the hollow. People called them sludge impoundments. I guess everybody assumed the dams that contained them were safe, or at least the people who were in charge of regulating them took their jobs seriously to protect us."

Her voice seemed to raise an octave, as if she was talking like a little girl again, trance-like, channeling the child of her youth.

"As we drove back down the hollow, we got to a place where there was a view of town. There was a loud rumbling and it seemed like the ground shook. Daddy stopped the pickup and we watched this crazy, massive wave of black water rush above where the creek was through town. Daddy yelled, 'Holy shit,' and gunned the engine.

"We drove the last mile into the main valley so fast and I was so scared. We could see our house being overwhelmed by the water. It began to buckle and then move with the current, first slowly and then faster. A few hundred yards downstream, it smashed into the railroad bridge and disintegrated into a thousand white plank sticks."

"Jesus. What happened?" Pug asked, innocently.

"The impoundment dam broke. Actually, three of them broke. There were three impoundment dams upstream on one of the several heads of the basin. The top one was built eight years earlier to contain and filter the water that is used to clean coal after it is mined. Then they built two more on the same drainage. They were built of slate, rock, and leftover coal. The top one gave way and then the wave of water swept over the middle one and its dam collapsed, too. Then the same with the third; it collapsed, too.

"Coal mines generate lots of rock and dirt waste; up to a quarter of what's brought up. You know that. Coal preparation plants use enormous amounts of water to separate the proverbial wheat from the chaff, meaning the coal from the rock waste. What's left over is a dark, black slurry. Sometimes people call it 'gob.' Mining companies use tailing ponds where the impurities can settle out from the water. The company that owned this mine was Pittston Coal. When those dams broke, over 100-million gallons of black, slimy crud flowed into the valley."

Pug watched two more black vultures soar overhead, gracefully in the cold, still air. He wanted to comment, but was compelled to stay quiet as his kin continued.

"Anyway, the street we were on began to be overwhelmed by water, too. Daddy tried to turn the truck around, but it was pushed over an embankment by some floating debris. Daddy grabbed me by the arm and pulled me out his door and we barely made it to a higher place before the water swept over the truck bed and swamped it completely. We saw several other people running away from the water for their lives, but we knew lots of people weren't going to make it. The water kept getting higher and we kept backing away from it.

"Oh, it was awful! It was raining and cold and we were

already wet and filthy dirty. Stuff started floating by in the flood, basketballs and refrigerators and broken boards. I remember watching the cars. They were bobbing along like beach toys. I saw a trailer float by and then get caught by a tree where it wrapped itself completely around before it came apart. I saw a body floating by, a boy about Stuart's age, trying to swim but getting sucked underneath the goo. It was horrible. I was too shocked to cry."

A hound dog ran in front of Pug's truck and he braked quickly and instinctively to miss it.

"I looked at my daddy's face and he was horrified. He didn't say a word about Momma or Stuart; we both knew they were gone. We never spoke about them again. I had always thought of my life as being happy until that moment. My parents loved me; at least I thought they did. My brother was a brat, but I loved him still. I had friends and I loved school. I loved reading history and I loved being a West Virginian. But I have never had a happy day in my life since."

She took out a cigarette and lit it, not asking Pug's permission. Under most circumstances, he would have said no, but he couldn't get himself to ask her to put it out.

"The flood was crazy; it took some houses and left others untouched. We were taken in for awhile by some friends of Daddy's whose house was intact. At some point, we moved into a trailer up the valley near where our house used to be. But nothing was the same; even the landscape had changed. There were piles and piles of junk strewn everywhere. The little creek behind the house where I used to play with my dolls was still there; somehow, even my favorite doll that I'd left there the day before. But nothing else was around. Everything changed. I was disoriented; everybody was.

"The people who moved into the trailers near us were strangers. We used to have visitors come over and we'd go to family reunions. The people around us weren't friends or family or anything. There was no privacy. The trailers were packed so close we could hear what was going on in the next one. People were angry and sad, and the couple next to us yelled at each other all the time. Listening to them was like daggers in my ears. It wasn't insulated and there was no way to keep it warm enough. I remember being freezing cold for weeks. When summer came around, it was broiling hot in there. But there was nowhere else to go. We used to sit on the porch swing in the summertime before our house got swept away – momma and me. But the trailer didn't have a porch and momma was dead.

"There were rats everywhere. The trailer had cockroaches and mice and ants. We didn't have a yard to play in. There were three rooms in that cracker-box: mine, daddy's and the living room. We felt like we were in jail. We had no room to move around. It wasn't a house. It wasn't our house. It was just a place to stay until things got better, but people didn't think things would get better.

"People were just changed. Nobody seemed to laugh any more or tell jokes. Kids didn't get along. Nobody wanted to do anything. When I grew up and studied psychology, I realized what was going on; everybody was depressed. Nobody called me 'honey' or 'sweetie' or anything kind any more. People seemed to sit around aimlessly."

Pug was mesmerized by his cousin's story, hoping she would stop and the pain would soon end, but he didn't ask her to stop.

"Part of that depression was that everybody lived in fear. They feared rain and wind and snow. Even when months went by, they didn't buy new things or decorate or move on with their lives. Everybody was in suspended animation, with no new hopes or dreams for the future. We all had a past but nobody seemed to have a future. If you've ever lived with a depressed person, you know how debilitating it can be. Imagine an entire depressed community.

"Most of my friends were either killed or moved away.

Most were killed. 125 people died that day. I heard that somebody had found my brother's body, naked, in a tree. Momma's body was never found. They put a coffin in the ground for her anyway; I'm not sure what sense that made. So that tombstone has Stuart's body in a coffin and an empty coffin beside it. I try to convince myself that Momma is in there, rather than being covered by flood scum. I agonize that someday her skeleton will surface again in another flood.

"Over 1000 people were injured in the flood and over 4000 of us were homeless. I remember that survivors mulled around for hours, wondering what to do. Some people said we were the lucky ones. But I didn't feel lucky. I don't think too many of the other survivors did, either. I think we felt guilty that we were alive and they weren't.

"We didn't have school any more that school year. It was the saddest and loneliest months of my life. It was too cold to play outside until spring, but I had nothing to do inside. I read every book I could find, but there was no library and the trailer didn't come with any books."

Pug's mind drifted to a book he'd read years earlier about Holocaust survivors, who after their liberation weren't elated as the rescuers expected them to be, but were so horrified that they never recovered emotionally and were scarred for life.

Zola continued, "It seemed like Daddy clung to me harder and tighter than before. He had never cooked anything and had no idea how to do it; I don't think he knew how to boil water. So we had beans and meat from a can almost every night. I tried to teach myself how to cook and remember how Momma used to do it. Daddy always looked at my face, long and hard, as if trying to see Momma's face in mine. Daddy would lay in bed with me when I went to sleep, which for awhile I thought was comforting both to him and to me. He called me his 'special little gift from the Lord.'

"Within a year or so, I entered puberty and the incest

started."

She stopped talking for a moment and put her hand to her mouth, as if steeling herself from recounting the horrors. Then she sniffled, took a deep breath, and continued. "He would begin to rub my breasts as they grew, and he would get excited. I didn't know what was going on; I was just a little girl. I knew it didn't seem right, but I had nobody to talk to about sex."

Pug came to an intersection and had forgotten the route. Without saying a word to her, Zola pointed to the left and said, "That way."

She took a deep breath, seemingly trying to decide how much of her life story to reveal. Then she continued, "When I was thirteen, my breasts began to get swollen and tender. I woke up sick and raced to the toilet several mornings. Then one morning there was a massive, bloody discharge in the toilet. It scared me to death! In hindsight, I know exactly what had happened, but it freaked the hell out of me at the time. There were no counselors. I really had no motherly figures to help me through any of this; they'd all been swept away. And I never became pregnant again.

"I've always told myself that the Lord knew I should never become a mother. Daddy started drinking more. When he had too much, he was too drunk to come to me. So I did everything I could to make sure there was always enough whiskey around the trailer. I ran away with a boy when I was sixteen. Daddy finally died of cirrhosis of the liver. I suppose I helped kill him by feeding his alcohol addiction. But in a way, he died the same day as Momma and Stu."

Pug shuffled in the driver's seat, uncomfortable with the conversation.

Then she continued, "You know, it's West Virginia's cruelest stereotype."

"What's that?" he said.

"Incest. Somehow, I don't mind all the other jokes people

make about us. I've learned not to be too sensitive. I'm comfortable with who I am and there are lots of redeeming qualities about the people from West Virginia. But not incest. It isn't funny."

She stopped talking as quickly as she'd started. A few minutes later, she began again as if in mid-sentence from earlier. "I married a boy when I was 17. But he was abusive to me and I ran from him two years later. I married again when I was 22. We stayed together for four years, but he left me when I couldn't bring him children. I told him when we married that I was sterile, but he never believed me.

"During all this time, I got my GED and I kept reading everything I could ever lay my hands on. I got four Associates Degrees from the community college system, one in history, one in psychology, one in biology, and one in environmental sciences. I began to read more and more about the history of West Virginia, particularly about the rapid industrialization that happened here when coal was discovered."

"It is all starting to come back to me," Pug said in a flash of recollection. "Buffalo Creek! I heard about the flood at Buffalo Creek when I was, like, twelve. I knew it was somewhere else in West Virginia, but I never knew where. And I never knew you went through it. I just heard that your mom and brother died. I guess I assumed it was a car wreck. I'm sorry that happened to you."

"Nobody," she said, wiping her hand unselfconsciously across her bald pate, "should have to live through what I've been through. Why did I live and they die?"

"Was your father ever compensated for the loss?"

"Fuck no. If it was anything, it was a pittance. Pittston Coal called the flood, 'An act of God.'"

"That's absurd."

"Of course it is. Everybody knew it and Pittston's saying it was made everybody furious. For years before the dams broke, people complained that they thought they were inadequate.

But a federal mine inspector declared them satisfactory just four days before they disintegrated. He died in a mysterious accident a few years later.

"There are still dams like this all over West Virginia, over a hundred of them," she continued. "There are more in Virginia, Tennessee, and Kentucky. I think about them all the time, the risk that tens of thousands of West Virginians have living downstream. There are two huge impoundment dams up the creeks that feed the Jacobs Fork in War, so I'm living in the shadow again now. The whole town is.

"Anyway, the survivors sued Pittston and settled a couple of years later for a few thousand dollars each. The state of West Virginia also sued them for $100 million for damage to state infrastructure. But the governor at the time, Arch Moore, settled for only $1 million three days before his term ended in 1977. West Virginia had voted for this man for governor twice consecutively, then again a few years later. He was later convicted of corruption and served three years in prison before he was released. There's nothing politically that ever happens in this damn state that surprises me any more. Everyone in our government is in the pocket of the coal industry."

Her eyes scanned the scenery passing by and she changed her subject. "You know, it's shit-bleak around here in McDowell County. But for some reason, even in the dead of winter, I still think it is beautiful."

Raindrops began to splatter on the windshield. She spoke again, "Even today, when it rains, I still get antsy. I love snow. It makes everything so pure and white and new again. But I hate rain. If I didn't feel called to put an end to mountaintop removal mining, I'd move to Nevada."

They reached the edge of War and Pug drove over the railroad track that marked the north end of town. "Do you want me to take you back home? I don't think I ever asked where you live."

"Daddy's house, my house now, is near the elementary school. The furnace doesn't work very well. Mind if we just sit together for a bit longer? I'm happy to be warm in here. Say, I've been running my mouth ever since we passed Iaeger. Tell me more about yourself."

He told her about his career in the textile industry and the closing of his factory. He spoke more about his growing disillusionment in the way so many good American jobs were being shipped away to the Far East and his anger at the fate of so many of his friends.

She asked about his wife.

"When I met her, I thought she was a goddess. She was from Tennessee and I met her in college at West Virginia University. She turned out to be a crook. We had moved to Martinsville and I was working myself to death in those days, sometimes 13 hour days. I started to suspect her of cheating. One day, she was gone. Our checking and savings accounts had been closed and she'd taken our money. She took my boys, too. The state of Virginia is very sympathetic to women and although I'd never done anything wrong, I got screwed. That was seven years ago. My sons are on their own. I think I may have mentioned that one is in Texas and the other is in South Dakota. I never see them."

"So you've faced some demons, too," she sighed.

"Damn straight. I was drinking myself to death like your daddy for a few years. I got some help and now I'm sober, but I'm still mad."

"Who are you mad at?" she baited him.

"The Man. For years, I was a staunch conservative. Everyone in my family was, except my mother. I was mad at the freeloaders. The slack-bastard parasites. The welfare people. The 47-percenters. The Food Stamp scums. They were bringing down the working people and the whole economy. Over the past few years, my views began to change. I like to say I saw the light."

"How so?"

"The system is rigged. I've never begrudged rich people. If people make money the old-fashioned way through hard work and ingenuity, God bless 'em. But when factories in Martinsville started shutting down, first the others and then my company, I started to realize the deck was stacked. The playing field wasn't level. My company brought in a new president from Wall Street. He didn't know jack-shit about textiles; all he knew was the bottom line. My workers were skilled people who worked hard and took courses at the community college to improve their skills. Guys who had never touched a typewriter learned how to use computers. They worked harder than mosquitoes in a nudist colony and were making $15 per hour, which in this country will keep you above water, but just barely. The company figured out that they could get workers in Guatemala to work for $2.35 per hour. Then they figured out they could get goddamn Chinks to work for $0.85. So the work left and the factories shuttered."

"It's kind of an irony," she stated.

"What's that?"

"They expect the workers who have lost their jobs to somehow find the money to buy the products they're now making overseas."

"They don't think about that. The industry uses illegal immigrant workers in Florida and Alabama to grow cotton. They treat them like slaves, constantly threatening to deport them if they unionize or cause any trouble. They ship the bales to Southeast Asia where they make socks and sweatshirts and pillowcases which they then ship back to the United States. Somewhere in this country there are enough people punching keys at computers shuffling money around who have enough dough to buy this stuff. And now the rest of the world is becoming as consumer-crazy as we are. The guys on Wall Street are vultures, pure and simple."

"It sounds like you're as angry as I am."

"Damn right," he shrugged. "If I'm not there yet, I aspire to be."

+ + + + +

Meredith Goldschmidt went to the hospital again to stand vigil with Arnie by his bedside. Under the rhythmic beat of the electrocardiogram, she dozed off. She was awakened by a nurse who said, "Mrs. Goldschmidt, Mr. Tingley asked me to tell you if you came in today that he'd like you to call him."

She dialed the number the nurse gave her. Tingley's wife, or so Meredith assumed, answered cheerfully, "Merry Christmas." Meredith could hear children squealing in the background. Meredith told the woman who she was and then asked to speak with Tingley.

He answered, saying, "Hello Madam Secretary."

"Mr. Tingley."

"I won't keep you but for a moment. The dead woman's fetus has a DNA match from your husband."

"Yes, Mr. Tingley. That has been my expectation. Thank you for letting me know."

"Yes, ma'am. I'm very sorry."

"I am, too. Merry Christmas to you."

"Merry... well, goodbye Madam Secretary."

Meredith took another look at her unconscious, unfaithful husband, and left.

She drove to the marina beyond Saluda and walked purposefully through the gate, gesturing to Morris, the manager. She unmoored her yacht and backed it carefully away from its slip. It was a cold winter day with a brisk wind and high choppers on the Rappahannock, but she was a worthy seaman and she steered the boat into the rolling water. She drove southeast, around the tip of Windmill Point and into the rougher waters of Middle Chesapeake Bay. She sailed to the east where she spent the night nursing two bottles of wine and a bag of pretzels anchored in the lee of Tangier Island.

DEC 27 Friday

Delores Graham, Pug's mother, was nearing 80 years old, but was still surprisingly self-sufficient and spry. Pug started helping her with shopping each week, but on many Saturdays like this one, Pug's nostrils filled with the nostalgic scents of bacon and eggs before he even opened his eyes.

"Good morning, mom."

"Did you sleep well, honey?"

"I've had a lot on my mind, but yes." He told her about the trip he'd made with Zola the day before and her stories about surviving the Buffalo Creek disaster. He didn't mention the incest or Zola's miscarriage.

"There are a couple of things I need to mention today," Delores said. "First, I'd like your help please with my typewriter." She wiped her hands on her red and white checkered apron, seemingly the exact same one she wore when he was growing up. She was a small woman, shorter with age, but imbued with a great inner strength and clarity of soul. She was a stay at home mom when he was young, but finished her degree in English at Bluefield College and got a job as the High School librarian after he and his brother had left for college. She was busy working on a manuscript, a memoir, plucking away on an old Smith-Corona typewriter. She needed to have a new ribbon installed.

"The other thing is that your dad is having a visitor this morning. Do you remember Estell Hazelwood? He was in the Boy Scouts, a few years before you were. Everybody calls him 'Red,' even though he's black."

"Yes, I remember him."

"He's been coming over from time to time to play checkers with your dad. I seem to recall that he told me

Emmett once did him a favor and he felt like his visits were his way of paying back. Frankly, it's been so long I don't even remember what the favor was."

"How old is he these days?"

"Oh, I suspect Red is around sixty. He's a reporter at the Bluefield Star Sentinel. He'll be here after noon. Once we get daddy up and fed, will you set up the card table in the living room?"

"Sure."

They ate breakfast together, Dolores and Lucas "Pug" Graham, talking about old times and reminiscing about his childhood days and her memoir. They spoke about the foods she'd raised him on, pinto beans, fried taters, green onions and corn bread. Cornmeal gravy. Garden tomatoes. Squirrel meat. As he rose to put his dishes in the sink, he decided to broach a subject he'd been avoiding.

"Mom?"

"Yes, honey."

"About Mill."

"Honey, Millard just didn't come home after work one day. He's a grown man and your daddy and I don't watch his comings and goings too closely. But when his car was still gone in the morning, I called Lacey and he found it at the mine. Lacey called the sheriff's office, but they had no idea where to look. They sent a deputy around, asking questions. Here's his card. Doug Webber. He said to your daddy and me, 'Maybe Mill just went hunting or something.' I said, 'No, he would have told me.'"

Pug recognized the name on the card; Webber was the cop who'd hassled Zola at the café.

"Mom?"

"Yes?"

"How long has it been?"

"Seven weeks, I think."

"We, well, at some point we have to assume he's dead."

"I know, honey." She wiped a wisp of grey hair back onto her forehead. Her blue eyes were still clear, as her mind seemed to be. "Your dad, I've tried to talk with your dad about it, but he doesn't have much of an attention span these days. What do you think we should do?"

"I don't know, mom. I'm guessing he may have a will. Have you spoken with Mary?" Mary was Mill's only daughter. Mary left home at sixteen and Pug was sure she and Mill were estranged. Mill's wife had died of breast cancer years earlier. There were no other heirs.

"Let's get through the holidays, honey. Come next week, if there is still no word, why don't we see if we can find an attorney or talk with Lansing Turner at the funeral home and see what steps we need to take."

"Mom, I think I may go see Lacey myself this morning. I'd like to see what he knows, if anything."

They helped Pug's father Emmett into some clothes and positioned him at the kitchen table with his oxygen tank nearby. Dolores was feeding her husband of 62 years when Pug walked outside into a 25F morning. Frost clung to every blade of grass, and as he walked across the small lawn it crunched under his shoes.

He backed the Sienna to the turn-around, being careful of the edge, which had an 8-foot drop. He drove down Maple Street into town, and then turned northwards back towards Yukon and Lomax where he passed the day before. Lacey was splitting wood outside his simple, brown home. Being just after the winter solstice, the winter sun had left most of War in the shade in the morning hours, but the sun was shining on the black asphalt shingles of Lacey's roof and the mist streamed skyward from the melting frost.

"Hey, Pug. What brings you this way?"

"There have been some things on my mind. You got a minute?"

"Sure." He swung his axe into a stump where it stuck with

a thud.

"You're pretty astute..."

"I wasn't born yesterday. I've seen it all," Lacey hockered and spit on the ground.

"How long have you worked for Mill?"

"Gosh, it must be 26-27 years now. I worked for your daddy when he was still in charge. When Mill took over, I've worked for him."

"You must be past retirement age," Pug guessed.

"I'm 69. I retired when I was 65. I sat at the house for three months living on the check. I heard my wife complain to her friends that she had three times as much husband for a third the money. I was bored to frustration. I asked your brother if I could come back to work. He's had me do less strenuous work, which was kind of him. Some folks like to sit on their ass and do crossword puzzles and watch TV. I like to work."

"I know what you mean about work," Pug said, shuffling his weight onto his right leg. "Mom was telling me the other day about one of her cousins who was lazy as hell. He got on disability at age 33 from a mine accident that broke his arm and limited his use of it. But that was the extent of it. From that time on, his big accomplishment was getting himself out of bed. His yard was full of trash and he never bothered to clean it. Mom said she went into his kitchen a couple of years after his disability, and she said dirty dishes filled the sink and the dust balls in his hallway were as big as softballs. He seemed healthy enough, or could have been, but he died at 53. She said it was boredom."

A blue jay landed in the rhododendron bush nearby, its leaves shriveled closed in the cold.

The muscles in Pug's upper arms spasmed as he unsuccessfully tried to envision a softer way to ask what he'd really come for. Then he blurted, "What do you think happened to Mill?"

Lacey paused, evidently thinking through plausible answers. "Lemme say first, I don't know. He didn't have too many enemies. Most of the guys in the mine liked him."

Pug took that as a tacit insinuation from Lacey of foul play.

Lacey continued, "There were some harsh words with the manager down at the Bradshaw tipple where we take our coal for processing. I overheard Mill talking with Gloeda about the tipple not weighing our coal accurately. There's been a new mine inspector, Merritt Lawton, who's got a craw up his ass. He's been assigned to the mines around this area for about three years. Every mine operator in town hates that son of a bitch. But there's a lot of stress everywhere in the coalfields these days. When people's livelihoods are threatened, they can do some ugly things."

"What do you mean?"

"You want the short version or the long one?"

Pug grabbed two nearby lawn chairs, wiped off the film of frost on each and handed one to his employee. "Fill me in."

"Mining got cranked up in these hollows in the early part of the twentieth century, as soon as the railroads arrived. The miners needed the trains to carry off the coal and the trains needed the coal to fuel them. I suspect if these hollows had never had coal in 'em, most of this region would have become a nature preserve; it's that fertile. The coal has been a blessing and a curse.

"When we have wars and booming economies, the country needs more coal and workers flock in. When we have depressions and recessions, people leave. But nothing was like the exodus that began in the 1950s when coal mining became mechanized. I know you know this stuff."

"Yes, but I still want your take on it," Pug insisted.

"I'm an old country preacher. I never get enough of my own voice. Anyway, the population of McDowell County plunged from a high of almost 100,000 people crammed almost toe to toe in these hollows to under 22,000 now. You can imagine how depressing and debilitating that is for the folks left here. The good people, smart kids like yourself, went away to better opportunities. Not many come back. The people who stayed seem to fall into just a few categories. There are the guys and a few women who still mine coal. They make good money as you know."

"Yeah, I was looking at our payroll the other day."

"Then there are the older people who are not financially or emotionally ready to start over somewhere else. Then there are the people who for whatever inexplicable reason have this place in their blood. And at the bottom, Lord strike me down for saying so, are the mentally deficient, the welfare cases and the drug addicts. And there are more of them than you know. War has been written up in national magazines for having the worst prescription drug problems in America."

"How's that?" Pug queried.

"People are addicted to opiates like Oxycontin. People call it 'hillbilly cocaine.' It's a pain killer. It comes in a pill form. I've heard that some of the addicts will heat it in a microwave oven, then freeze it, then grind it into a powder, the microwave it again, and then once it cools, snort it."

The old man sniffled, and then continued, "My grandson died of an overdose. Twelve people die here on average each month. Three-quarters of our kids live in houses with unemployed parents. Kids everywhere seem to be born with optimism, but it gets sucked out of them here by the time they're three or four; you can see it in their eyes.

"There are people around here who make a decent living dealing drugs. Except invariably they get hooked themselves. You can tell the people on it. They look like hell. Their speech is so slurred and incomprehensible they're hard to understand. Our state leads the nation in drug opiate addiction. We lead the nation in obesity, too.

"McDowell is the bottom of the bottom at the bottom

of the state. For fifty years, since Lyndon Johnson's War on Poverty, there have been economic development initiatives brought here. They've all fizzled out, when newcomers got bored, frustrated, or went broke. McDowell County is where anti-poverty programs go to die.

"Our schools can't find teachers to come here. If you were 22-years old and fresh out of Duke or UVA or Ohio State, would you come here? Teachers here are more like social workers than teachers, with so many kids hungry or orphaned. Ain't we got reasons to be proud?" he shrugged.

"Anyway, back to coal. The machinery revolutionized mining. One continuous miner could do the work of fifty men. Back in 1950, there were 40,000 miners in this county and today there are around 1200 and we mine more coal today.

"But as efficient as these machines are, we were still falling behind the productivity of strip mines like they have out in Wyoming. I heard tell there was a railroad train that goes from one of the big strip jobs in the Powder River area of Wyoming to a power plant on the other side of Nebraska every day with 100 or more cars. That one power plant burns 100 railroad cars of coal every day. And there are hundreds of power plants."

Pug took a moment to envision this, but Lacey continued.

"Now we're seeing strip jobs all over the place here in Appalachia. One of the astronauts wrote that they were so big and so many of them now that he can see them from the space station. They aren't as dangerous for the miners, because they basically use giant earth-moving equipment. They sit in their climate-controlled cabs, listening to country music on the CD changer. But real miners take a dim view of those guys. To me, it ain't mining if you don't get dirty.

"In the past few years, the market has really plunged. The tree-huggers want to kill coal because of how dirty it is. The gas drilling guys have some new technologies that are flooding the market with cheap natural gas. Nobody wants our coal, at least not as much. What's a man going to do around here if we can't mine coal?"

"You sound like you really like mining," Pug noted.

Lacey stood up and walked back to his ax. He pulled it from the stump and set a log to split. "I moved away from McDowell County when I was 27. I landed in Cleveland, Ohio. I worked in retail, in construction, and I drove a truck. I even did some reporting for a local newspaper. I hated it there. The weather was stifling in the summer and dismal in the winter. The racism and crime were awful. People were selfish and suspicious of one another. Everybody locked their house; I'd never owned a key to my house before. One time I ran out of gas and it took two hours before anybody stopped to help me, and he was from West Virginia, too. It didn't feel like there was any nature to be seen. I'm a West Virginia boy. I missed these hollows. I had to come home."

Whack!

"Thanks, Lacey. I'll see you Monday."

"Why don't you come to my church tomorrow?"

"Thanks for the invitation. I think I'll pass this time."

"Yeah, 'this time'!" Lacey shrugged. Whack!

Pug got up and walked towards the Sienna. "Lacey?"

"Yeah?"

"Is my brother dead?"

"I don't know, but I suspect so. I'll be praying for him tomorrow. You know, these mountains are like Swiss cheese with all the mines. If a man wants to hide something that will never be found, McDowell County is his kind of place."

Pug put the car in reverse and backed away, then headed back to War.

+ + + + +

Reaching the house, he saw an old, dirty Honda Civic

in the driveway. The rear bumper was dented and dangling three inches lower than it belonged and there was a crack across the front windshield. He remembered that his mother told him company was coming. He found his father seated in the living room across a card table from their visitor.

"Pug," his father wheezed to begin an introduction, not wanting to take too deep a breath before the oxygen in the clear hoses to his nostrils refilled him.

Pug introduced himself, not wishing to wait, "Hi, I'm Lucas Graham."

"Hi, I'm Estell Hazelwood. Folks call me 'Red'." He stood and extended his hand.

The man whose hand Pug shook was a light-complected man with Negro blood, but clearly mixed race, with white hair and white wisps of eyebrows. Pug wondered where the nickname had come from.

"Folks call me 'Pug'. Seems like nobody goes by their real name around here."

Red was of average height and had a slight paunch. He moved a black checker across the board and returned to Pug. "Your dad was my scoutmaster years ago. He took care of me when my dad wasn't really in the picture. We've stayed friends."

Pug remembered that his dad became a scoutmaster when he and Mill were kids, but forgot he'd stayed on to influence other boys as well.

"Where do you live?" Pug asked.

"I'm over in Abbs Valley, in Virginia. I work in Bluefield at the Star Sentinel. We only have two reporters left. How about you?"

Pug told him about moving from Martinsville to help out. "You know my brother Mill is missing?"

"Yes, I wrote a short article about it a week or so after his disappearance. Not much to write about. 'War man disappears. Police have no clues.' Do you know if there's anything new on the case?"

"No. I spoke with the sheriff over in Welch a few days after I got here. They have it in their files, but they don't really have staff to look into it."

"You didn't hear me say this, but unless your brother magically reappears, he'll never be found and nobody will ever be held responsible. Welcome back to Southern West Virginia."

Pug walked to the thermostat and turned it down from 74F to 70F. He heard the furnace kick off. "You want some tea, Red? Sweet?"

"Sure. Sweet."

Pug returned from the kitchen with two glasses, one for Red and one for his father. Then he got a third for himself.

"Where's mother?" he asked his dad.

"Out."

Red said, "She left an hour ago. She said she was going to a friend's house, Claudia Wilmer, I think."

Making conversation, Pug said, "How's the newspaper business?"

"Sucks. Journalism is dead in America, at least local journalism. Circulation is down, readership is down. Everybody is getting their news on the Internet or Fox TV. The big newspapers are in trouble all over the country. Nobody's doing any real investigative reporting. We're barely hanging on. I've had my benefits cut until there's almost nothing left. My pay is the same thing I was making 15 years ago and I have to buy my own gas to report on a story. This area used to be in our coverage area, but we don't even technically have a reporter covering it."

"Lemme ask you... I noticed a CB radio antenna on your car."

"Yeah, your dad got me interested when I was a kid. Taught me all kinds of neat things. "

"Dad got me into radio, too. I was poking through the

attic last week – I'm trying to get a handle on what dad will leave behind when he passes – and there were lots of old radios. Let me show you what I found."

He walked into his bedroom and emerged with an Astatic Power D-104.

"That's an old set, on 27 MHz as I recall," Red said. "A friend in Bluefield has one, too. He showed me something interesting; you can reverse the channels and that lets you talk on the receive channel and receive on the talk channel. Your messages aren't encrypted, but nobody thinks to listen there so it's pretty private. Most new CB radios are channelized but in the old days, you could switch them. Old hunters used to do this. They'd switch the send crystal with the receive crystal, and then they could discuss where the prey was without being detected.

"We had a lot of fun with them," Red reminisced. "There's no privacy in our world any more, but we could talk with each other and know nobody was ever listening." He moved another checker and then walked outside. When he returned a moment later, he held another radio. "Do you mind," he asked Pug, taking his radio from him. With a screwdriver he had on his key-chain, he opened a cover on the radio and he switched the position of two wires. He turned on both radios and spoke into his. The voice came through on Pug's. "Don't bother with a phone; call me here if you ever need anything."

+ + + + +

Meredith Goldschmidt drove back into the capitol city in the late afternoon. Traffic was lighter than usual given the holiday break. Her plan was to visit Arnie at the hospital, but she was drawn to the National Cemetery across the Potomac in Virginia in Arlington. She walked to her father's grave in a driving, chilling rain. He had been a decorated airman in World War II and was honored by his country to have his final resting place in the most revered of burial grounds. His heroism had always inspired her, and throughout her life while she constantly strove for excellence, her quests were always more motivated from the fire that burned in her own viscera than from any exhortations from him. But she knew where the pride had come from. She spoke aloud and openly to his tombstone, finding comfort in the only true friend, or so it seemed at that moment, in this angry, suspicious, cutthroat city.

She drove to Sibley Memorial to see Arnie. Again, his condition remained the same. Her thoughts were not with him, but instead with the parents and friends of the dead mistress. But she would not seek them out. What possible words of comfort could she give them? Scenarios played out in her head:

"I'm sorry my husband killed your daughter."

"I'm sorry my husband impregnated your daughter."

"I'm sorry your daughter had her mouth..."

She stormed out of his room, determined not to visit again until he regained consciousness, if ever. Bastard!

DEC 28 Saturday

After breakfast, Pug's mother reminded him that he'd promised to replace the ribbon in her typewriter, so he walked into the den where he found the machine sitting atop what used to be his father's desk. There was a piece of paper in it where the type had become so dim that he could barely read it. He took the new ribbon cartridge and attempted to place it in the holder, but realized that it was incompatible. In the bottom desk drawer, he rooted through some miscellanea until he found an unopened box that contained another cartridge, still wrapped in cellophane. It had a price tag marked "Piggly-Wiggly $0.39". He checked the compatibility and was delighted it fit, knowing the difficulty he'd have finding another for such a dated machine.

While installing it, he noticed a pile of typewritten sheets, which were evidently his mother's work. She walked in as he was completing the ribbon installation. "What's all this, mom?"

"I've been typing away the past few months. It's sort of a personal history. Sort of a community history. I started when your dad became more incapacitated and I couldn't get out and about as much. I didn't think I had much to say, but as I really started into it, the dam sort of broke. Every few nights I'd spend a few hours on it. I'd like to do some more tonight, with that new ribbon."

"Do you mind if I read it?" he asked.

"Oh, not just yet." She pushed her wire-rim bifocals back up her nose. "I'm not real confident with my writing. Maybe when I finish. Or when I pass."

Pug knew she was being modest. She had been a librarian and knew what good writing was. She was probably better than she was letting on.

"Let me make some more progress. I'll share it with you someday, I promise."

"I look forward to it," he noted. "Say, Mom, do you know if Mill's 4-wheeler is still around?"

"I imagine it's right where he left it, in the shed beside his house."

"I'd like to take a ride."

"We have keys to his house and his car on the peg by the back door. A week after he disappeared, I turned off his water and gas and emptied his refrigerator. I suspect if you root around, you'll find a key to it."

Pug packed a paper sack with some snacks and a couple of plastic bottles of water. Then he walked up the hill behind the house to Mill's small home, a mobile home. Letting himself inside, he was spooked by how quiet it was. Everything was apparently just as Mill had left it the day he disappeared. He picked up a couple of invoices from the kitchen table and made a mental note to share them with Gloeda. On a hook by the door, he found a key to the padlock on the shed. The 4-wheeler's key was in the ignition. He turned it, hit the starter, and the machine rumbled to life. He stashed his lunch under the dashboard and backed it out. He closed the door, and then headed down the hill into War. He thought for a moment about whether it was legal to drive an unlicensed vehicle in the road, but had seen several other 4-wheelers being driven on the highways and convinced himself it would be fine. He filled the tank with regular at the Hillbilly Mart, where he paid in cash to an androgynous clerk who was so morbidly obese as to be unable to stand from the reinforced wooden stool with an old pillow duct-taped to it.

He drove past the City Hall which was housed in a former railroad depot. A large green sign with white letters was tacked beside the front door, "CITY OF WAR". On the other side was another sign containing the Ten Commandments, municipal admonishments to the townspeople of one of America's poorest places.

He turned on the road to Warriormine and then past William Pokey Hill Road, and found a jeep trail he remembered as a boy. He passed the skeletal remains of several homes, now deeply engulfed by foliage. He marveled at the choking fecundity of the area, knowing the rapidity with which garden crops grew in the nutrient-rich ebony soil. He remembered the potatoes in a wicker basket, bigger than any he'd ever seen in the supermarkets, sitting in the outdoor closet behind his parents' house unwashed with black dirt clinging to the skin.

One house had a collapsed roof and a tree as big around as his thigh growing through it. Another had a porch laden with rubbish, including an old hand-cranked washer and piles of automobile tires. The thought swept through his mind that antique hunters would probably be mining this area decades after the coal all played out. Tiles of vinyl siding lay loose from the exterior wall and sheets of fiberglass insulation flapped in the gentle breeze. All the windows were broken. A car battery lay on its side, leaking its toxic stew of chemicals into the groundwater.

As he climbed higher, the road became increasingly narrow and rutted. He slowed to walking speed as the machine angled steeply upwards. It was bumpy but fun. He was amazed at the steepness the machine could climb. Several other dirt roads snaked off in various directions, the whole mountainside seemingly having been traced by bulldozers, as if by ants in an ant farm.

Nearing the top, he saw a pumpjack well pump gently rocking back and forth, pumping natural gas to a waiting pipe. The walking beam rocked slowly, rhythmically, and reminded him of the teeter-totter at the school playground he used to enjoy so much as a child, swinging up and down with Mill or another friend on the far end. He watched for a few moments, and then kept driving.

He saw a wooden sign tacked to a tree that had carved into it, "Ross Semetary" and the misspelling caused him to chuckle under his breath. He parked the Kawasaki and walked an overgrown trail 50 feet from the main jeep trail to a clearing where several dozen headstones poked above the abundant, lush foliage. He walked among them, finding the markings on most already eroded away. He almost missed a row of fifteen or so makeshift tombstones, really only slate rocks, some still vertical and some fallen over. He could read a few inscriptions. None marked anyone who had lived for more than two years; these were the eternal markers of the family's infant deaths. The largest stone had inscribed, "Wilgus Earl Ross, Born May 12, 1904, Died February 4, 1968. God is good."

He felt guilty that he might be standing over a grave, but they were tightly packed and generally strewn about making avoiding them impossible. He walked back to the Kawasaki and motored on.

He came to an area where clearly people had parked 4-wheelers before. He parked his and walked to the south to the edge of a cliff face. There was a grand view into the chasm below. He could see the main highway from the south, SR-16, snaking up the forest-clad canyon. A car made its way along, looking slow in the distance. There was little to look at besides the highway, a ribbon of rail, and below everything a creek. Three buzzards rode thermals below his elevation. It was beautiful in a stark, austere way, the brown forests and leafless trees.

His gaze shifted to his same level, where the mountainsides were remarkably consistent in height. He remembered from his college geology class that these mountains weren't really mountains at all, but the remnants of an eroded plateau. The layers of rock, interspersed with layers of organic material, had been laid down in successive layers only to be carved into these narrow hollows and chasms in the most recent geological upwelling.

It was a chilly day, 45F he guessed, but the sun shining on the southern-facing cliff made it seem warm and not uncomfortable. He gave up smoking years earlier, but picked up an open pack at Mill's house and he lit one, hoping it would ease his anxiety.

The situation that confronted him filled his soul with torment.

His father seemed to be nearing the end of his earthly journey. His father had always considered Mill to be the favored son. Pug always tried to do his best, but it never seemed like enough. Pug told himself that his return to War was heroic, helping his mom and trying to solve his brother's disappearance and mining company problems. But it seemed like a retreat, a surrender to the forces against him. His college degree brought him increasingly diminishing career opportunities. His personal life was hollow and unproductive. He had no hobbies and did no charity work.

Worst of all, everyone around him was, at best, worried, and at worst filled with detestation and loathing. Zola had endured a life of pain which didn't seem likely to abate. He puzzled over her angst, but realized he felt a greater sympathy for her positions now than he might have earlier in his adult life. He had grown up with a conservative bent, buying into the myth of personal responsibility, that everyone had the opportunity to better himself or herself. That notion had been steadily annihilated through his experiences in Martinsville, where he watched countless friends' lives be ruined by the forces of unchecked corporatism. He had watched several corporations close their plants, staffed by hard-working, honest, loyal and dedicated people who were demoralized emotionally and fiscally. One plant had achieved the highest level of productivity in its 72-year history the year before it was shuttered, then dismantled, and then demolished. Martinsville had the same shuttered stores and empty houses as War. But War was physically more depressing, drearier, more choked with almost jungle-like vegetation, and had more of a craniated, inside-the-earth feel.

He flicked the expired but still lit cigarette over the cliff.

Making matters even worse, one of his employees, and by the nature of a small business' relationship between owner and worker a friend, was grieving over the death of his family. And the company mine was apparently in dire financial straits in ways he was yet to fully grasp.

A jet stream stretched across the sky above him, its contrail left by what he envisioned as a corporate jet, filled with executives and Wall Street brokers on their way to vacations in Cancun or Waikiki or the Maldives. He seethed with discontent and loathing.

He drove the Kawasaki back into town and parked it like a car in front of the War Room Café, finding Zola at

the same booth where he met her before. He invited himself
to join her, and then chatted about his discontent until she
interrupted him with her own musings.

"We live now in a sacrifice zone," she claimed.

"What do you mean?"

"The state of West Virginia has been completely sold to
corporate America. Corporations don't care about people.
They don't care about nature. To them, there is nothing of
intrinsic value, like a free-flowing stream, a songbird, or a
scenic vista. Everything is fair game to being overwhelmed
and consumed. There is a constant and deliberate effort by
the coal companies to create a permanent underclass, so
distressed as to treat a job, any job regardless how menial,
poorly paid, and inconsequential, as something to be coveted
and fought for. Labor unions were places where oppressed
people could collectively bargain and petition for better
treatment. But they've been annihilated and now people sulk
alone in their homes eking out a meager existence, making
money selling drugs or scavenging things."

She put a bookmark in her book and set it down. Then
she continued, "For things like textiles, the corporations
moved the jobs to the lowest workers on the planet, people
who historically have no power and no history of the quest
for it. Here in the coalfields, the corporations employ
tactics like mountaintop removal mining that fulfills several
objectives. It destroys the landscape permanently. It reduces
the workforce. It impoverishes the residents because it
destroys any equity they may have. Then when the coal is
played out, the workers themselves are cast aside and a
spoiled landscape is left behind, unable to sustain anybody.
Wholesale destruction of entire landscapes and ecosystems
has become commonplace and accepted."

She lit a cigarette, blew some smoke out of the side of her
mouth, and coughed.

"Our politicians are owned by the coal companies. The

media is owned by the corporations. The media never comes to tell the rest of the nation what's going on here. They feed us the most inconsequential, trivial bullshit masquerading as 'news'. When I was younger, universities were the sources of free, spirited thought. They have been de-funded by the states and the professors scrap for corporate support, teaching the kids only what the corporations want taught. The kids are learning to be little capitalists, desperate to fall in line, get in debt, and become slaves to the system themselves."

He said, "When I was in Martinsville and corporate America was destroying that city, I could see that most people, even those affected, were passive and largely oblivious to the causes of their misery. They're only interested in their next tattoo and smart phone. Huge swaths of formerly industrial cities are abandoned to vandalism and decay and nobody on Wall Street seems to care. The assault on our middle and lower classes doesn't seem to matter to them."

"Yeah," she agreed. "The saddest thing is that even people who are paying attention and understand the encroachment of corporate dominance somehow think the destruction will stay isolated, confined to various places around the country like here. They have no idea. It is a plague and it will never stop until everything is consumed. I'm surprised the mining companies aren't mining the Grand Canyon."

He said, "I figure it's only because they haven't found anything there they want yet."

She coughed and nodded in agreement.

He wished her well, finished his coffee and departed.

DEC 29 Sunday

Pug awoke to a breakfast of white toast and grape jelly washed down by black coffee, prepared by his mother as she flitted about, getting Emmett situated before she departed for church. Pug didn't want to go, but his mother's insistence was palpable although unspoken.

Sitting inside the church beside his mother, watching the eager acknowledgements of other parishioners, sent him back into the reflection on the cliff from the day before. He had seen in Martinsville how the former employees of destroyed companies never wavered in their religious beliefs, no matter how dire the situation inflicted upon them became. Whatever happened, for better or worse, was God's will.

An exultation of preacher Karwoski, a man as old as Pug's father, interrupted his reverie with his dramatic changes in pitch and emphasis. "And another year is set to pass, a year of blessings of the Lord, and the hope of eternal life beside Jesus Christ! Our struggles are mere practice for the days of reckoning. How can faith give you a blessed New Year? How can the coal that awaits our extraction bring us renewed prosperity? In the same way saints of old were blessed, in their unwavering faith of salvation, the gift of our great and merciful savior, Lord Jesus Christ, who grants us the mercy of God forevermore."

Pug's mind filled with illusions and abstractions, images of holy ghosts and winged angels, images reinforced by the murals and stained glass panels of his church in Martinsville which was substantially more ornate and opulent than this poor, tiny sanctuary in War. His concentration was lost and he squirmed on the uncomfortable wooden pew in the dim, poorly heated room.

He returned home with his mother and they found his father, slumped and asleep in his motorized chair. Pug sat across from him, staring curiously at his wrinkled face and features that mirrored so many of Pug's own. His father's bald head had unsightly moles and discolored splotches, punctuated by defiant strands of individual hairs. Pug realized, through his closest kin, his own mortality, a thought that startled him.

Suddenly, his father's head shook as if banishing a bad

dream. His eyes opened, looking clearer to Pug than he'd seen since he'd arrived.

"How was church, son?" Emmett whispered.

"Fine, dad. How are you doing?"

"I had a little nap. I enjoy my naps. (Cough.) In my dreams, I'm still a young man, sometimes a child. I remember when my legs were strong and I could breathe freely, without (Cough.) so much pain."

"You sound good, dad."

"(Cough.) You're kind to say so, but I don't have much time left. I'm ready to join my maker." He smiled, showing yellowed teeth. He had patches of stubble where his mother's shaving of him hadn't gone well.

"Son," he continued. "I was harder on you than I should have been. (Cough.)"

"Dad."

"Let me finish. My father was an absolute dictator, a real jerk. I was determined when Millard and you were born to be a better father. But I'm not sure I ever was."

"You did fine, dad."

His father's eyes drifted shut and he fell back to sleep.

DEC 30 Monday

The next morning, a Monday, Pug set his alarm and woke before sunrise, wanting to be the first person to arrive for the daily shift at the mine. He wasn't sure whether the Getgood twins would report for work, but he wanted to speak with the others.

The Getgood twins did in fact arrive, earlier than most. Pug asked everyone to gather for an informal company meeting before donning their mining overalls, boots, helmets, and other gear. He expressed his wish that they had a good Christmas, notwithstanding of the tragedy that befell Ronnie. He mentioned financial difficulties, on which he was trying to get a handle. Curtis Sparks, a miner Pug didn't know well but everybody called, "Mousie," said, "They're g-g-gonna shut us d-d-down, aren't they?"

"Who?" Pug asked with sincere curiosity.

"The EPA. The F-F-Feds. Whoever r-r-r-regulates mining at the g-government."

"I don't know," Pug replied, earnestly. "We seem to be getting more than our share of fines lately. I don't know if the feds are cracking down on coal mining in general or if we just have an asshole inspector."

Mousie was a young guy, filled with piss and vinegar. "My daddy tells m-m-me that in his day, n-n-nothing was regulated."

Lacey said parentally, "Yeah, but we lost thousands of miners every year in accidents. And everybody had black lung."

Mousie said, "When I went to the d-d-doctor last time, I read an article that said black lung d-d-deaths were increasing anyway. N-N-Nobody gives a sh-shit about us m-miners."

Pug said, "I watched the president speak the other night at a campaign rally. His energy policy is 'discover, dig, drill, and de-regulate'. So maybe things will get easier for us."

"Easier?" observed Lacey. "Hell, nothin' ever gets easier for coal miners of West Virginia. We're a forgotten, forsaken species."

Pug told them that they'd be working all day and then a half-day the following day, New Year's Eve, then off on that Wednesday, and then back on Thursday and Friday.

"Let's get to work, shall we men?" Pug instructed. "Donnie, you and Ronnie hold up a minute. Everybody else, go on inside."

The men gathered their gear and shuffled into the carts that would take them into the mine.

"It's fukkin sick, is what it is," Donnie sighed to Ronnie and Pug after the others had left.

"What he's sayin' is..." Ronnie began.

"My baby and my wife, they never needed dying." Donnie said. "Somebody's gonna pay."

"Have the authorities come by to speak with you?" Pug asked.

"Fuck no," Donnie yelled. "What authorities?"

"We figured somebody would come by sometime to see, to see Donnie," Ronnie clipped an electrical cord to his headlamp.

"I guess I did, too," Pug agreed. "Come the first of the year, I'll make some phone calls."

"I'm 'bout to explode," Donnie shouted.

"He's gonna explode," Ronnie seconded. "He's gonna kill somebody. I might just kill somebody, too. We do everything together, most things anyway."

"You two feel like working today?"

"Hell, yeah," they both said, almost in unison. Donnie, "Maybe taking chunks out of this mountain will soothe my nerves."

Pug spent much of the afternoon trying to install a new set of brushes and a winding on the back-up stepper motor for the conveyer. To finish the job, he needed to drive to Beckley for some parts. It took almost four hours to drive there and back on winding Route 16. When he returned, he entered the office to find a man he didn't recognize. The man was in his late thirties, tall and overweight, with a crew-cut and what appeared to be a perpetual sneer. He spoke first, saying, "You must be Lucas."

"Who the hell are you?" Pug demanded, angered by the impertinence of the man before him in his own office.

"Lawton. Merritt Lee Lawton. Federal Mining inspector. Pleased to make your acquaintance."

"I wish it was mutual," sneered Pug.

"You'd best not be so hostile. You'll be seeing lots more of me. I'm in charge of mine inspections here in McDowell and Wyoming Counties. I found seven infractions today. I've just finished the paperwork." He handed Pug a thin stack of papers. "Your fines are detailed. They're payable at the courthouse in Welch within ten days. But I'll be back within seven to make sure you've corrected them. Good afternoon." He walked out the trailer door, leaving it for Pug to close against the cold.

Gloeda, who had been watching the exchange, said, "That's the way it works, Pug. Inspectors come any time they want, without notice. They find anything wrong they can. You can fight these in court, but you'll lose."

Pug looked through the pages. "Violation section 33:12: Leaking oil from differential cover on continuous miner #221. $821." "Violation section 10:42: Missing screws over electrical box cover on rooftop bolter #19. $532." "Violation section 4:21: Inadequate limestone dusting on wall in corridor 43B. $392." There were seven sheets, totaling $3920.

"Shit," Pug said. "What right does he have to do that?"

"Every right," she said. "Like I said, you can fight it, but you'll lose. I work for lots of small mines around the area, and this one is as clean as any, but Lawton seems to really sock this one with fines."

"Why do you think that is?"

"If I didn't know better, I'd think he was trying to run you out," she said. "He and Mill constantly banged heads."

Pug and Gloeda decided they would sit down after New Years to see where they could scrape together the money to pay the fines.

DEC 31 Tuesday

The men at Graham Mining worked only a half-day on New Year's Eve. When the guys began departing for home, Lacey said to Pug, "Follow me home, would ya? I've got something for you."

Pug drove the Sienna down the mountain behind Lacey's Chevy S-10 pickup. At Lacey's house, he parked and Lacey motioned him inside. It was raining steadily, with a temperature just above freezing.

"I don't envy your position," Lacey said bluntly. "I wasn't born yesterday and things don't look good at the mine right now. I don't see the books, but I can tell. Listen," the older man continued, "here's a bottle of whiskey. I was going to give it to your brother around Christmas. Somebody gave it to me years ago, but I don't drink no more." He brushed some dust from the top.

"Thanks. You said something the other day when we talked..." Pug began.

"It's over for us, us miners in West Virginia," Lacey asserted, leaving Pug wondering what Lacey thought Pug was implying. "We've always been pawns in the rich man's game. It's like that everywhere, from the silver mines in Bolivia to the gold mines in Australia to the diamond mines in Africa: the owners are kings and the miners are slaves. We've produced more coal in McDowell County than any county east of the Mississippi, and yet we're by far the poorest county in the second poorest state in the nation. Why do you think that is?"

As Pug scrambled to answer his question, Lacey continued, "It's because coal has made us poor. In the 1920s, people came from all over the world to work underground mining coal. It was a great equalizer, blacks and whites. It was one of the only places in the country where a black man could make the same wage as a white man for the same work. Since then, working conditions have improved all across the country, except here. Here we're still slaves. The money is good, at least for those of us who have jobs. But everybody is sick.

"I watched my granddaughter die a few years ago. She was three. She had stomach cancer. Three years old! We sat by her bedside at the Cincinnati Children's Hospital for two weeks before she passed. There were tubes running into her carrying chemotherapy poison. She had no hair. She had the cutest smile. There is nothing sadder than losing a child. I can't tell you how much we cried. I almost lost my faith in the Lord. Then I realized it wasn't the Lord's fault. It was the coal companies that killed her.

"For decades, everybody who ever worked underground in coal died prematurely. But now, everybody else dies prematurely, too, with all the pollution. Every family on my street has somebody with cancer or some digestive disease. One woman on my street died last year from pancreatic cancer. She was 46. Another girl at my church died with uterine cancer. She was 29 and had two children.

"We had a baby born a year or so ago who had deformed genitals. Another baby was born with most of her digestive system deformed. She only lived for a few days. Some of the streams around here run orange. I tell you, pollution kills people. For the coal companies, it is nothing more than numbers on a spreadsheet.

"When I was a boy, like I was saying, there were 100,000 people crammed into these hollows. But you know what? We still had some nature. There were raccoons and bobcats and squirrels. There was deer and bears. We could do subsurface mines and if we followed the rules, we could limit the damage. The new mines, they're strip jobs, mountaintop removal mines, and the destruction is complete. People call them moonscapes, but that's hardly a strong enough description. Do you know that when a bobcat is chased from its territory, it's dead? Cats are territorial and the next bobcat isn't just going to share. The bears are the same way. We see a lot more bears in town, rooting through the garbage and killing pets because we've run them out of the mountains. A bear needs fifty acres to feed.

"The mountains were wild with fruit, blackberries and

gooseberries. People had apple trees and there was more apples in the fall than anybody could eat.

"These strip jobs are huge! That's their vision of West Virginia. Our state used to be a sea of green. Now it's like zits on a teenager's face. The Bible tells us we have dominion over the earth, over the fish of the seas, and the birds and the livestock. But God never wanted us to ruin everything so completely."

Pug was surprised that a lifelong miner would be opposed to mining, but understood that it was only about strip mining.

"Nothing is going to improve. Our state government is totally in bed with the big corporate mining operations. And the President is no better; neither is the Vice President. I can't even describe that seething pile of bovine excrement."

Pug thought back to what Zola had told him, much the same stuff.

Lacey was on a roll, "In my daddy's day, the companies took care of everything. For better or worse, they built completely dependent societies. They paved the streets; they built the water plants and the water lines. They built the schoolyard ball fields. Then there was some point, I can't really put my finger on it, when they stopped caring. They stopped maintaining things. They let the water plant deteriorate. They stopped re-paving the streets. They stopped building ball fields and basketball courts. Everything is about the money now.

"Life expectancy in Southern West Virginia is lower than almost any place in the country. People are poorer. A shameful number are addicts and we see overdoses all the time.

"Employees are the costliest part of any business, and the coal companies need fewer employees to do strip jobs than you need for an underground mine, production tonnage being equal. You know, over half as many people work for Wal-Mart in West Virginia today as in underground coal mining. Yet you'd think coal ruled the world. Anybody who talks about monitoring or regulating mining operations is demonized. A 'war on coal'. You tell me what sense that makes. It's like a 'war on terror'. Terror is a tactic. How can we have a war against a tactic? Coal is a rock. How can anybody wage a war against a rock?

"The coal companies are buying out everything. They already own over 90% of the land in this county. Even the people who do own their own house often don't own the ground underneath it. The coal companies, if they can't buy people out, they'll run them out. Can you imagine living under the specter of a rock fall, like the Getgood boys? There's blasting going on all the time. Chimneys crack and separate from the walls. Pictures fall off walls. Dust settles on everything. People have to breathe it. The streams and wells are polluted and nobody can drink anything but bottled water. Kids get sick at the elementary school when they play outside. Children get cancers of the lungs and the brain. If you had a family, would you want to raise your kids here? You're lucky you got out when you did. More left than stayed.

"Did you know there's a community, Lundy, up in Boone County that Bessie Energy flat-out destroyed? They came to town and told the residents that they were going to strip-mine the mountain above town and everybody had to leave. They didn't want any residents left when they destroyed everything in sight."

"Can a private company do that?" Pug asked, incredulously.

"Not legally, but yeah. They offered what they considered a fair market value for the homes, which of course is well less than the residents needed to find another home somewhere else. You tell me what a fair market value is for a home in a community where nobody wants to live. Anybody who refused could stay, but Bessie told them they would make their lives a living hell. Only a few stayed. Bessie said they were doing the residents a favor by buying them out before they destroyed everything–the buyout was 'protecting them'.

One resident was packing up to move out and she died on the front porch of the house. The medical examiner called it a heart attack, but everybody knowed it was a broken heart.

"But you know what? They've done killed themselves, the coal companies. The cost of doing cleanup and remediation has made coal more expensive and they have massive obligations, assuming they're ever forced to live up to them. They have even greater obligations to retired miners on their pensions. Do you know what they do?"

"No. What?"

"They merge with other coal companies, then they gather all the obligations together and spin them off into a new company, then they let that company go out of business so they don't need to pay anybody anything. So all those ruined lands and all those retirees need to be taken care of by taxpayers.

"The best, easiest coal to mine was taken out of here decades ago. Now, natural gas is getting cheaper all the time. More electricity is made now from natural gas in this country than from coal. The coal companies have demonized anybody who stands in their way, but their real enemy is technology. Time has marched on but they're stuck living in the past. No wonder everybody is so angry."

"Speaking of angry," Pug said, "what do you think of the Getgood boys?"

"They've tried to be good boys, all their lives. But I knew their pappy. Let's just say they haven't had much in the way of good role models."

"Are they dangerous?"

"Right now, I think everyone is dangerous. People can only deal with so much abuse."

On that note, Pug thanked Lacey again for the gift. "Happy New Year to you."

"Likewise."

Pug walked back to his car. The rain of the morning had

intensified, and the ground was soggy under his feet.

+ + + + +

On this and the prior several days, Meredith had stayed home from the office. Washington was a ghost town, as many legislators and their aides had gone to their districts for the holidays. It had been several days since she'd gone to the hospital. There had been no calls from anyone at Sibley, which she took to mean that there was nothing to report. But on New Year's Eve, she went anyway, just before dinner time. She found Arnie's condition substantively unchanged. She sat by his bedside for an hour, mesmerized by the flickering colored lights strung alongside the building outside the window.

She became increasingly revolted by his presence, her heart filling with hatred. She took one last look at him and left, deciding that she never wanted to see him again.

+ + + + +

That evening, Pug sat up with his parents in their living room, planning to watch the traditional ball drop at Times Square in New York City on television. He and his dad played checkers, but his dad's breathing seemed particularly labored. Pug must have dozed off himself and he awoke to the sound of cheering coming from the TV. He glanced over to his mother. Her head bobbed gently and he could hear her snoring, although she'd not removed her glasses. Then he saw that his dad's head had slumped over into the cushioned wing of his upholstered chair. His eyes were open but pale and blank in expression. He neither moved nor was breathing. Pug reached across the card table for his father's wrist where he checked for a pulse, unsuccessfully. On their television screen, the ball reached the bottom, fireworks went off, and the crowd erupted in cheers.

Pug went into the kitchen pantry where he found a plastic sheet that he thought his mother used to cover the kitchen table when peeling apples. He took it into the living room and spread it on the floor near the bookcase. He removed the breathing tubes from his father's nostrils and shut the valve on the oxygen tank. He lifted his father's body from the chair and placed it gently on the plastic sheet. He went into his parent's bedroom and found a blanket in the closet which he used to cover the body. Then he woke his mother with a gentle nudge. "Mom."

"Oh, honey, I must have dozed off. Did I miss the New Year?"

"It was a few minutes ago. Mom, Papa died." He pointed at the blanket-covered body.

She placed her hand over her mouth and surveyed the scene. She took Pug's hand between her own. Hers were bony, with wrinkled skin, and were cold to his touch.

"It's okay, Lucas. Please help me up. I'd best be getting to bed." He walked with his mother into the bathroom and he handed her her nightgown from the hook behind the bedroom door. Once she was done, he prepared himself for bed as well.

Part 3

JAN 1, Wednesday

ON THIS NEW YEAR'S DAY, Pug awoke with a hangover not of alcohol but of the pall of death. It was still dark outside, but he walked into the living room where his father's corpse lay. He had left a light on overnight, but he turned it off, hoping it would help him contemplate the day. It was New Year's Day, January 1, a traditional day of new beginnings. His father was dead. His brother was presumed dead. Rain continued to fall, streaking the windows.

His reverie was shaken by a light rapping at the front door. At first, he doubted whether he'd actually heard anything at all. He turned the light back on and went to the door. Opening it, he found a wet figure standing in the rain.

"Please, Zola, come in." As she entered and unwrapped the wet woolen scarf from her bald head, he said, "What brings you here at this hour."

"Premonition," she said succinctly. "I have premonitions when it rains like this. There is death here. What has happened?"

"My father. He died just before midnight last night." He pointed at the body.

She gave him a loose hug, resting her bald head against his cheek. "I'm sorry."

"We all knew it was coming."

"What's next?"

"I don't know. I don't know if Lansing Turner will be at his funeral home today or not. I figured I'd wait until at least 9:00 a.m. to give him a call."

He went into the kitchen to heat some water for coffee.

She followed and sat in one of the metal-framed Naugahyde chairs. At her encouragement, he told her some of the stories from his childhood, of his father first taking him into the mines, of scouting and hunting. Her presence soothed him and her insistence on him telling stories of his youth made him feel better about his father's passing.

Once his mother awoke and joined Pug and Zola, conversation continued with reminiscences of Emmett Graham. The rest of the day was a blur to Pug, as staff from Turner's Funeral Home came to carry the body away for embalming and Turner himself came later for signatures on the death certificate.

JAN 2, Thursday

Pug and his mother had breakfast together quietly. She fixed him ham and eggs, with onions and Velveeta, which he always liked. They agreed to go to the funeral home to make some arrangements with Lansing Turner. The visitation would be that same evening, at 6:00 p.m. with the funeral the following day, Friday January 3, commencing at 10:00 a.m. at the town cemetery. There wasn't much in the way of formal announcements, with there being no newspaper or radio stations anywhere nearby, but the community had long employed informal communication networks for spreading important news like obituaries.

Pug took his mother home and dropped her off. He put on work clothes and made his way to the mine. He took one of the low-slung carts inside and found Donnie and Ronnie working together on the roof-bolter. He watched them work for several minutes oblivious to his presence. Ronnie operated the controls to the machine. It had a large, electric-drill like chuck that held a foot-long drill pointed upwards. Under his controls, the bit spun and while the chuck moved upwards, drilling a hole in the rock on the ceiling of the mine. As the chuck reached within an inch of the ceiling, he lowered it to the ground. The chuck and drill stopped spinning and Ronnie loosened the chuck and removed the drill bit. Then he placed an extension rod between the drill bit and the chuck, then raised the chuck again to the ceiling. He repeated this maneuver 5 times until the hole was approximately 5-feet deep. Then, he shoved a bolt, a piece of steel looking like rebar into the hole, bending it by hand as he inserted it as it was longer than the height of the mine. Along with the bolt, he shoved into a hole a long, rubber balloon-like sheathing which contained two compartments, one each holding resin and hardener, the compartments being split and the materials being allowed to mix as the bolt was spun, again by the chuck. Then, at the bottom, the exposed end of the bolt was affixed to a steel plate with a hole in the middle, set flush with the roof rock material. All of this work was done while Ronnie was essentially laying on his side because the roof was so low. Donnie stayed nearby to assist, handing Ronnie materials as he needed them. The work seemed extremely strenuous. The twins traded positions every half-dozen bolts so neither man became overly fatigued.

When they took a break, the three men spoke and shared condolences about the recent deaths in both families. Then Donnie said to Pug, "I've been thinking a lot about your brother."

"Yeah?"

"I don't think..." Donnie began.

"None of us think," his twin interrupted, "that he's still alive."

"That's kinda been my conclusion," Pug sniffled. "Y'all have any ideas?"

"Our mines have always been tightly inspected," Donnie said, wiping some dust from his eyes with a dirty handkerchief. "But I was talking with Gloeda. She said fines have gone up. This new mine inspector, Merritt Lawton, is a horse's ass.

Mill had said some pretty nasty things about him after his last couple of inspections."

"Yeah, he was still here when I got back from Beckley the other day."

"He's a snarly character," said Ronnie. "Reminds me of a copperhead. He's a punk. Seems like he grew up angry. When he got some power he decided to take it out on everybody else."

Donnie, "I've never seen him smile."

"Do you think he's responsible for Mill's disappearance?" Pug said sarcastically.

"Hard to say," Donnie chimed.

"Hard," Ronnie agreed. "But it wouldn't surprise me."

Pug walked, bent over with his helmet scraping the ceiling, over to where the other guys were working. Each expressed sympathies about Pug's father's death. The continuous mining machine was stopped because the conveyer system that carried the coal from the mine became jammed. Pug worked with his men to clear the jam and production was restored.

That evening, he ate supper with his mother before walking her to his car in the continuing rain to drive her to the funeral home. It was a cold, wet, dreary night and he held a large umbrella for her and steered her around the mud puddles as she entered the passenger seat.

Approaching the funeral home, he thought it looked like the most profitable business in town. Inside, he and she stood abreast near the open casket where his father lay, eyes glued shut, with rouge making his wrinkled face look younger and more vital. Pug sensed some unfamiliarity with his father's face, seeing it for the first time in years without breathing hoses bringing oxygen to its nostrils.

A line of perhaps 35 people total came to pay their last respects, including all of Graham Mining's employees and several spouses. The experience was a blur to Pug, with spatters of remembrances and long, familiar faces. He was embarrassed on several occasions when people recognized him but he couldn't place them at all, as if he'd been living in a separate reality for decades.

Ronnie and Donnie, the identical twins.

Lacey. And his wife – couldn't remember her name.

Gloeda Spangler. "I always liked your father. He was a kind man; a good man."

Zola Wilkerson. "I'm so sorry for your loss, Pug."

"It was his time, Zola," Pug said.

"He suffered for so long," said a man who looked close to death's doorstep himself.

Red Hazelwood. "I'm glad I had a chance to see him that one last time."

Mousie Sparks. "He was the b-b-best b-b-boss I ever ha-ha-had."

Pug thought he heard someone in the line talk about possible flooding, something that happened too often in these narrow hollows. Somebody said something about the Upper Horsepen impoundment dams on Horsepen Creek, near the strip mine at the state line. Pug was distracted by a visitor and never could determine exactly what was said about it or who said it.

JAN 3 Friday

Pug was awoken by the ringing telephone at 7:27 a.m. "Hello?"

"Pug, it's Lansing Turner. We've got the grave dug and a canopy and some chairs set up at the cemetery. It's still raining pretty hard. You want to postpone the burial?"

"Is the rain a problem?"

"Not other than discomfort for your mourners. And some folks get upset when we lay a coffin into a hole with a pool of water in it."

"What's the weather forecast for the next few days?"

"As you know, Hurricane Thad has stalled over central North Carolina and that's why we've seen all this rain over the past few days. According to the reports I've seen, it's going to get worse, at least until Monday or Tuesday. Can you imagine? We never used to have hurricanes this late in the year."

"Then let's go through with it. I'll see you at the cemetery at 9:45."

"Very well. See you then."

He hung up the phone and knocked on his mother's door, waking her. They got dressed and had some breakfast, and the drove to the cemetery. There were only a handful of people attending, sitting on the dozen chairs under the canopy. The casket, now closed, had been placed on 4 X 4 pieces of wood on the grass, with two long, nylon straps underneath. A hole had been dug already by the Caterpillar tractor parked nearby. A pile of slate-black dirt sat beside the hole, streaked with rainwater. Incessant rain splashed off every horizontal surface.

Preacher Karwoski had a few final words, and then one of Turner's employees, dressed in a yellow plastic sheet he used as a poncho, fired up the Caterpillar's motor and swung a metal hook chained to the bottom of the tractor's scoop over the casket. Turner took the two nylon straps and looped them over the hook. The diesel engine revved and the scoop lifted, bringing the casket with it. He swung the casket over the hole, and then lowered it down where it splashed the muddy-black water at the bottom. Then they removed the straps and Turner handed Pug a ceremonial shovel, which he used to toss some wet dirt onto the wooden box below.

Then Lucas "Pug" Graham and his mother, Dolores Graham, went home.

Pug changed his clothes, had a bite to eat, and then prepared to drive to the mine, as it was payday.

His mother kissed him and said, "I'm going over to see Claudia Wilmer. She's not been well and I know she would have attended the funeral today if she'd been better. She'll want me to tell her about it. I'll be back before dinner."

"Be careful, mom. The roads are slick with all the rain."

"You be careful too, son. Goodbye." She gave him a light kiss on his cheek.

His front-wheel-drive Sienna slid several times on the muddy dirt road to the mine office. It was still raining hard as he walked from his minivan to the office. Gloeda had delivered the paychecks to his desk earlier in the day, so he could pay his men at the end of the shift. She also left the year-end financial statements for his perusal, along with a note on a yellow snippet of paper taped to the folder which said, "This is the last of our cash. We need to talk on Monday."

He picked up the paychecks and drove a cart into the mine. He found the twins turning wrenches on the conveyor, extending it 20 feet to correspond with their progress with mining the seam.

As he turned to leave, he saw Lacey running towards them, hunched over but still moving quickly. Breathlessly he yelled, "There's been a problem outside. The valley has been flooded."

"What happened?" Pug shouted.

"I was half-listening to a radio station out of Charleston. There was a news bulletin. One of the dams above War has ruptured. Much of the valley has been swept away."

"Fuck!" Donnie yelled.

The men dropped what they were doing and raced the carts outside the mine. Pug reached the Sienna and drove at breakneck speed down the dirt road, nearly losing control twice, as his company miners drove behind him in their vehicles. As they reached the edge of the main highway, a horrific scene of devastation met them. The waterline had extended over the highway where all manner of debris was being deposited. The creek itself, normally not 20-feet across was now 150-feet across, a roiling black mess, littered with all manner of man-made stuff: cars, trailers, toys, and parts of houses. It had evidently already receded from its maximum intensity, as there were items discarded on the hillsides below the current level of the tumult.

Pug emerged from his minivan and Lacey raced to his side. Lacey mumbled under his breath, "God have mercy."

Pug's thoughts went to home and his mom. His home, up a side hollow, would be safe, but if his mother had left for Mrs. Wilmer's house right in town, it would undoubtedly be gone. The men stood immobile, gobsmacked by the turbulent bedlam playing out before them.

The twins stopped behind him and emerged from their vehicles to stand by the maelstrom's edge. Donnie yelled, "My truck! I'm driving to War. Get in."

Donnie reached for the driver seat of the custom raised pickup and his twin Ronnie sat beside him. Pug and two other miners jumped into the back. Donnie drove the pickup into the flowing black bedlam, pointing upstream. He drove 200 yards to where the water's edge revealed the highway again, as floating flotsam slapped against the truck's grill. At one point, the water was higher than the tailgate and the entire bed of the truck saturated with six-inches of water, wetting everybody's shoes and pant legs. The engine seemed to skip a beat, but Pug realized it was as the exhaust pipe went underwater and the sound was muffled. Finally, the truck churned through the mess and emerged on dry land, with water streaming out of the bed and the doors of the cab and steam from under the hood.

Back on unflooded pavement, Donnie raced the curvy road the two miles southward into War. He stopped just short of the waterline, 50-feet before where Pug knew the railroad tracks lay, now inundated. They were confronted with a scene of utter devastation. The receding waterline painted black the sides of the few buildings still standing, with the water now 4-feet lower than the zenith. Two dozen people stood nearby, palms covering their mouths as they recoiled in shock and helplessness. Rain continued to pelt them.

"Buffalo Creek," Pug mumbled to himself, remembering the disaster he'd just recalled with Zola. He took off on a trot towards his home, jumping over fences and running through yards to stay out of the water. He reached his hollow and ran uphill, slowing to a walk to catch his breath. Reaching his door, he chastised himself for his urgency; either his mother was inside and safe, or not. He burst inside, "Mom! Mom!"

There was no sound. He ran from room to room, futilely. "Mom!" She was gone, likely forever. He walked outside again towards Mill's house and saw Zola. "Thank God you're safe," he yelled, and ran to embrace her.

"Where's your mother?"

"I don't know. I'm going to look inside Mill's house. If she's not there..." his voice trailed off.

He broke inside and his worst fears were confirmed. She was nowhere to be found.

Pug and Zola ran back downhill towards town. The water was receding rapidly but the damage had been done, as if a single, massive tsunami had swept through. They saw a car, swept into a tree, listing upside-down. Thankfully, it was unoccupied. Nearby, an entire two-story house lay crumpled. An older man yelled from inside, his body wedged between beams, his legs broken. Pug assembled several people nearby, some he recognized and some not, to assist pulling the beams and extricating the man. Pug, Zola, and a man he recognized but whose name he couldn't remember, carried the broken, now unconscious man to the shelter of an open garage beside an unscathed house. The other rescuer began mouth-to-mouth resuscitation but was unsuccessful; the injured man died on the cold cement floor beside an oil-stain. Zola found a tarp folded on a shelf and she covered the man.

Pug shivered convulsively, realizing that his flannel shirt was soaking and he was wet to the bone and cold. Still, he and Zola and the other man returned to the receding water's edge. Two men approached them, both carrying dead children.

"It's the school," one of them said. "The school was swept away."

Pug's heart, already at a depth he'd never experienced, sank further. His mind flashed back to his own children, playing on the playground swing and teeter-totter. Now, the children of War – all of them – were gone.

"Put them in that garage," Pug pointed uphill from where he'd come.

Debris, combinations of plank wood, cars, trees and limbs, and appliances lay in horrible, unimaginable piles, some as big as houses. He thought he saw a doll, wedged tightly between a washing machine and the door frame of a wrecked house. A head and shoulder emerged from the wreckage, and he could see it was a child, a girl of perhaps 7-years. He used a nearby wooden beam to leverage the washing machine upwards as Zola pulled the body away. The girl had blonde hair. Her skull was cracked and she was naked, the force of the water having ripped her clothing from her body. Zola carried the corpse up to the garage while Pug searched for any familiar landmarks, hoping to find a shred of good news about his mother and her friend Claudia Wilmer, who she had gone to visit. Alas, Wilmer's house lay in a massive tangle, 200-feet downstream of the now flooded basement and foundation.

Four bodies lay nearby, clearly left by another rescuer, both with drapes of whatever cloth materials could be found over them. Pug knew instantly that the nearest one was his mother, because her shoeless feet were still clothed by the type of stockings she always wore. He lifted the rain-soaked blanket over her torso and head, and was relived that her clothing was still intact and her dress covered her body, sparing her the indignity of the nudeness of the dead schoolgirl. He sat on the wet ground beside her for moments until rivulets of water still cascading from the relentless sky sent a compulsive shiver down his spine. He covered her and began moving aimlessly again.

People, wet and shell-shocked, drifted to the water's edge, all with vacant, mile-away stares. Pug saw an older woman, lying dead, but looking peaceful as if napping, wedged against some building debris. A mud-covered sheltie collie sat near her, licking her face, trying to clean the mud from it. He approached, but the dog growled and Pug retreated, figuring the time would come when the dog would resign itself to its master's fate.

Pug wandered to his church, which, situated on a slight rise, had providentially been spared the scouring effect of the floodwaters, although the low chain-link fence below it was a twisted wreck. He entered the building behind three other people carrying a woman's body. A young woman carried a dead child over her shoulders towards the door. Inside, he saw that the wooden pews had been commandeered for the repositories of the dead. One woman sat on the floor beside the dead body of her boy and wailed. Pug reunited with Zola and he suggested that they return to his house and retrieve some dry clothing, as many of the survivors were soaking wet and hypothermic in the forty-degree rain.

They never spoke as they entered the house, found two wicker baskets that they filled with clothing from his parents' closet, and returned to the church. But Pug knew what she must be thinking, that this tragedy was eerily similar to her nightmare of forty years earlier.

A woman was crying and shouting to anyone who would listen, venting her anguish. "I was on my way to pick up my daughter from school. She, she... I was taking her to the dentist. I rounded a bend and saw a wall of water, like 20-feet high, smash into the school. At first, I thought the building would survive, the water plowing into it and spreading around it like a rock in a mountain stream. The glass windows all burst at once, like an explosion inside. The building held on! But then it crumpled, brick walls and all. The roof split into three enormous slabs, floating down-river. The water ate everything in it. My baby! My baby is gone!" Her wail sent his spine into convulsions.

"I'm going back outside," he told Zola.

He walked upriver, assisting people wherever he could. He pulled a family of four, all dead, from the inside of a swamped, overturned car. He was grabbed by a stranger, "Please help!" They ran to a tree where the body of a girl, perhaps a teenager, was pinned against three split limbs. She wore nothing but panties and her left arm was wrapped across her face. She didn't look too bad, until he walked around the base of the tree and saw that the other side of her body was gashed open, her entrails drooping from her slashed abdomen. He and another man who happened by climbed the tree and extricated her from her death perch. Attempting to lower her gently to the ground, the man slipped and fell, and as he did, her corpse fell from Pug's grasp and smacked the ground beside its intentioned rescuer. Pug scurried down and found the man unconscious and bleeding on the ground from a head wound. Pug attempted resuscitation but it was fruitless; he was as dead as the girl he'd tried to rescue. With the help of others, Pug carried the girl's body, then the man's back to the church. At the church door, the wife of the deceased man was assisting someone else, but then saw her dead husband. She shrieked into a sickening wail.

Pug and Zola continued to work wherever they could, late into the afternoon. As darkness began to descend, the rain abated and the sky began to clear. Pug realized that there was no electrical power in town. Back at the church, Pug ran into the reporter, Red Hazelwood. "What are you doing here?"

Red was covered in mud and clearly uncomfortably cold.

"I was working on a story here in town of another business closing. When the flood approached... you know, somehow I could feel it coming. The woman I was interviewing, the china in her breakfront began to chatter and a piece of crystal fell from a shelf and broke. I grabbed her by the hand and literally dragged her out her back door before the wave smashed into the house. We were ten feet from her back door when the wave hit us, carrying us against her chain-link fence. I crawled across the fence, pulling her by the collar of her blouse, until we escaped the water. My car was in front of the house and it was swept away. Looks like I'll be here for awhile."

"We need to get you into some dry clothes," Pug said. "Let's get up to my house."

As they turned to leave, the twins drove up in Donnie's pickup. Ronnie said, "They're gone. My wife, my girls; they're gone. Elsie was substitute teaching at the school. All the teachers and children are dead." He sobbed openly and his brother wrapped his arms over his twin's shoulders to console him. Pug realized that both men had lost their entire families within the span of one horrific week. But then again, so had he. He also realized that Donnie's, Ronnie's, and Zola's homes had also been swept away and he would be sharing his home with them.

Pug convinced his friends to accompany him back to his house to have something to eat. Pug found some candles, which he lit with a cigarette lighter. He found three flashlights. Nobody spoke. It was so quiet Pug thought you could hear a mouse sneeze.

Pug knew everyone was as shell-shocked as he was. He was disoriented, walking as if dizzy and drunk. He was dead tired but he continued to move about the house, shuttling clothing to his friends, catering to their needs before realizing how cold and wet he was himself. Finally, he asked the twins to bring some firewood from the porch and start a fire in the chimney insert, so at least they'd have some heat.

He dug out some cold food from the refrigerator, which was now inoperable. He opened a can of beans that they ate cold. He looked around the room at Ronnie, Donnie, Zola, and Red, empathizing with the profound grief each person was internalizing. The former three were in some sort of catatonic state while Red seemed to be composing words in his mind about what he'd seen, his eyes darting to and fro in the dimly lit room.

Suddenly, as if a marionette having received a tug on his strings, Donnie sprung to life. "I'm going to kill...

"We're going to kill," his twin intercepted, "the some-bitches that done this."

"As God is our witness, "Donnie continued, "whoever's responsible is gonna die. If it takes us to our own graves, we'll get revenge."

Pug could feel the gaze of the twins on him, as if searching him for his reaction. He said nothing, sensing the futility of argument.

"Let's get back to the church," Zola broke the silence. "I'm sure there's more work to do."

They put the remaining food away, blew out the candles and walked downhill to the church again, Pug carrying with him another load of clothing to give away. By this time, the first of the rescue vehicles had arrived, large-wheeled camo covered Army trucks with Red Cross symbols painted on the sides. The trucks had evidently driven over the mountain to the east as Route 16, the sole highway into town, had been rendered unusable due to the loss of four bridges, three upstream of War and one downstream. Several people had brought camping lanterns and work was being done inside the small church to identify the dead and console the survivors. Pug ran into Lacey who cried that his home, with his wife in it, had been washed away.

Pug and his new house guests – Zola, Donnie, Ronnie, Lacey, and Red – eventually returned to his house, exhausted and terrorized, and each found a place to sleep. He put three more split logs on the fire and went to bed.

+ + + + +

Meredith Goldschmidt was returning from a meeting on Capitol Hill, listening to WAMU Public Radio when their classical music programming was interrupted by a news bulletin. She was lost in thought, waiting at a traffic signal at the corner of Constitution and 12th NW, when the male announcer began blurting out details of an emerging catastrophe in southern West Virginia. Details were sketchy, but apparently a remote valley, called a "hollow" in that area, had been swept away by flooding. It was one of many communities that were suffering from floods in the wake of the hurricane, but the death toll, estimated at over fifty, was appalling to her. "Stay tuned for further developments, reported by NPR when they happen."

When she reached her office, there was no particular alarm about the event in West Virginia. She put it out of her mind, anticipating a shopping trip in the morning to take advantage of some of the after-Christmas sales, which would end that weekend.

At the end of the workday, she bought dinner for herself at a Taco Bell where the plump, black woman who took her order never made eye contact and carried on a brisk conversation with the other clerk about her date the prior evening. Meredith sat alone and ate her Spanish rice and bean burrito. She noticed the people around her were almost all overweight and most had unsightly tattoos, some on their necks and faces. One black boy stood and as he walked towards the door, the top of his shorts was so low that three inches of his underwear were revealed, barely covering the crack in his ass.

Two hours later, Meredith was at home alone, comfortable

with most of a bottle of port already consumed, her pink nightgown draped over her, and an old Katherine Hepburn movie on TV, when the phone rang.

"Hello?"

"Madam Secretary, this is Frank Manning from the White House. There has been a tragedy in West Virginia."

"Yes, Mr. Manning. I heard about it this afternoon."

"Madam Secretary, as you may know, President Cooper is in Saint Petersburg, Russia, for the G10 Summit. He would like you to go as his representative."

Scheisse, she murmured under her breath.

"Excuse me, madam?" He said, apparently straining to hear her.

"Sorry," she stammered. "When?"

"In the morning. Our office is working on tickets to Charleston, the capital, for you and Jennifer Wilkins; we assumed you'd like to have her along. I'll call you back as soon as we have confirmed reservations."

She hung up and dialed Jenni, who had to leave the theater where she and her fiancé were watching the latest Hobbit movie, in order to answer. "Pack your bags, sweetie. We're leaving in the morning for West Virginia."

"Ma'am?"

"You heard me right. There's been a tragedy. We're being sent as President Cooper's representatives."

"Where again? Virginia?"

"No, West Virginia. You know, 'mountain momma, country roads, take me home'."

"When do we leave?"

"First thing. Pack your bags."

"Yes, Madam Secretary."

Moments later, she heard from Manning again with ticket information. "Departure is 10:25 from Reagan. You'll be changing planes in Detroit."

"Detroit? That's further from here than Charleston."

"Yes, Madam Secretary, but there are no flights to Charleston from here. You'll have a layover of 3 hours. You'll be in Charleston in time for dinner."

"Damn, I could drive there quicker."

"With all due respect, have you ever driven in West Virginia? It's slower going than you might think. We have you booked at the Hilton, downtown. Sunday morning, a West Virginia state trooper will meet you in the lobby at 9:00 a.m. and will drive you to the affected community. It is a town in the southern part of the state called War."

"Excuse me?"

"Yes, Madam Secretary, it's War. There really is a town called War." He was quiet for a moment. "Or at least there was until yesterday."

He gave her further details, what was known of the flood and disaster, including the details on the failure of the two impoundment dams and the known casualty numbers, already over 180.

JAN 4 Saturday

Pug awoke before daybreak to rustling in the living room, where apparently most of his guests had crashed. He was unsure whether anyone had used his parents' bedroom, a logical place to sleep but perhaps still heavy with the scent of his recently deceased father. He threw on a bathrobe and entered the living room where the Getgood twins were lacing on their boots to return to the madness outside his doorstep. Zola had already departed to rejoin the relief efforts.

Pug managed to get Lacey and the Getgood twins to eat a slice of bread and have some orange juice before departing. Then he dressed and scurried downhill towards what once was his hometown.

The nightmare of the previous day had in no way diminished overnight; in fact things seemed worse. A pall of death had swept the narrow valley, with a musty, rotting smell permeating the air. The force of the flood had played weird tricks on the landscape. In some places, the ground was scoured of topsoil down to rock layers, pebbles, and gravel, as if sprayed by a powerful fireman's hose. In other places, the grass was merely swept over by the water, and was already rising again towards vertical. Rain continued to pelt down and the entire region was shrouded in fog, lending a Gothic, morbid, sinisterly claustrophobic feel.

Before Pug reached his church door, he was commandeered away by several people looking for help to remove the debris of a collapsed home a mile upstream, which covered at least two people whose fate was unknown. A dog had been found scratching at a collapsed roof and workers determined there were people underneath, either dead or alive. With two chainsaws, some crowbars, and lots of muscle, Pug worked with several other men to extricate three people, all adults: one dead man of about 60 years, one dead woman of about 75 years, and one woman of about 40 who was near death, unresponsive and unconscious. Pug watched as a woman rinsed the mud from the victim's mouth and performed mouth-to-mouth resuscitation on her. Pug was pulled away on another rescue before he could learn of the sufferer's fate.

Further up the valley, he watched as a bulldozer operator worked on a huge pile of debris. The driver was skillful, working quickly and gently at the same time, removing piece by piece, where other people walked to and fro looking for people, dead or alive.

Nearby, he saw a young, pregnant woman who looked to be no more than a teenager hunched over the dead body of what Pug assumed to be her husband. She wailed audibly and pushed away a woman who tried to comfort her.

It seemed that few people were injured. People were either dead or unscathed. It seemed like the same with the structures. If the tsunami hit a house, it was splintered to bits. If it didn't, it looked exactly as it had three days earlier.

Pug assisted in pulling two dead children's corpses from beneath a tangle of debris, including two large trees, parts of a house, and piles of what appeared to have come from someone's large mining equipment warehouse. He worked with three other people to fashion a stretcher from a couple of shirts and fence poles. Then he and a man he recognized but didn't know carried one of the two bodies back to the makeshift morgue at the church.

Outside the church were three huge National Guard all-terrain vehicles, painted in camouflage. Pug learned from the chatter the cause and status of the disaster.

The dam break was in the two tailing ponds below the mountaintop removal mine at Upper Horsepen near the Virginia state line near Bishop. The flood swept northward, down Cucumber Creek at Newhall, at the confluence of Cucumber Creek and Dry Fork, scouring the corridor of SR-16 through Newhall, Cucumber, Rift, into War, the area's largest and most important community. From there, it continued its devastation into Yukon, Lomax, English, and through Bradshaw and beyond. Highway 16 was open from Caretta to Welch, but from Yukon all the way to Newhall, it was obliterated. The dense fog was preventing relief efforts from arriving by helicopter.

The death toll was estimated at 195 and rising, mostly children from the school. Nobody was even guessing about the number of lost cars and homes, and homeless people.

The Army vehicles had driven first from Bluefield to Welch, then south to Caretta, and then over the mountain on narrow, steep roads commonly only used by recreational 4-wheelers. They brought in cases of bottled water, Army ration canned food, blankets, cots, tents and medical supplies. Three Army medics arrived, but found few injured people to assist. What they needed were morticians.

As Pug reached the church, the Army commander emerged

from the building carrying a bullhorn. Pug continued to carry the corpse inside, but could hear the commander's speech as he left the body inside. The commander introduced himself as Major Wardell of the West Virginia National Guard. The commander was discussing the staging of outside relief efforts as Pug emerged again.

"... with my unit from Bluefield," Wardell continued. "We will be setting up communications here at the church to monitor rescue activities. Shipments of food and drinking water are en route. FEMA will be bringing in other relief supplies over the next few days. Authorities in Charleston are coordinating with FEMA in Washington.

"Sometime tomorrow afternoon, a delegation from FEMA and the Department of the Interior will be here to address recovery concerns."

"What the heck happened!" somebody shouted.

"There's no misunderstandings about the flood," the Major shrugged. "There was a dam break on the upper and lower impoundment dams near Bishop. The flood has impacted communities all the way through Bradshaw. We're just getting a handle on the death toll."

"We fuckin' know that," the same man yelled. Pug had seen him around town before but didn't know his name. "How the fuck did the dam break?"

"Sir, I don't know the specifics. I'm a guardsman. You need to ask the mining company people and the mine inspectors. My job is to begin helping you people. You can ask the authorities when they arrive tomorrow."

All afternoon, work continued to find the few injured and help them in any ways possible and to locate the dead and bring them back to the church. Major Wardell's men loaded nine injured people on the Army trucks for evacuation to Welch for evaluation and treatment, a task normally handled by helicopter but impossible due to the dense fog. Someone had started a list of missing people on three large sheets of paper tacked to the wall of the church sanctuary. Whenever somebody had been found, his or her name was crossed off, with either a "D" for dead or "A" for alive beside them. Those not crossed off were still missing.

Pug occasionally saw Zola, the Getgood twins, Lacey, and his other miners. He also ran into Red Hazelwood. He had already called in one story by radio to his newspaper in Bluefield. He asked Pug if he could crash at his house for the foreseeable future, until the world knew what had happened. Pug said, "We'll squeeze you in somewhere."

Pug returned to his house as darkness set. The steepness of the mountains nearby always made the days shorter, with only a few hours of direct sunlight hitting the hollow this time of year. But the rains continued and the darkness kept getting more odious and pervasive. Walking up to the house, shivering in the wet, Pug thought about the sick ineffectuality of rains that continued even after the flood, and he chuckled to himself over the macabre futility.

When he entered, Zola was inside already. She had lit some candles and had removed some food from the thawing refrigerator. He was dead tired, filthy, wet, and dirty. He wanted a hot shower, but with no running water and no working water heater, he knew that was not to be. He took off his wet clothes anyway and put on some dry ones, dragging other clothes from his own and his parents' closet so his guests would have dry clothes as well. There had been a small gas-powered electric generator at the mine, and, someone, perhaps one of the Getgood twins, had retrieved it. Pug connected it to the refrigerator and then to an electric griddle so they could fry some hamburger meat and not eat another cold dinner.

The Getgood twins and Red Hazelwood arrived at about the same time, each one with faces washed in despair. The twins were mumbling with expletive-laden incoherency and matching tones of desperation in the dimly lit room where

Pug couldn't even tell which twin was which.

And then the idea hit him.

Perhaps there would be an outlet for their frustration, his too. It was an audacious idea, one that ricocheted around his head like the little white plastic balls in the lottery machine. It was an angry, scary, forbidden idea, and it prickled his skin to be thinking it. But in his anger, resentment, and animosity, his resolve steeled as quickly as the idea congealed.

"Zola, come in here, please. Everybody listen up." And then his idea spilled forth. The others quickly acquiesced. Scenarios reverberated through the room for two hours more, as plans were made, then discarded, then revised, and then rebuilt, fortified. Emotions were palpable. Raw. Intense and angry. Vengeful.

Tomorrow they would take action.

Pug and Red worked well into the night, synchronizing the radios to allow for communication on a CB band that was unlikely to be tapped.

+ + + + +

Meredith Goldschmidt met Jennifer Wilkins at their office in the Department of the Interior building on the historic Washington Mall at 7:15 a.m. where they packed some paperwork. Meredith drove her Lexus to Reagan Airport and caught an on-time flight to Detroit. The remnants of the hurricane had reached the DC area and the trip to Detroit was in a driving storm, with the jet buffeted until it rose over the clouds. The skies broke over Lake Erie and they landed a few minutes late, but given the long layover, they had plenty of time for their connection to Charleston. The airplane back to the south was a small, 16-passenger prop-jet. Never rising over 15,000 feet, it was a hellacious flight, with Jenni vomiting into the barf-bag.

It was raining hard in Charleston, a deep, chilling rain, as they took a cab downtown to the hotel. Goldschmidt was in full victimhood mood, as she hated all funerals and tragedies, and being forced by rank to take on the President's obligation to attend, angered more by knowing the President would have his own helicopter ride and Secret Service accompaniment while she and Jenni traveled in discomfort and anonymity.

JAN 5 Sunday

Meredith Goldschmidt and Jenni Wilkins finished breakfast in the hotel's restaurant and moved to the lobby to await their escort. Right on schedule, a law officer entered the room. He was a huge black man, she guessed 6'5", with a noticeable paunch. He tipped his trooper's hat, covered by a clear plastic rainguard, and a stream of water spilled onto the floor in front of him. He spoke with a languid, flowing accent that she had trouble discerning immediately.

"You the Secretary of the Interior, Goldschmidt?"

"Yes. This is my assistant, Jenni Wilson."

"Ma'am," he nodded in mock respect to both of them. "I'm Trooper Coles, West Virginia State Police, Welch division."

She immediately decided from his condescension that he was misogynist, and she disliked him.

"I'll be drivin' you ladies to War. Y'all ready?"

"Yes," Meredith said.

He turned and walked away, leaving their bags behind. Meredith looked at Jenni. Both shrugged, then picked up their own bags and followed.

He held open the right rear door to the police vehicle. Meredith shoved her bag into his midsection until he grabbed it, and then did the same with Jenni's bag. Then she got inside and Jenni followed. Coles shut the door behind them. He sped away with his lights flashing. She was relieved there were no metal gratings in the passenger area and there were door handles on the rear door, allowing her to open her own door at their destination.

"Ma'am, we're headed first to Welch. That's the seat, the county's seat. You'll be joining two other men and their escort, a county deputy. One man is Alvin Youngblood. He's the owner of the mines and the impoundment dam that broke. The other is the inspector, Merritt Lee Lawton, whose job it was to inspect the area's dams and mines."

Meredith for the first time felt anxious about the task and facing a community of grief-stricken citizens. "Do you think the survivors will be very receptive to these men? Or me?"

"Hard to say, ma'am. I suspect they might be a bit testy, frankly."

"Will we be in any danger?"

"That's why I'm here, ma'am," Coles boasted, fist-bumping his chest.

+ + + + +

The Sunday morning began much the same as the prior days since the disaster, except the Getgood twins were notably absent when Pug awoke, already making preparations for the day's plan. Red, Pug and Zola went to the church to see that the corpses were being wrapped in Army body bags and placed outside in the cool air, now just above freezing. A light dusting of sleet covered them and the many piles of debris still littering the valley. Much of everything else, including Main Street through town was now dry again, as was the railroad track. However, the track had been destroyed both below and above War, so there was no possibility that any trains would be arriving for some time. The only non-resident vehicles in town were those over the mountain used by the Army and National Guard trucks. FEMA still hadn't arrived.

Uncharacteristically, the fog was utterly persistent,

hampering any rescue from the air, as helicopter pilots still couldn't navigate the tight valleys without visual aids.

Red approached Pug and said he'd been offered a ride to his office in Bluefield. The two men synchronized plans for what they hoped would happen later that day, and Red departed.

Inside the church, Pastor David Karwoski was presiding over a brief service, which Pug and Zola attended. Pastor Karwoski read from a list of the names of the known dead, loudly and with poignancy and reverence. With each name Pug recognized, he felt as if a new syringe, laden with poison, was being injected into his gut. Zola was overwhelmed with grief, and she sobbed loudly and unabashedly. Pug knew, but he understood that he couldn't really fully know, how horribly reminiscent this disaster was to the event decades earlier that had destroyed any chance for her of a happy, fulfilling life. He dwelt in his rage, knowing that a healthy dose of righteous indignation and fury was something he desperately needed, an essential element to his part in the scheme he and his compatriots had sketched out for that evening.

Amidst the ongoing recovery work, he returned to the house to establish radio communication with Red and the Getgood twins. Rumors circulating through town were that the dignitaries would be arriving by car, perhaps late in the afternoon. The delegation would likely include a FEMA official, a representative of Bessie Energy who owned the collapsed dam, and the United States Secretary of the Interior, a woman named Goldschmidt. The highway department was doing emergency reconstruction of the destroyed bridge downstream of town, to allow vehicle access from Welch and the outside world. From Pug's perspective, everything was going according to plan.

+ + + + +

The escort for Meredith Goldschmidt and Jenni Wilkins left Interstate 77 south of Beckley and soon were on the curviest road Meredith could ever remember. As the car swerved to and fro, Jenni looked as ill as the day before on the airplane, so Meredith left her alone. The two federal bureaucrats and their chauffeur did much of the three-hour journey in silence. They passed through several small towns, most of which seemed to have more commercial buildings vacant than occupied. There was a palpable sense of descending into the narrow confines of the hollows. In many places, the stream, which each road seemed to parallel, was roiling with murky brown to black water. Streams of paper and cloth debris hung from overhanging shrubs. The rain continued and the fog became denser and more oppressive.

Finally, they arrived at the town hall in Welch, a single-story brick building shared with the public library, surrounded by a perimeter brick wall. There, they encountered the rest of their delegation.

A big man, stocky, with a balding head and fleshy face forced his right hand towards her, grabbing hers. "Alvin Youngblood, at your service, Madam Secretary. I'm president of Bessie Energy. We own most of the land in Southern West Virginia. Nothing happens in this state without my approval," he said boastfully.

"Charmed," she growled, taking her hand away from his puffy, domineering grip.

The other man was Merritt Lee Lawton. He was taller in stature and much younger, she guessed around 40. He had brown, beady eyes, and a sinister expression. She thought he looked like a man who hadn't smiled since childhood. She was also introduced to McDowell County Deputy Doug Webber, who never shook her hand nor gave her any eye contact. They chatted briefly about the order of their comments, then got into the cars of Coles and Webber and continued the 20 winding miles southward to War.

As the vehicle in which Goldschmidt and Wilkins were being escorted rounded a bend two miles beyond Caretta, they encountered the first signs of the destruction. Goldschmidt was horrified by the immense piles of mud-stained debris alongside the creek bed. Even with the closed windows, the smell of musty death permeated her olfactory. She covered her nose, revolted.

+ + + + +

Notice of the upcoming visit of the still unnamed dignitaries had traveled informally up the affected valley, and a crowd began to assemble by mid-afternoon. Pug had received word from Red that the delegation would likely be late, and would include the assistant to the director of FEMA – the Director was in California overseeing efforts at an earthquake that happened the day before the War flood – and various assistants, the Secretary of the Interior of the United States Meredith Goldschmidt, and an aide. The representative of Bessie Energy would in fact be Alvin Youngblood its president. Youngblood was widely known and despised throughout the coal region, for although he was a West Virginia native, he was notorious for his manipulative and mean-spirited dealings. He would likely be traveling with a state-assigned bodyguard, anticipating hostility from the community.

Just before 5:00 p.m., Donnie Getgood radioed Pug from his vantage point downstream of War near the newly reconstructed bridge with an update. "There are three vehicles. One is a state police car, flashing blue lights like a Christmas tree. One has FEMA decals all over it. The other is a big SUV."

"I'll report back when I see these guys," Pug replied. It was getting dark and the fog was increasingly enveloping.

A few moments later, the police car, the FEMA vehicle,

and the SUV arrived at the church. Several people emerged, to Pug's eye all looking professional and conspicuously clean. One tall, striking woman with auburn hair and designer glasses scanned the devastation and brought her hand to her mouth. A younger, smaller blonde woman stood by her side, also seemingly shocked, especially as four townspeople carried the corpse of a teenage boy right past them. A state policeman with "Coles" on his name tag brushed by, leading the delegation towards the church. One of the men Pug recognized as Merritt Lee Lawton, the mine inspector. Pug scolded himself for not realizing sooner that Lawton was likely responsible for the inspection of the failed impoundment dam.

Then Pug recognized another person from newspaper articles. The big, stocky sixties-ish man with the crew cut and fleshy, snarling face was Alvin Youngblood, the president of Bessie Energy. He had a bulbous nose, with abnormally knotted veins showing through the skin. A hero to some, a pariah to others, Bessie under his watch had for years run the most dangerous mines in the three-state mining region, and Youngblood had been habitually unapologetic about the myriad of accidents and abuses. Youngblood had appeared in Red's newspaper two weeks earlier for giving away Christmas toys at a free event, presumably buying favor among the young people who would someday become advocates for his mining abuses.

Pug radioed Donnie with an update, as promised.

Officer Coles produced a bullhorn and proclaimed from the church steps, "Y'all just be patient. These folks are going inside for a few minutes and they will make a statement."

The crowd made nervous, anxious gestures. Chatter picked up, but people stayed peaceful. Moments later, the dignitaries emerged. The tall woman took the bullhorn. She wore a pair of slacks and a jacket that said, "United States Department of the Interior" on a patch. The younger and smaller woman stayed close by her side.

The older woman said, "Ladies and gentlemen, my name is Meredith Goldschmidt. I am the Secretary of the Interior of the United States. I am here as a special representative of President Cooper. The Department of the Interior oversees mining operations throughout the country, so accidents like this fall under my purview. This is my assistant, Jenni Wilkins." She nodded to the younger woman. "Jenni and I will be setting up a recovery operation in Welch to coordinate efforts here in the flood area. What has happened here is so tragic! We know the strength and resolve of the people of West Virginia. Please be assured that the President of the United States has empowered my staff to do everything possible to mitigate the ongoing tragedy.

"With me today is Alvin Youngblood, president, Bessie Energy."

A chorus of boos rose from the testy crowd.

"He would like to say a few words."

The big man with the snarl took the bullhorn. Pug looked at Zola who was visibly scowling at Youngblood.

"Y'all," he began, with a pronounced drawl, "This is real damn awful what God made happen here."

"You son of a bitch!" somebody yelled from the crowd.

"Settle down!" Youngblood snarled back. "We do everything by the book at Bessie Energy. Our dam was inspected just last week and was certified sound. Nobody could have ever known God could pour so much water into that pond."

Splat! Someone threw an egg at Youngblood. It missed, falling short and hitting the railing instead, showering the dignitaries with yellow yoke material.

Wilkins wiped some splatter from her face; she was visibly shaken.

Officer Coles took the bullhorn and shouted, "No more of that!" He scanned the crowd but in the fading light couldn't see who the perpetrator was. "This man, Aubrey Jones, is from FEMA. He and his assistant will be staying here to coordinate relief directly." Coles looked at Jones as if asking if he wished to speak. Jones shook his head. "Listen, y'all. That's all we've got to say for today. I'll be bringing Mr. Youngblood and Secretary Goldschmidt back here from Welch in the morning."

"When's the damn electricity coming back on?" a woman yelled.

Coles looked at Jones who shook his head again. "We'll do an assessment and have a statement about that in the morning," Coles said through the bullhorn.

The delegation of Office Coles, a McDowell Sheriff's deputy, Youngblood, Secretary Goldschmidt and her assistant, and Lawton the mine inspector, strode to the awaiting cars. The officers got behind the drivers' seats. The others got into back seats.

Pug reached his Sienna as the two cars began their drive away. He radioed Donnie, "They're pulling out now. There are two officers, one state and one county, driving. You won't believe this; ole Alvin Youngblood is here. Youngblood and Lawton are in the back of the county car. Two women are in the back of the other car."

"Yee-haw!" Donnie shouted. "We'll just be a-waiting for them!"

"Over and out."

+ + + + +

Pug and Zola got into the Sienna. He started the engine and waited exactly two minutes, then followed the police cars. Zola placed a stocking she'd taken from Pug's mother's bureau on her head and handed one to Pug which he placed on his head. He drove slowly on the curvy road northwards towards Caretta. He felt his heart race as he rounded the bend and saw the scene unfolding just as he'd hoped.

Ronnie had parked the huge coal truck askance in the road, blocking both lanes. As Pug came to a stop some 40 yards away, the blue flashing lights came on the police car and the two officers of the law emerged from their vehicles and walked towards the truck. Pug extinguished his lights. He and Zola pulled the stockings over their faces and emerged from the Sienna. The two conspirators walked forwards as quietly as possible, she armed with a Glock handgun and he with a rifle Ronnie had given them.

"You can stop right there," rang out a voice from the dark towards the officers. Pug was sure it was Donnie. "Hold your hands high!" Both men raised their hands.

Ronnie opened the door to his truck and turned to descend to the pavement. As he did, the deputy sheriff in an instant had unholstered his gun and shot Ronnie in the back. Just as quickly, the deputy was felled by a bullet from the dark, hitting him in the cheek. His face exploded as his body recoiled and sank to the ground. The sound echoed throughout the valley.

"Damn it," said Lacey Reedy, emerging from the dark wearing a miner's hat and coveralls, his face purposefully smeared with coal dust.

The dignitaries emerged reflexively from their cars. As they did, Zola approached the federal government representatives and said, "Hands on the car please, ladies." They complied, as did Youngblood and Lawton when Pug approached them. Meanwhile Lacey handcuffed Officer Coles' hands behind his back as Donnie's rifle was pointed at his temple. Lacey then delivered four more pairs of handcuffs to Zola and Pug and they secured their prisoners in a like manner. Zola intertwined the cuffs of Goldschmidt and Wilkins, securing them together, as did Donnie with the three captive men. Then Lacey produced five blindfolds, which they affixed over the prisoners' eyes.

"Let's get out of here," Pug said.

"I'll do some cleanup," Donnie said. "I'll meet you at the mine."

The big man, Youngblood, yelled, "What the fuck you think you're doing?"

"Shut up," Pug said.

Although Youngblood couldn't see, he apparently sensed that Pug was nearby, and kicked hard in Pug's direction, connecting with a glancing blow to Pug's left shin. "Damn," Pug winced. Angered, he swung his fist into the captive's solar plexus as hard as he'd ever hit a man. Youngblood crumpled to his knees.

The tall woman, Goldschmidt, strained to maintain her composure. "I am an official of the Government of the United States of America and a member of President Cooper's cabinet. You must release us this minute."

Zola said, "Lady, look around you."

Pug laughed inside, knowing that Goldschmidt was blindfolded. Lacey laughed aloud.

"We have two hundred dead around here, maybe more," Zola said. "The rest of us feel guilty that we're not. Somebody's got to pay for what happened here."

"No more talking," Pug said, his heart racing. "Next person who opens their mouth gets shot. That understood? Z, you take our lady guests to the four-wheeler. L, you and I, let's get these gentlemen, if you can call them that, into the van." Pug purposefully used an initial rather than a name. "D, we'll see you there."

Zola escorted the two women to the four-wheeler where she helped them into the cargo area.

Pug, Donnie, and Lacey shuffled the blindfolded, handcuffed men into the back of the Sienna where the rear seat had been removed. Then they loaded the dead deputy into the patrol car and placed Ronnie's body into the passenger seat of the 4-wheeler. Donnie then got into Ronnie's truck and straightened it in the road, allowing Pug and Lacey to drive their vehicles forward and towards their destination. Before driving away, Pug watched as Donnie used the huge truck to push the deputy's car, then the government car, over the embankment and down the steep ravine. Then Pug sped off.

"I know who you are," Lawton the inspector proclaimed.

"Z," Pug replied, "Please shoot that man in the head," Zola turned in her seat and cocked her handgun.

"Sorry, please!" Lawton implored, fearful of his life. "I won't say another word."

Eight minutes later, Pug left the pavement and drove a short way on dirt, extinguishing his lights 100 yards prior to parking. Lacey drove in behind him.

By the time the prisoners were outside of the vehicles, Donnie arrived in another 4-wheeler. The kidnappers put hardhats on everybody's head and battery-powered lights on their own.

Goldschmidt said, "I don't know what you want from us, but you don't need my assistant, Ms. Wilkins."

Wilkins sobbed anxiously. Pug looked at the terrified, pretty young woman, clearly facing a situation her life had never prepared her for.

Pug thought about it for a moment. He looked at Lacey who shrugged back at him. Zola and Donnie did the same. Pug said to Zola, "Keep her blindfolded. Drive her someplace where somebody will find her in the morning, but make sure she has no idea where she is or where she's been. Or who you are. Then tie her to a tree and come on back." He gave her a length of rope that he'd brought along, about the diameter of a child's pencil.

"No worry, boss!" Zola said.

"God, thank you!" Wilkins cried, the first decipherable utterance she'd made. "Secretary Goldschmidt, I..."

"Don't worry," the older woman said reassuringly. "Once these folks get what they want, we'll be fine."

As Zola led the younger woman to the Sienna and drove it away, Pug and Lacey cuffed Youngblood to inspector Lawton and secretary Goldschmidt to Deputy Webber.

"Okay, folks," Lacey said, "We're gonna take you on a little walk."

The entourage walked uphill, then level, through the darkness, illuminated by the kidnappers' headlights. Each of the prisoners stumbled several times, being still blindfolded. At one point, Youngblood fell on his face, taking Lawton down with him. Pug, Lacey, and Donnie all strained to get the captives back on their feet. "Let's keep moving, please," Pug said.

Moments later, the group was brought to a stop at a point where musty air hit them in their faces. Pug spoke again. "Okay, ladies and gentlemen, or I should say lady and gentlemen, y'all will all need to lean over for the rest of our walk."

"Where are we going?" Goldschmidt asked.

Pug sensed the other prisoners knew the answer already. "Ma'am, we're going inside."

"Inside what?" she asked with astonishment.

"Yee-haw! We're going coal mining!" Donnie yelled.

They moved forward and immediately Webber's hardhat smacked into the roof of the entrance, knocking him back. "Dammit!" he screamed.

"Take these infernal blindfolds off," Youngblood implored. "We need to see where we're going."

"Fine enough," Pug said, removing the prisoners' blindfolds. "But let's get an understanding here. You four are going first. We're behind you, holding lights on you and pointing our guns at you. Don't try anything."

"Where are we going?" Goldschmidt asked again.

"We have a little hotel set up for you. You'll be our guests for a few days," Lacey said, mocking politeness.

"Maybe longer," Donnie sneered.

"The roof of this mine is an almost uniform 4' 8" tall," Pug said. "Y'all bend over and go on in."

As advertised, the mine roof was low enough that everyone walked at a crouch. Youngblood was clearly laboring, given his heft and the recently inflicted damage to his gut from Pug's punch. The pair of Youngblood and Lawton went first, followed by captors Pug and Lacey. Fifteen feet behind, Webber and Goldschmidt were escorted by Donnie. Lacey shouted out directions as they came and passed intersecting corridors. Pug recognized early on that Lacey was taking everyone in circles, deliberately confusing them. Working mines have cables with one-way thimbles strung near the ceiling to be used by escaping miners in the event of a fire or power failure. In places, the cable was still in place but in others it had been removed. In other places, the thimbles had been reversed. Pug was convinced that anyone lacking light would never be able to find his way out and would have a difficult time if they did have light.

As they marched the prisoners around and around for seemingly an hour, hardhats often clanging against the low ceiling, Pug sweated profusely even in the cool, damp air. In places, they walked through standing puddles, wetting everyone's shoes.

At one point, Youngblood implored for a break. "Go to hell, Youngblood. Keep moving," Pug insisted, poking him hard in the back with the barrel of his gun.

Finally they rounded a corner where they emerged into a larger room, perhaps 20' X 10', but no taller than the rest of the mine. A matrix of bolts held 8-inch square steel plates affixed to the roof of the mine, imbedded in the hard rock ceiling. On one end sat the cannibalized remains of a continuous mining machine, a hulk of immobilized machinery.

"Here we are," Donnie proclaimed eagerly, "Casa Oscuridad," using Spanish for house of darkness that Pug figured Donnie had learned in the military.

Pug saw that Donnie and Lacey had prepared the room exactly as they had discussed. There were several folding Army surplus chairs and cots resting against a wall, along with a pile of clothing and blankets. There was a portable latrine against another wall. In a touch of superfluous decorating that amused Pug, there was a West Virginia University pendant in blue and gold with the word "Mountaineers" tacked to a wall of rock and a matching throw rug on the dry floor.

"Welcome to your new home," Pug said to the captors.

"Here," Pug said, handing his gun to Lacey. He then worked with Donnie to place a heavy metal ankle shackle on each prisoner, starting with Youngblood, then Lawton, Webber, and then Goldschmidt. Each shackle was connected to a steel bar on the continuous miner by a six-foot length of heavy chain.

"What now?" asked Webber.

"We're getting back to work in War, burying the dead," Pug sneered.

"What about us?" Goldschmidt pleaded.

"You'll be staying here for awhile," Lacey said.

"I hope you find the accommodations comfortable," Donnie added.

"How long?" Youngblood asked.

"As long as it takes," Pug insisted, unfolding chairs for his guests.

"As long as it takes for what?" Youngblood growled.

"Let's go, y'all," Pug said to his fellow kidnappers.

"Wait!" Goldschmidt implored. "Are you just going to leave us here in the dark?"

Donnie snickered.

"That's the idea," Lacey said. "There's some blankets and cots. There's some water over there," he pointed at some jugs. "That water comes right from our War municipal water supply. It's got heavy metals in it. It's disgusting, but it's all we got. 'Course, you'll need to find everything in the dark, 'cause we're not leaving any lights."

"Sweet dreams," Donnie said sarcastically.

"We'll see you in a few hours," Pug said.

Youngblood shouted angrily, "You will all burn in hell!"

Lacey fired back, "If you get there first, would you warm up the place for us?"

Pug, Lacey, and Donnie, turned to go, their lights now illuminating the corridor in front of them but not the prison.

Youngblood shouted, "Just what the hell do you people want?"

The kidnappers stopped walking. Pug turned around and said simply, "Justice." Then they kept going.

As the new kidnappers moved towards the mine entrance, they congratulated themselves over a job well done. Nobody dared speak about the impending consequences.

Emerging into the dark winter night, Pug said to Donnie, "I'm sorry about what happened to your brother."

"Me, too. Thanks. My family is dead. His family is dead. I'm the only one left. I fully expect that within a week or two, I'll be dead too, or in prison for the rest of my life."

"What did you do with his body?"

"I hoisted it onto the truck. Then I drove the truck to your mine. I took his body into the workshop shed and hid it under some tarps. Then I got the 4-wheeler and drove here. I need to drive it back to the mine and retrieve his body. I'm going to hide it in the mine for a few days. I'm afraid if I bury it at the family cemetery, somebody might notice and would suspect me of the kidnapping and then come after us."

Pug looked at all three co-conspirators, "Does anybody think we left any clues behind?"

Lacey said, "Not that I can tell. But for what it's worth, Lawton knows who we are."

"That's true," Pug said.

"But," Donnie said, snickering, "He's only got three people to tell."

Pug drove the Sienna back to War, driving past the kidnapping scene. There were no vehicles there. He went inside his house and radioed Red Hazelwood. "Our mission is underway," he said.

"What's the status?" Red asked.

"We have four prisoners. Youngblood is the president of Bessie Energy. Lawton is a mine inspector for the state. He's the guy who's given me such grief at our mine. We have a county mountie named Webber. And we have a woman named Goldschmidt. She's Secretary of the Interior."

"Holy shit!" Red exclaimed. "Of the United States? Shit, you kidnapped her? She's on the President's cabinet!"

"Yeah, I know. We let one person go, an aide to Goldschmidt. Somebody will find her in the morning, but she won't be able to identify us."

"Any casualties?"

"Yeah. There was another officer, name of Coles. He's dead. We lost one of our guys, Ronnie Getgood. His twin brother Donnie is with us. We dumped Coles over the embankment in one of their two cars. Donnie has Ronnie's body stashed away."

"Won't people be suspicious when they see Donnie around town and not Ronnie?"

"We talked about that on the way here. Donnie is going to try not to be seen at all. Most folks can't tell them apart. If he is questioned, he'll say that Ronnie is missing in the flood. We have so many other people missing around here that nobody is going to worry about one more. At least we hope."

"So what now?" the reporter asked.

"We all just do our thing. We're all going to go back to work in town on the recovery. You just report what you know for now. I'm sure within a few hours, somebody will figure out there's been a kidnapping, that five people are missing on their way back from War. Somebody will find the cars over the embankment by morning, along with the girl we released.

So for now, you don't know anything more than any other reporter. We'll make a statement that you can distribute within 24 hours. So stand by."

"Pug?"

"Yeah?"

"This is serious, man."

"Yeah."

"I mean, you've committed a federal offense. You'll get a death sentence. Maybe me, too."

"You'll be fine, Red; you haven't done anything wrong. I know what's at stake for me. We already have 200 or more dead here. Any more, I don't give a shit about myself. Over and out."

+ + + + +

Within minutes, the men began talking about their escape as Goldschmidt listened with a detached desperation. She shivered convulsively in the damp, cold grotto, unable and unwilling to join their scheming. Her captor's final word, "justice," ran over and over through her thoughts, wondering what that meant to him. She began shuffling around in the dark, an amazing, primordial dark she'd never before experienced, feeling her way towards the pile of blankets. As she took the one on top to cover herself, the men began talking about the captors.

The voice she recognized as Lawton's said, "Lucas Graham is the ringleader. They call him 'Pug'. After I got rid of his brother, Pug came back to town and took over."

"That's the mine just north of town, ain't it?" Youngblood asked.

"Yeah, it's one of the mines you paid me to put under."

Meredith pondered what the men meant, feeling as marginalized as she'd felt at the recent Presidential cabinet meeting where she'd been so ruthlessly verbally abused by the Vice. Youngblood even began to resemble the Vice in his depreciatory, sneering manner. She felt a strange detachment, as if in the total darkness her fellow captives had quickly come to completely discount her very presence.

The men continued conversing about the others, with Lawton having recognized the other two men and Webber having recognized the woman as one of the mountaintop removal activists. They talked about each kidnapper's weaknesses, agreeing that none except the Getgood boy would probably have enough guts to kill anybody. When the time came, they would use that to their advantage.

It was wickedly unsettling, with Meredith eavesdropping on a conversation happening in her immediate midst, yet not having the ability to see anyone or anything. She knew they knew she was there, but nobody asked her for any input or opinions.

A visceral pall of damp, dark dread swept over her. Her unfaithful husband was comatose. Her sole offspring was literally on the other side of the world. Her parents were dead. Her bosses, the most powerful people in the world, treated her like chattel. She was in a dungeon worthy of the most despicable fairy tale, perhaps soon to die and never be seen again. And she was in the company of assholes.

At least Jenni was safe, or so she hoped. She removed her wet shoes and socks, and lay back on the cot, covering herself with two blankets. Her bones ached in the cold, but her exhaustion was profound and eventually sleep overcame her.

Part 4

PUG AND ZOLA WOKE just before dawn, with Zola sleeping in Pug's parents' bed. Having lost his home in the flood, Lacey had spent the night at Pug's place, too. Donnie, seeking privacy, had moved out, having taken up residence in the cabin on the mountain. Pug and Zola gathered some food, including some Army rations taken from the relief stores the day before, and loaded them into Pug's Sienna. They drove past the kidnapping scene where a tow-truck was pulling the government vehicle back onto the road from where Donnie had pushed both the night before. There was a cop directing traffic but few other vehicles. Nobody stopped Pug or Zola or asked where they were going.

Pug placed the food items and Donnie's Glock handgun into a knapsack he'd hidden near where he parked the van, and then the two abductors began the hike up the mountainside over frosty mud to the entrance to the mine. They picked up the hard-hats they'd stowed the night before, switched on the electric headlamps, and walked inside, crouching. Twenty minutes later, they rounded the bend to find their captives lying on the cots.

"Rise and shine, my friends," Pug exclaimed, in mock cheerfulness. "Good morning, all! Hope everybody slept well."

"Well, well," Youngblood sneered, "If it ain't the Prince of Darkness. Get us the hell out of here."

"Not so fast, fatso," Zola said, removing her hard hat and wiping the sweat off her bald head.

Webber, mocking her as he'd done a couple of weeks earlier on the War Room, said, "Lookie here! Still no hair, my little Nazi?"

"Go to hell!" she screamed.

"Listen, folks," Pug said plaintively, "We don't need to like each other, but we should try to get along."

"I'll get along when you pull this fuckin' iron off my ankle," Webber sneered.

"Like I said, not so fast..." Pug began.

"With all due respect," Meredith Goldschmidt began, diplomatically, rising herself from her cot, "we know who you are. You're Lucas Graham. Folks call you 'Pug.' And you, young lady, are Zola Wilkerson. Inspector Merritt recognized you, Pug. And Officer Webber figured out who you must be, Ms. Wilkerson."

"Yes, ma'am," Pug said respectfully.

"My name is Meredith Goldschmidt. I'm the Secretary of the Interior of the United States of America. I am in President Cooper's cabinet. I am eighth in line for succession to the presidency. Kidnapping me is an act of treason. I strongly suggest you release me right away. And these gentlemen, too. What you've done has serious consequences."

Zola glared at Goldschmidt. "No, shit, lady! Consequences. Bah! Tell us one we don't know."

"What my friend is trying to tell you, Madam Secretary," Pug explained, "is that we're aware of what we've done and of the consequences. None of us has anything to lose. And that should make the four of you really nervous."

"With all due respect, Mr. Graham, you need to release us. I'll try to argue for leniency but this sham has to end."

"And with all due respect to you," Pug countered, "this is not a sham and I suspect it has only just begun." Pug opened his knapsack and set the food and the gun before him. He opened some rations for the prisoners, spooning some beans and franks on four plates.

"So what's your plan, Pug?" Youngblood asked, feigning cooperation. "Justice, you said. What's that mean?"

"Sorry to keep you in the dark," Pug began as Zola chuckled at the obvious reference, "but you'll be informed in due course. Right now, we encourage you to make yourselves at home and be cool."

Goldschmidt shook visibly in the chilly, confined space.

"We've got some victuals for you this morning," Zola spooned.

"Morning is it?" Goldschmidt asked.

"Yes, Ma'am. We can give you weather reports if you'd like them," Pug said, cooperatively, "but I don't assume you'd want to know what's going on outside."

"To the contrary," Webber the officer said. "I'm figurin' your murder of last night will be pretty well known by now."

Pug handed Goldschmidt a plate of beans. "Ma'am. Cuisine de la FEMA."

Zola placed another plate on the mine floor in front of Youngblood, barely within his reach.

Pug extended his hand with another plate towards Webber, but the tall, cat-quick officer grabbed Pug's hand and wrenched him off his feet and he fell to the mine floor, with Webber's hands around his neck.

"It's time for this charade to end, NOW!" Webber yelled. "Release us or I'll fuckin' break your neck."

Zola picked up the gun and pointed at Pug and the officer.

"Shoot him, Zola," Pug said calmly.

Webber yanked Pug towards him, attempting to use Pug as a shield. Then, an ear-splitting pop echoed through the shallow room. Webber released his grip as his hard-hat flew off his head, split in half by a bullet that grazed the helmet but somehow missed the officer's head. Pug scampered away from the officer's grasp, beyond the reach of the chained and shackled man.

"Thanks," Pug said to Zola. He retrieved the prisoner's hard-hat pieces. "Too bad, now. Looks like you won't have any head protection any more."

Pug resolved to keep better distance between himself and Webber in the future.

The kidnappers finished handing out the food and waited for their captives to eat, with nothing much said. They wiped the residue from the plates.

As the kidnappers started to leave, Webber glowered, "What are we supposed to do? Just wait?"

"You could watch some TV," Zola said, laughing.

"Do some painting!" Pug chimed, as they strolled away.

"Perhaps some knitting!" Zola trailed, jocularly.

They walked a bit farther and Zola said, "Pug, I've got another idea. I don't know how long these folks will be our guests, but they have no idea how fast time passes. If we really want to mess with them, we can accelerate the days."

"Good idea," Pug said. "For the next day or two, a day will pass in 20 hours instead of 24. It will make them that much more nervous that nobody is coming for them."

That evening, with Pug's approval, Zola gathered her few remaining things and moved into Mill's old house. With Donnie on his own at the mountain cabin, that left only Lacey still staying with Pug.

+ + + + +

Seven hours later, Pug woke Zola at 3:00 a.m. and they drove back to the mine in the dark. There was a light dusting of snow on the road, but with an early rising quarter-moon the road was easy to see even without the headlights that Pug had left off at first, then convinced himself he'd look even more suspicious without them than with.

They trudged up the hillside in the snow without their helmet lamps on. They walked quietly the last 50 steps to their makeshift jail, trying to see if their prisoners were asleep. Arriving near their destination, Pug extinguished his light and had Zola do the same. Then, playfully, he swung his hard-hat hard against the ceiling with a bang!

"Shit!" Youngblood shouted.

"Just having a little fun this morning!" Pug exclaimed.

The stench of excrement hit Pug's olfactory. He looked at the latrine and surmised that his captives had found it and done their business, even in the pitch darkness. Pug attended to the latrine, closing the soiled plastic bag and replacing it with a fresh one. He carried the old bag down the corridor.

While Zola was setting out food for the men, Goldschmidt caught Pug's ear and said quietly, "Listen, I don't know what plans you have for me, but could you do a woman a favor? Being in this cave is as close to hell as I've ever been. The fat guy snores something awful. I could use some privacy. When I have to defecate, I have to crawl over and figure out what I'm doing in the dark. I know the men can't see a thing, but could you give me some space here and perhaps my own pot?"

"Let me see what I can do," Pug said. He was beginning to feel some sympathy for the woman.

"We'll be back every 12 hours or so," Pug promised as they prepared to depart. "Speaking of which, anybody got a watch? If you do, we'd like them, please."

Nobody moved until Zola pointed the gun again at Lawton. He reached for his left wrist and unstrapped a cloth-strapped watch. Her gun pointed to Youngblood who took a shiny gold watch from his breast pocket and pitched it to Pug. Pug looked at it and Youngblood's initials "AY" were inscribed on the watch face which was studded with diamonds.

"Webber? How about yours?"

After Zola pointed and cocked her gun, Webber unstrapped his and threw it over, too.

"Oh," Pug thought out loud. "We'd like your wallets, too. And your cell phones. Y'all won't be needing them."

Again, nobody moved. Pug took the gun from Zola and sent a bullet into the wall behind Lawton's left shoulder. The sound was deafening and his prisoners reached to cover their ears, all too late to do any good. "I don't think I should have to ask twice, do you Zola?"

"No-sir-ree!" she exclaimed.

He re-aimed, this time at Lawton's nose. Everyone grabbed their wallets and cell phones and pitched them towards Pug.

"That's more like it. I appreciate the cooperation."

+ + + + +

Just after dark, Pug and Zola drove to pick up Lacey and then over to the mine again. In addition to more provisions, they carried some hand-wipes and small bottles of waterless antibacterial hand sanitizer that were now all over town. They found the captives right as they were left hours earlier. Pug wondered how they'd passed the time.

"I'm hungry as hell," Youngblood insisted. "I'm having blood-sugar problems. If you are going to keep me very long, you'll need to get me some of my diabetes medicine."

"Fat chance," Pug scowled, looking at the man's girth.

Lacey attended to the latrine this time.

While feeding them, Pug considered what to share with them and when. Would they demand ransom, as they'd discussed initially? Even if the ransom was paid, he wasn't sure what he'd do with Youngblood. And he had no idea what to do with the others.

Meredith Goldschmidt said, "How long do you plan to keep us?"

"We're not sure yet," said Pug, truthfully.

"What can we do to earn our release?" she plugged.

"Not sure of that, either. As I said, we're interested in justice. A terrible wrong has been done outside here and it must be avenged."

The distinguished woman, now wrapped against the

constant 53F of the mine with an Army blanket, stood and stretched, still bent over with her helmeted head resting against the low roof of the mine. She paced a few feet, clanging the chain strapped to the shackle on her ankle. She seemed to be considering her next tactic when she said, "I've never known darkness like this. When you are gone," looking at her captors, "I can put my hand in front of my face and I can feel its warmth, but I can't see it. My eyes want to make light where there is none."

Nobody said anything.

Goldschmidt continued, "What are those two red lights beside each other over there that occasionally blink?" pointing at a distant corner. "It beeps on occasion, too."

"Lady, that's a methane detector," Lacey said, returning from his housekeeping chore. "Miners use it to detect a flammable mixture of methane if it exists in a mine. Methane'll explode. That's why nobody smokes inside. Methane won't catch fire if there's too much and it won't catch fire if there's too little. It's the Goldilocks of flammable gasses; it needs to be just right!" he chuckled.

Pug continued, "This mine isn't ventilated any more. Whenever miners work an active mine, they're required to ventilate it with huge blower fans, aren't we, Inspector Lawton?" He looked Lawton's way, but got no reaction from his captive. "But since this mine was abandoned years ago, there hasn't been any ventilation. I suspect the methane will be pretty high. We'll keep tabs."

+ + + + +

The kidnappers finished their chores, secured the area and the prisoners, and then departed. On the way outside the mine, Zola said to Pug, "I never heard about methane detectors. Is that for real?"

"Absolutely. In fact, a buddy of mine worked in a Bessie

mine 'till he got so scared he had to quit. A supervisor put plastic bags over the detectors so they wouldn't properly detect the methane. The mine exploded and it killed 32 people. But to tell you the truth, I re-wired the machine to simply beep every 15 minutes to keep them on edge. Methane shouldn't be building at all because there is no more coal being disturbed, which releases methane. Lawton will probably know that, but I'm just trying to mess with their minds. It may not occur to him. Next time we go back inside, when they're not looking I'll re-set it to beep more often."

Back at his house, they had some food themselves and re-charged their helmet light batteries with the generator power.

+ + + + +

Meredith awoke from a sleep – like the rest of her naps with no idea how long she'd slept – shivering in a cold, nightmare-induced sweat. She dreamed of an albino cougar, prowling the underworld. It stared at her with two red eyes. It snarled, growled menacingly, and then retreated into the dark.

JAN 7 Tuesday

Back in town, Pug went back to the church to continue assisting in any way he could. Someone had brought a laptop computer and had achieved satellite Internet connection. Pug read an article from the Bluefield newspaper on-line with Red's by-line.

Officials kidnapped outside War

Last night, on State Route 16, four people were kidnapped from their vehicles. One person was killed, Vernon Dale Coles, Jr., a State Trooper from Beckley. His remains were found inside his police car in a ravine where the kidnapping was thought to have occurred, some three miles north of War.

The kidnapped individuals were Her Honorable Secretary of the Interior of the United States Meredith Goldschmidt of Georgetown, Washington, DC, Alvin Youngblood, president of Bessie Energy, Merritt Lee Lawton, a mining inspector based in Gilbert, and Doug Webber, a McDowell County Deputy Sheriff.

The officials were in War to coordinate relief efforts following the horrific flood of January 3 which killed 225 people in the War area.

Jennifer Wilson Wilkins, an assistant to Secretary Goldschmidt was released by the kidnappers and was found early this morning chained to a tree east of Carretta. She is suffering from hypothermia, having spent the night outside, but is recovering in Welch General Hospital. Her injury is not thought to be life-threatening. She is unable to identify her captors, only saying that she believed there to be four in number. She also believed that one additional captor was killed in an exchange of gunfire with Trooper Coles, but if so, his body has not been found.

No motives have been determined and no person or persons have claimed responsibility.

Anyone having any information about the whereabouts of the kidnapped victims please call 911 immediately.

The former townsite of War was buzzing with activity, although none of the buildings within 35 vertical feet of the creek remained standing. The old city hall, housed in the former railroad station, had been swept away, too. Bodies continued to arrive at the church, but not with the regularity of the prior days. With the road now open to Welch, a flow of rescue vehicles had arrived, including heavy earth-moving equipment. Piles of debris were forming around town, with new material arriving as soon as the contents could be assured free of living things, or dead. The stench in places was overwhelming, and people wore cloth masks over their mouths and noses. Pug saw several people sobbing. One heavy-equipment operator labored over a pile composed mostly of a collapsed house, picking skillfully and carefully over the shattered pieces. The only thing he found to break his work was a dead dog, a terrier, its hair matted and its back broken. The gruesome work continued.

+ + + + +

Pug made his next trip into the mine with Lacey, Donnie, and Zola. This time, Red Hazelwood came along, too, at Pug's request. Hazelwood wore a child's Halloween mask, a rubberized likeness of Ronald Reagan, to hide his identity. Pug also carried a small digital camera and the newspaper with Red's article.

"Good morning, everybody!" Pug shouted as he arrived. It was 9:30 p.m. but he was sure by now his prisoners were totally disoriented.

"Good morning, all. Did everyone sleep well?"

"Bastard," Webber grumbled under his breath, sending a wad of spit towards Pug, missing narrowly.

"Shut up, asshole," Pug responded. "The next stage of our operation is ready to get under way. We brought along a witness," he nodded towards Red, "and we're going to take some photos."

"You're going to ransom us," Lawton blurted, stating the obvious.

"Well, we're going to ransom you, Mister Fat Cat Industrialist," Zola said, staring at Youngblood.

Pug said, "Won't do us any good to ransom Ms. Goldschmidt, 'cause the Federal Government won't pay. And it won't do us any good to ransom you, Webber, 'cause McDowell County doesn't have two dimes to rub together. And it won't do us any good to ransom you, Lawton, because you're lower than pond scum and nobody gives a shit about you. We'd probably have to pay somebody, even your mother, to take you back."

Zola handed Goldschmidt the day's newspaper. "Say 'cheese,'" Pug implored. Meredith managed a wan smile and the flash scorched the room. "Hand that newspaper to Youngblood, please."

Youngblood grabbed the paper and began ripping it to shreds. He stopped and glowered at Pug, whereupon Pug snapped his photo. "You might as well start ripping it up," Pug said, "because it's all you're going to get for dinner."

Pug took photos of Lawton and Webber for good measure, making sure there was nothing in the background of any of the photos that would give away their location, other than that they were deep inside the earth.

Before leaving, Pug unshackled Meredith and moved her and her bed to another area nearby, equipping it with her own latrine, honoring her earlier request. Then he and the other kidnappers departed the prison area.

Two hundred yards away but still covered by a sky of 500 feet of rock, Red broke his silence and said, "What do you want me to report about the prisoners?"

Pug instructed Red to print an article showing the captives and demanding $1 million from Bessie Energy for the heirs of each victim of the flood, now $220 million total.

"Oh, one more thing."

Pug placed Youngblood's watch on a small rock on the floor of the mine. He took a photo of it. Then he smashed the crystal with another rock. Then he took another photo of it. He slid the memory chip from the camera and put in Red's breast pocket and smiled at him. They continued their egress.

A moment passed and Red said, "Pug?"

"Yeah?"

"Are you sure about what you're doing?" Red asked,

plaintively, his helmet resting against the ceiling.

"I don't think anybody is sure about anything any more, at least in War. But there's no backing out now."

After several hours of clean-up work around the former tiny city, Pug and Zola picked up Lacey on their way back into the mine, where Donnie met them at the entrance. Pug carried with him some clothes from his mother's closet to give to Secretary Goldschmidt, thinking she might appreciate having something clean to wear. In the mine, Pug attended to her while Zola and Lacey attended to the men.

Goldschmidt thanked Pug profusely, saying how relieved it was for her to have clean clothing, particularly underwear. Pug said, unshackling his prisoner, "I'm going to leave my headlight here with you. Call me when you're done changing and I'll re-attach this."

"Are you going to leave me here unwatched and unchained, with your headlight? I could escape."

"I don't think you'll be going anywhere. I'm sure you have no idea which way is out."

"Yeah, true enough. Anyway, thanks for the trust."

"Yes, ma'am."

He walked into the other prison room where Youngblood was increasingly petulant. "Dammit, Pug. Look, we know who you are. We know your plan. We've figured out all of you."

"Yeah?"

"Yeah! Release us and we'll do what we can to save your sorry asses. Otherwise, you'll die making heroes of yourselves."

"I suspect so," Pug sighed. "That's our fate, I suppose."

+ + + + +

Pug returned to Goldschmidt and re-shackled her ankle.

The once distinguished, accomplished woman had clearly been crying. "Look, I understand where you're coming from and what you feel you need to do," she said to him. "But I'm dying in here. I'm always cold. There's an incessant drip of water coming from somewhere and it's like a Chinese water torture. But what's really getting to me is the boredom and the darkness. The only thing I hear is the dripping water. Can you give me something to do or something to read? Anything! The Wall Street Journal. War and Peace. Mein Kampf. I don't care."

"Let me see what I can do," he said, cooperatively.

+ + + + +

On the way out, Donnie put in place just around the corner from the captives a three-stick wrap of dynamite, wired to a 3-minute timer. He had asked Pug for permission to have it in the mine as an ultimate doomsday device, should everything come apart. He showed Pug, Lacey and Zola how to arm it and set the timer in motion.

JAN 8 Wednesday

Pug and Zola woke a second time around 7:45. They had some food and again went to the church. As they walked inside, Preacher Karwoski was giving a brief sermon over an unidentified body. Somebody told Pug it was the remains of a teenage girl, but it was so badly battered and disfigured that nobody knew who she was. It had been sitting underneath a house that looked relatively intact, but nobody had checked underneath until a dog started pawing at the dirt and alerted rescue personnel.

Finally, the electricity was restored. Pug's attention was drawn again to a laptop computer that had this from the Bluefield Star Sentinel web page, written by the Publisher,

Red's boss:

Ransom note received in War kidnapping

At 2:00 p.m. yesterday, Bluefield Star Sentinel reporter Estell Hazelwood was contacted by an unidentified man who claimed to be a mastermind of the recent kidnapping of several officials. The kidnapper has demanded from Bessie Energy, $220 million, representing $1 million for each of the heirs of the known victims of the January 3 flood in War. Bessie Energy is the company that owned the dams that collapsed, causing the flood.

The ransom is for the safe return of Alvin Youngblood, Bessie Energy president, and the other captives.

Release of the hostages is predicated on the establishment of separate bank accounts, each devoted to the heirs.

According to the kidnappers, if the ransom demands are not fulfilled within 72 hours, the prisoners will be executed.

Meanwhile McDowell County coroner Raymond Cornelius has established death certificates and chains of custody for the flood victims. Cornelius reports that officially 228 people have been reported missing. There are 220 bodies identified, thus the ransom amount demanded from Bessie Energy.

Bluefield Star Sentinel reporter Hazelwood has been questioned by police, but has been uncooperative, stating First Amendment rights to source privacy.

Because one of the kidnapping victims was a federal official, Secretary of the Interior Meredith Goldschmidt, the FBI is now involved and agents are assisting state police in the search.

Accompanying the article was the photograph of Youngblood that Pug had taken.

Pug had only moments to consider the presence of the FBI until two agents with those initials embroidered on their jackets walked through the church. He avoided eye contact and went outside to resume his part in the community's dreadful work.

Word was that the Army was making a purposeful attempt to burn condemned houses and carry away crippled cars as quickly as possible before residents could salvage them. Pug also learned that several fundamentalists from a church in Missouri had descended on the community where they were spouting hellfire and damnation, as if the devastating flood was ordained by God for the sins of the citizens.

Near the site of the former elementary school, a pyre was burning with debris from several ruined houses. Pug overheard someone say that many people had brought dead pets to be consumed by the fire. While he watched the inferno rage at a comfortable distance, he overheard three men talking about the kidnapping and the ransom. One said, "If they ever release that bastard, Youngblood, I swear to God I'll kill him myself."

Pug was inwardly pleased by the surreptitious support. But his pleasure only lasted moments until he caught the scent of burning flesh and it nauseated him. His mind's eye flashed the images of the dead girl he'd seen a few days earlier. Waves of remorse, stress, and sleep deprivation swept over him. Metallic bile built up in his throat and he ran behind a wrecked car where he vomited.

+ + + + +

Back in the mine that evening, Pug attended to Goldschmidt first. She asked him, "How's it going with the ransom?"

"I don't know yet," Pug admitted.

"Keep me posted," the Secretary said.

"Excuse me?"

There was a clamor in the adjacent room and Pug broke away to see what was going on. Youngblood was in a rage. "I've had just about enough of this goddamn charade. Turn us loose NOW. I demand it!"

Zola replied calmly, "You don't seem to have a lot of cards to play Mr. Fat Cat Company President."

"Fuck you, baldy-bitch."

"In your dreams," she retorted angrily.

"Now, now," Pug interjected. "Let's just get along, shall we?"

Webber the deputy said, "You've already kept us in this hell-hole for what? Three days? Four? When are we going to be released?"

Pug knew Zola's accelerated time scheme was working.

"You people have caused the destruction of my community. Justice must be done. We're in no hurry."

"You'll HANG, all of you!" shouted Youngblood.

"Yessir, we expect so," said Donnie. "Yee-haw!"

+ + + + +

Pug returned to Meredith, where he produced a short stack of papers from inside his coveralls. "I brought something for you," he said.

"What is it?"

"Something my mother was working on for the past few months. You asked for something to read. It's a memoir or something. For the past several months, she's been typing away on an old manual typewriter some recollections from her youth and from her friends." He reached inside his coveralls and handed her several sheets. "I haven't read it. I'm too busy burying my dead neighbors. Maybe you can tell me what it is. I brought you a small, battery-powered light to read by. It has rechargeable batteries that I've only charged to 5%, so you'll only have a few minutes each day to read. But I'll bring another set next time and more papers if I can find them."

"Hey," she said.

"Yeah?"

"Thanks."

Pug smiled and then departed.

Meredith wasted no time diving into her reading material. She read with a frenzied panic, hoping to absorb as much as possible before her precious light gave out. It began,

My name is Delores Annie Winfield Graham. This is my story.

I'm here writing this because my friend, Claudia Wilmer… gosh, we go back to high school together, told me writing my story would be a good thing. "Take your mind off Emmett and his death, upcoming." She said, "Tell everything you remember, everything."

Folks always marveled at my sense of smell. I'm almost 80 now, but I don't like to count my years any more. I have more years behind me than ahead of me now, but I have no regrets.

First thing I remember in my life was riding home from the doctor in Bluefield on the train. I suspect I wasn't three or four. I don't know why mammy took me there or what my malady was, but I was a sickly child. I had a problem with my eyesight, too, not diagnosed until I got to school. That's why folks said I smelled things.

My husband Emmett has black lung, pneumoconiosis. He will die soon, likely within the year. I suffer his every breath. When we sit together at night, I turn off all the sounds in our house.

I swear I could hear a mouse sneeze. I
listen to him breathe. I listen to the air
rushing down into his lungs. His lungs
work hard, sucking in this air. I see
in my mind's eye all those cells in his
lungs, coated by black filth, that prevent
them from absorbing the oxygen he needs.
He has been my lifetime companion, and
that film of coal dust is suffocating him,
slowly and painfully. I try to breathe for
him, to smell for him. I figure there's
goop in my lungs, too, but I still smell
stuff. He tells me he can't smell any
more. I ache for him. But he will die and
I will live on with the memories of his
death and so many painful deaths before
his.

Meredith took a deep breath, smelling the musty, earthen
smell that permeated the mine, and wondered about the level
of coal dust. She continued reading.

Anyways, I remember that train pulling
into the station at War and even before it
did, I remember smelling War.
Places have their smells. I guess in
hindsight, War smelled like everywhere
else in Southern West Virginia, but it
seemed strangely, pungently dark, thick,
and industrial. It smelled like burning,
but a wet burning, the soot-laden air
belching from the steam locomotive's snout
mixing with the sulfuric smell of burning
coal.

Burning. Always, something was
burning in War. When I was a child, the
locomotives that chuffed through town were
steam. They were belching monsters, white
steam flowing out the sides and coal smoke
pouring out the top. Slate dumps burned,
often for years, with an awful smell and
choking air quality. All the miners used
carbide lamps on their hard hats in those
days which burned acetylene created by a
reaction of calcium carbide with water.
Adults smoked, most of them, the women
smoking cigarettes and the men smoking
cigarettes and pipes. There was always a
fire going in the kitchen stove, even on
the hottest days. The coke ovens were the
worst, with a choking, heavy, irritating
carboniferous stench a body can never
forget.

I have always been fascinated by the
stories of the coalfields. I don't even
like the word. There are no fields around
here. Everything is hills and hollows.

The coal mining regions - I like
that better - have from the earliest
days harbored stories of death, injury,
hardship, and destruction. But most of the
stories are from the men's perspectives.
What about the women?

Don't get me wrong. Men suffered
enormously, down on their knees working
the coal. They lost limbs. They breathed
dirty air. They got black lung. They died
prematurely. But the women suffered too.

Men crawled through tunnels of coal. But
their job was to bring it out. Onced they
did, then the women dealt with it too.

Meredith unconsciously rubbed her left hand on her left
knee, wondering if she'd ever stand straight and walk on it
painlessly again.

Let me tell you about my Indian
ancestry.
My people descended from the Cherokee.
Mine is a matriarchal bloodline. What
I know about my lineage is always the
traditions of our women.
When I sat by myself at our creek in
the hollow we now call Gary as a child,
I envisioned the mother of my people,
my great-grandmother, a Cherokee named
Chanchala, the unsteady one. My women
have always been somewhat unsteady, or
as we say now restless. We were edgy. We
yearned.
Chanchala lived in the tall mountains
of North Carolina, born on the cusp of
the American Civil War. Was hers a happy
life? I can only imagine. I know in my
heart she lived with the deer, the bear,
and the wild turkey. She watched the raven
and the buzzard swoop overhead. We visited
her homeland on vacation back in 1974 when
the boys were young. It still had deer and
bear and turkey, in fact more deer than
ever.
Her family avoided the War by exploiting

the isolation the mountains provided.
They would have been Unionists, I'm sure,
knowing the horrors of slavery from
experiences in their past.

Chanchala married an Irishman, O'Byrne,
around 1875. They struggled to provide for
their family of girls, they were dirt poor
as literal as the word can be. Blanid was
born in 1875. Finola was born in 1876.
Ciara was born in 1878. The youngest, Dae
was born in 1880. Dae was the only one to
survive childhood.

Dae married a Scotsman, Campbell, in
1901. With the soils depleted in the rocky
Blue Ridge, he moved her to Gary Hollow,
West Virginia, to where coal was beginning
to be mined. He needed work. Lots of
people did.

Then, the light went dim. She folded her sheets of reading material and put them inside her coat by her breast. Her eyes remained wide, processing nothing.

+ + + + +

Late that evening, the kidnappers met at Pug's house, joined by Red Hazelwood from the newspaper. Pug asked everyone to get together because he felt some possible dissension in the ranks. He wanted to ensure that they were all on the same page.

Donnie's rage was palpable. "Let's just kill them all," he sneered. "My brother is dead. My family is dead. My brother's family is dead. I don't give a shit no more. I'll be dead soon."

Zola intercepted, "Please, not yet."

"Why the hell not?"

Pug stepped in. "We've demanded ransom from Youngblood's company. We're claiming they were negligent and deserve to pay for the deaths."

Zola said, "I was a victim of the Buffalo Creek Flood forty years ago. It destroyed my life and the lives of everyone I knew. The goddamn mining company never paid the victims nothing."

"Pug's right," Lacey claimed. "We ain't doing this for ourselves; it's for the victims."

Donnie nodded his head, apparently mollified.

"What's going on with the ransom, Red?" Pug asked.

"I met with a lawyer this morning. He's trying to figure out how to set up the accounts where the money would land. The problem is that if the money is extorted through ransom, the Feds might find a way to get it returned. So the lawyer is trying to get accounts in a bank overseas, likely in Switzerland. He's amazingly cooperative. Under his breath, he said he wants the victims to be compensated as much as we do."

"Do you think Youngblood's company will pay?" Pug queried.

"I have no idea. I suspect if they relent, they'll need to pull the money together somehow."

Zola scoffed, "They were a $4 billion company last year. They'll find it."

Pug said, "I'm sure they've made it in profits, but they don't have over 200 million bucks lying around."

Donnie laughed, "If they don't want to see their CEO dead, they'll come up with something pretty quick. I'm ready to kill the bastard."

Pug continued, ignoring Donnie's threat, "I'm optimistic. I figure Bessie will wire the money directly to the bank we give them, again assuming they cave," laughing at his own mine reference.

"So what happens if they pay?" Lacey asked.

Pug looked at the others for some non-verbal feedback. Donnie chewed on a fingernail. Red wrinkled his nose dispassionately. Zola brushed a hand over her head where her hair had once been, then sniffled, then drew her hand across her throat, as if slashing it with a knife. "None of us are coming out of this alive," she concluded. "Why should any of them?"

Donnie looked up and nodded. Lacey nodded, too.

"Okay, then," Pug announced, "Look, let's cross that bridge when we come to it."

They spent the next few minutes discussing plans for the next couple of days of dealing with the prisoners and their bodily needs.

Then Zola said, "I was doing recovery work earlier today, up the hollow from where the school was. I saw some of the FBI agents, and they were walking with Goldschmidt's assistant, the one I released after the kidnapping. I recognized her but I don't think she recognized me. But I have a feeling that they'll want to chat with me sometime, given my history of protests. I have an aunt over in a nursing home in Welch. She's got dementia. I'll tell them I was visiting her when the kidnapping happened. But seeing those thugs was damned unnerving," she admitted.

"You okay?" Pug asked, paternally.

"Not really. But I'm determined."

Everyone responded with a collective moan of resignation. Red said, "With the FBI here in town and with my contact with 'the kidnappers' known, we'd best not be seen together again."

Pug agreed.

Everyone departed.

+ + + + +

Meredith Goldschmidt put her left hand to her face, unconsciously. The touch of her hand on her cheek and of her cheek on her hand surprised her, in a darkness she had only ever envisioned of outer space. It was an odd, almost foreign sensation, her pinky on her lips and her index and middle fingers on her closed eyelid. She opened and closed her eyelid, feeling the eyelashes brush gently against her fingertips. She could see nothing. Nothing at all. Her lips were chilly, but so were her fingertips. Her mouth opened and she bit her pinky lightly, feeling the delicate pain. Her molar, with what was surely a growing cavity, throbbed.

When would she ever see the light of day again? Would these kidnappers ever release her? None of them seemed ruthless or pitiless, but more desperate. She took stock of each. The one they called Donnie scared her the most. He was hillbilly wild and the most despairing, like a caged tiger. The woman, Zola, had the most lasting, pent-up anger. Lacey seemed almost kindly, and harbored difficult to read motivations. Pug was clearly the leader, but she failed to perceive any real vindictiveness in him. She scolded herself for her innocence, her long-held tendency to look for the best in people, knowing her life was in his hands and not really knowing what kind of man he was. Yet she thought she saw a glimmer of sympathy in his eyes if not for the others, perhaps for her.

She thought about her visit, fifteen years earlier to the Kreditbanken at Norrmalmstorg, Stockholm, Sweden, where in the early 1970s, several bank employees were held hostage for six days in a bank vault during a robbery. Upon their release, they sided with the robbers and pleaded for leniency, in an act later described as the "Stockholm syndrome."

Her mind swept back to DC, and a pall of animus swept over her. She pictured her husband, still comatose, lying on his hospital bed, perhaps with the dead woman's tooth marks on his manhood. She remembered her tearful respite on the

White House commode after her browbeating by the Vice only a week before – could it have only been a week? – with a pervasive sense of loathing. If she ever escaped from this gelid jail, she convinced herself she would never set foot again in Washington. She shivered convulsively in the cold, dark, subterranean dampness, reaching for her blanket in the dark and pulling it over her shoulders.

+ + + + +

Returning to his prisoners, Pug went to Goldschmidt's area first, "I brought you more of my mother's work."

He reached to hand it to her, but she put her hand on his. Hers felt cold to him. He took both her hands and held them together, inside his. He looked towards her and her eyes softened, as if pleading. In the dim light, her pupils were dilated, but her irises were a clear, azure blue. For the first time, he saw her as an attractive woman, and he felt sympathy for her. Quickly, he released her and walked away, lest he drop his guard.

Returning to attend to the male prisoners, Pug placed a bowl of rice in front of each.

Youngblood said, "Look, let's make some sort of deal. What good is it for you to keep us in here? How much ransom did you ask for?"

"Can't tell you. I won't tell you."

Pug looked at Webber's forehead. The bruise there showed some dried blood and Pug was sure he'd hit his head on the ceiling multiple times.

"Listen," Youngblood offered, "If you'll guarantee to turn me loose, I'll get you $10 million dollars."

"I don't want any money," Pug insisted.

"What do you want?"

"Restitution. I want money for the families who have lost members."

"Bring me a typewriter," Youngblood ordered. "I'll get you your money."

Pug was incredulous that the big man had offered his assistance with his own ransom. "Why would you help us?" Pug asked him.

"You're as inept as a drunken skunk," Youngblood screamed. "You could mess up a wet dream. If we wait for you to do something, I'll die of boredom in here."

+ + + + +

After Pug had left, Meredith returned to her reading of Pug's mother's memoirs, combining the new sheets with the old.

Coal defines our life here.

Coal is a noun, a verb, and an adjective. Coal is energy and power and tragedy, life and death. Coal is past, present, and foreseeable future.

Coal permeates every aspect of the lives of the women in my life from the day they were born or arrived from somewheres else. Coal is in the gardens. Coal is in the sinks. Coal is in the living rooms and on the sheets and in the beds.

Coal is on the newborns. Heavy. Black. Gritty. Deadly. Coal is in the food and in the water. Coal is under everybody's fingernails. In every coal camp or town in West Virginia, the economy, the culture, the destiny, and the providence is coal.

Gary was founded in 1901, named for the president of U.S. Steel Corporation. By the 1920s it was rapidly industrializing, with hoards of second-rate people being indentured into debt servitude as they landed at Ellis Island. Poles, Slavs, Hungarians, Czechs, they all came to the hollow where they owed the company money before they even arrived, indebted for the trip itself, enticed by the promise of income. Negro people came from Alabama, Louisiana and Mississippi, promised equal pay for equal work to the whites.

There was always tension and men was always fighting. Grammammy used to talk about walking the streets and hearing all kinds of languages she didn't understand. Security came from the guns people toted. The Baldwin-Felts men, company thugs, roamed the streets, supposedly keeping the peace. But they were there to prevent the men from unionizing, to get rights and fair pay.

Men were paid in scrip rather than dollars. Much of each man's paycheck was siphoned off to the company before the scrip was ever handed to him. He had to pay for his tools, had to pay for their oil lamps and the oil to light them, had to pay to get them sharpened, and had to pay for rent for the home the company rented to them. He even had to pay into a burial fund to pay for his own burial expenses. If he was killed in the mine and his fund wasn't up to date, expenses would be deducted before his widow would get the final paycheck.

They were paid by the ton produced. Some companies was good, fair and honest. Some cheated the miners, claiming that rocks or clay was in the mine cars.

Gary Hollow was a bustling, beautiful, tragic, angry, convoluted place. It was owned, or it seemed so, by United States Coal & Coke Company, a subsidiary of United States Steel Company. They did everything, provided everything. They built the houses. They built the schools and the ball fields. They built the company store. They built the churches and the dance halls. They built the water plant and the electrical plant. Nothing happened without their heavy hand. And generally nothing happened that they didn't want to have happen.

Most coal operators were a ruthless lot, greedy, of an iron-willed breed, dominant, aggressive, and evil-spirited.

Dae was my grandmother. Betty was my mother. Alice was her sister, my aunt. They're all gone now. Alice and Betty were both born in Gary Hollow, Alice in 1904 and Betty in 1907.

Here's what Grammammy Dae told me.

Gary was what we call cosmopolitan now. Neighborhoods were segregated, not just with the Negroes but the Poles, the Slavs, the Hunkies, and the Czechs. The men mostly worked together and the immigrant miners eventually learned English. But lots of the women never did. They were

isolated and I suspect lonely, especially
in the smaller camps.

Exotic smells poured from the kitchens
into the streets. As a child, I played in
the streets with their kids and we learned
enough of their language and they learned
ours so we could communicate and have some
fun together.

The coke ovens at the edge of town
filled the hollow with smell and smoke
continuously. Once the smell of coke
enters your nostrils, it never leaves.
Dae could never keep her draperies or
upholstery clean.

It wasn't a hard life. It wasn't an easy
life. It was just life. People were always
on edge. The work the men and boys did was
dangerous. Men got crushed by rock falls.
Mines exploded.

People had different expectations then.
Dae's people had been hunted down and
murdered and drived from their lands for
so many generations that they were happy
just to be in one place and have food to
eat, and jobs.

Dae's husband, Campbell, was a drunkard,
a slackard. Dae's fate was of servitude
and abuse, even before his death, early,
in a killing.

The company store was fortified like
a citadel, engineered to enforce the
company's domination over the people of
the town. Almost nothing owned in town
was bought anywhere else. They sold

canned goods. Most women grew their own
vegetables and most had chickens and a cow
for food. They sold clothing and fabric.
They even sold live canaries that miners
took into the mines to die first if there
wasn't enough breathable air. Their tiny
lungs couldn't process the poisonous
gasses, the "black damp", and they'd die.

The store was octagonal in shape, with
looking like two stories on the outside,
with gables on the first roof that gave way
to the second story. It had an elevator
in the center, which traveled up from two
levels in the basement to the first and
second floors, then to a hidden attic.
There was really a middle floor between the
first and the second. Dae, she called it
the rape room.

The elevator took women – and women did
all the shopping – from the first to the
second floor. It was also used to transfer
merchandise. At that middle floor, they
stored the coffins. There was always a need
for coffins. Regularly, you'd have a few
people die every week. When there'd be a
mine accident, they'd need a dozen or two
at a time. I'm talking about the nineteen-
teens, now. Every coal town and many of
the camps had a coffinateer who constructed
the coffins.

The front counter was near the center
of the room, adjacent to the elevator.
It always had a store clerk and another
man who looked like a clerk but was

really a Baldwin-Felts security agent.
His job was listening. Listening to the
conversations of the women, who knew about
any unionizing activities. The walls of
the store were shaped to echo back to
the counter, so he could hear most of
anything.

The foreign people were segregated into
their own neighborhoods or conclaves and
were never taught English, particularly
the women. This was to keep them from
organizing with other miners. The
women were particularly isolated and
marginalized.

For the Negroes, it was the worst. They
had only certain hours and certain days
they could shop at the store. There was a
window on the side of the store where they
would hand their list of what they wanted,
but lots of them couldn't read or write.
The clerk would then hand their stuff out
the window and take their scrip. There
were only a few hours each week they were
allowed inside.

It's funny now that I think about it,
but the Negroes had their own schools and
churches, but not their own stores. And
the adults worked together, the blacks and
whites. It seems strange now but I never
thought about it then. Lots of my friends
were prejudiced, but we were always taught
that everybody is the same in God's eyes,
even the coloreds.

Meredith began to shiver. The temperature of the mine was far from freezing, but it was cold nonetheless, particularly given her extended entrapment. It was a pervasive, invasive, persistent bowels-of-the-earth cold. It was a damp, clammy, snail cold. She began to shiver, first in her arms, then her upper legs, and then a spasm of frigidity swept her body so strongly her head shook violently and her cheeks bounced against her teeth. She nearly dropped the papers, but instead put them aside and wrapped her coat and blankets tighter, pulling the blanket over her head and face, feeling the fleetingly warm mist of her breath settle on her numb cheeks.

God, she was cold! Miserable. She ached to see the sun again and to feel warm rays of light on her skin. She wondered what her skin even looked like, having not seen anything other than her dimly lit hands as she ate by artificial, ephemeral light.

She got up and tried to stretch, her statuesque height as always bound by the mine's low roof. She paced a few steps each way, trying to revive circulation in her fingers and toes, but determined to spend what little time she might be allotted to continue with her reading. She sat again and resumed.

One time, Grammammy Dae was wanting to go to the second floor to do some shopping for shoes. The elevators were not self-service, so a clerk accompanied her and another enticed Betty and Alice with some candy to stay on the first floor. Dae was young and pretty. The clerk led her to a fitting room that had a cot where she could sit while she tried on the shoes. As she was trying on shoes, he closed and locked the door to the room. He raped her on that cot. How do I know? Because she told me two years before she died. What could be going through her mind as she suffered through that indignity, and then had to ride that elevator back down with that animal to her awaiting children?

Did she ever tell Campbell? What would he have done? There was no police protection, only the Baldwin-Felts thugs, paid for by the company. Did her Campbell complain? All she knew is that within weeks of her rape, he was killed by gunshot in a skirmish at the mine.

Campbell and Dae lived in a company house, and after his death, they were evicted. The mine company needed the house to bring in the next miner and his family. It was well known that the company treasured their mules more than their workers, because the mules cost them money and the miners could be easily replaced by new immigrants, "yearning to be free."

The rape room became well known to the women of Gary, and they avoided that floor of the store entirely. Story goes that the main perpetrator of the rapes was himself killed by gunfire, presumably by an angry husband. Many of the women made their own shoes out of whatever materials they could find: leather straps, cardboard, rubber scraps, anything to stay out of that store.

Grammammy Dae told me about other women whose men were indigent or crippled. Those women had to feed their children. There was no paying work in the coal camps, but women have always had assets, physical assets, that the Baldwin-Felts men and the company men found valuable. They issued credit to these women who sold their bodies, they called it Esau, which comes from the Bible. In the 25th chapter of Genesis, a starving hunter Esau stumbles into his brother's home begging for food, but giving up his birthright.

"Once when Jacob was cooking some stew, Esau came in from the open country, famished. He said to Jacob, "Quick, let me have some of that red stew! I'm famished!" Jacob replied, "First sell me your birthright."

"Look, I am about to die," Esau said. "What good is the birthright to me?"

But Jacob said, "Swear to me first." So he swore an oath to him, selling his birthright to Jacob.

Forfeiting on the Esau agreement meant for the destitute woman, the miner's wife or widow, submitting to the sexual ravages of the company strongmen. Grammammy's friends became sexual slaves, all to keep her children fed and housed.

After her eviction, Grammammy apparently got lucky, as she and her two daughters were taken in by the town's casket maker and his wife. They had lost their only daughter to the flu epidemic of 1918, and Grammammy became a permanent boarder and found work alongside the woman of the house, sewing interior linings for the more opulent caskets.

One friend of Grammammy's lost her husband in a mine disaster and would have lost their home as well, were their nine year old boy not available to take his place. So that little boy became a man at age nine and went to work mining coal so his family had a place to live. A company that would send a nine year old into the mines thought nothing of abusing his mother.

The entrenched power structure kept the workers pockets empty, the options nonexistent, and the spirits broken. Raw profiteering, ruthless exploitation of mineral and human resources, turned entire communities into biblical Esaus. To these powerful and ruthless elite, we have since named our universities, towns, hospitals, banks, and even churches. What robber baron could stand at the twilight of his life watching a church be named for him while knowing he enslaved children as he was systematically and repeatedly raping their mothers, then face his maker at the altar above?

Spoils ripped from the coal mines of West Virginia built the grand universities and libraries and museums of Cleveland, Pittsburgh, Baltimore, and New York, enriching the lives of the gilded while impoverishing the lives of the serfs toiling underground in the black depths below Gary, Davy, Capels, Shaft Hollow,

```
Bishop, War, and so many more. I learned
in high school that at one time there were
10 incorporated cities and towns and 85
unincorporated communities in McDowell
County. I bet half of them don't even
exist any more. Imagine being from a place
that doesn't exist any more!
```

As Meredith pondered that unhappy thought, her light went out while the cold persisted.

JAN 9 Thursday

The following afternoon, Pug found this article that appeared on the Bluefield Star Sentinel website:

Exclusive:
Bluefield Star Sentinel reporter visits kidnapping victims

Early this morning, Bluefield Star Sentinel reporter Estell Hazelwood was allowed unfettered access to the victims of last week's kidnapping outside of War. The victims are US Secretary of the Interior Meredith Goldschmidt, Alvin Youngblood, president of Bessie Energy, Doug Webber, a McDowell County Sheriff's deputy, and Merritt Lee Lawton, a Federal Mine Safety Engineer.

Citing First Amendment rights with respect to the privilege between a reporter and his sources, Hazelwood has refused to cooperate with law enforcement officials. He did admit that the victims had not been removed from McDowell County, but gave no further details on their whereabouts.

According to Hazelwood, all of the victims are healthy and are fed and attended.

+ + + + +

That evening, Red called Pug on the CB Radio and told him about the article, which Pug said he'd seen. Pug said that the FBI agents were waiting for him at the newspaper office, but he hadn't detected being followed. "I suspect I'll be followed everywhere I go now."

Pug concluded, "It's probably only a matter of time until they find us."

"Pug, have you thought about turning them loose and skedaddling?"

"Nope, not even once. I'm in this until the bitter end. And I don't think it's going to be pretty."

+ + + + +

Then Pug went to the area containing the male prisoners. He handed Youngblood what looked like a suitcase.

"What's this?" Youngblood asked.

"It's what you wanted. Open it."

Youngblood raised the latches and from inside he extracted Pug's mother's Smith-Corona manual typewriter. "Well, well. Looks like I'm writing my own ransom note."

Pug said, "There's some paper in the cover pocket. Turn it around and I'll shine my light on it so you can see to type."

Youngblood got to work, typing awkwardly with only his puffy index fingers. The slap of the keys echoed off the stone walls.

```
Abe Cohen
Cohen Brothers, Esq.
4764 Broadway, NY, NY

Dear Abe,

I am being held prisoner. Please coperate
with whatver parties present this note to
```

you by placing $50,000 randsome for each
lost soul in the account of his or her
heirs. Please tranfer the funds from the
account of:

Bessie Energy, Alvin Youngblood custodian
Account number 920443, Bank of the Caymans

Please transfer the money to wherever
insttructed by the kidnapers.

> Yours sincerely,
> Alvin Youngblood

Youngblood ripped the sheet from the machine and tossed it towards Pug, where it landed on the floor becoming slightly damp and dirty. He said, "There you go. Now get me out of here."

"Not so fast," Pug said, stashing the sheet in his jacket pocket. "Let's see what kind of results this gets. Then I'll have my people back in touch with your people." He had no idea what he would do with it.

Pug had slipped Meredith a new battery for her lantern and once the kidnappers secured the prison and departed, she returned to Pug's Mother's memoirs. She quickly deduced they were written on the same typewriter Pug had just brought Youngblood.

+ + + + +

Around 1930 in the height of the Great
Depression, my mammy Betty and Alice
married twin brothers from War, Tom and
Ken Harrison, and became double-kin. Both
became young widows.

Betty and her husband, my father, Tom
Harrison, got a house in Gary. I was born
in 1934. The country went to war in 1941,
but daddy didn't go. Mining was as valued
a service to the country during the war
as was fighting, as the country needed the
coal to make the coke to fuel the ovens
that made the steel that won the war. And
it was almost as dangerous. Miners were
finally paid a competitive wage, but safety
was on nobody's mind as production demands
were paramount.

I was six in 1942 when daddy was killed
in a mine explosion.

After daddy's death, mammy moved to War
to live with Aunt Alice and her husband
Ken Harrison who had moved there from
Gary to work for another mining company.
Ken led a successful effort to begin
the unionization of the mines in War
just after the Second World War. He was
arrested for a petty larceny at a mine
where he was organizing, and was murdered
under mysterious circumstances while
awaiting trial in the late 1940s.

So like I was saying, both mammy and
Alice were young widows. Alice had two
boys, my cousins, but they moved away
decades ago. They used to come home on
holidays when Alice was still alive, but
I haven't seen either of them in years.
Maybe they'll come back for the funeral
when my Emmett dies.

Grammammy stayed in Gary, so we didn't

see her as much. It was only 19 miles
away, only a dozen by the crows flying, but
we still didn't go much because the going
was so slow on all the curvy roads. And
neither Alice nor mammy had a car.

That's another memory, our trips back
to Gary. Grammammy and mammy used to make
homemade jams and jellies, and I'll never
forget how good the kitchen smelled.
Sometimes at Christmas they'd make peanut
butter fudge or chocolate fudge. Yummy!
Those were the good smells. But I always
got motion sickness, so the vomit smells
were just as stuck in my memory.

I remember only a few trips back there.

Folks said Gary was the prettiest place
in all of McDowell County. It was more
open, wider, with lower hills and more
sunlight. The churches were awesome, with
the onion-top churches of the Eastern
Europeans. War has taller hills on both
sides, limiting the sunlight to midday
hours. It was deeper, darker, and more
oppressive, especially in the winter.
It was wealthy, too, with rows of fancy
houses.

By that time, the women were working,
Alice as a cook in the high school and
mammy as a nurse in the hospital. The coal
companies were diminishing in importance
and were divesting of some of their
holdings. Between their two salaries and
the income from various boarders, they
were able to buy their house and keep it

until they died. Neither remarried.

Both women were avid readers. Betty worked with the school librarian to form a partnership with the public library in Welch to keep the high school shelves filled with an extraordinary collection of books, which Betty was able to borrow and read, and share with Alice, and eventually with Johnny and me.

Dinnertime conversations were completely unlike those of my friends' homes. We talked about religion, philosophy, and politics. When I visited with friends, their folks talked about the weather and gossip, or the price of coal.

Betty wrote under a pen name and convinced the editor at the War Herald that he should publish her commentaries. She called herself Justus Writeman. She was very opinionated, especially about what the coal companies were doing to the communities.

Johnny, my only brother, was born in 1934. He was shipped off to Korea and he died in a helicopter crash. We have no idea why he, or anybody else in America, was there. I hear tell there was never a peace treaty signed, so technically we're still at war with the North Koreans.

As I said, Aunt Alice was a cook but mammy cooked for us at home. Our kitchen was always filled with wonderful smells. We had some chickens out back and got fresh eggs. One time, mammy cracked a spoilt egg and it stunk like crazy.

Mammy roamed the hills behind our house and found mushrooms and especially greens – creasy greens and mustard greens, collards, turnip greens, and kale. I always looked forward to springtime because that's when the greens were coming in. Mammy always seemed to have a big pot on the stove and she cooked with ham hocks. In the wintertime, we'd have fried chicken and fried cabbage and lard biscuits. We also grew a little vegetable garden out back with the biggest potatoes you've ever seen. They'd last in the root cellar until May or June.

As I was saying earlier, outside was filled with smells, too, but not so good. In War, the coal company built the roads and the schools and the company houses but they never built a sewer system, so everybody's sewage was straight-piped right to the creek. The creek had huge fish in it, but of course nobody ate them. The creek always smelled something awful, excepting after a big rain. We had severe flooding every ten or twenty years, and all the businesses in town would need to spend weeks cleaning up to reopen. There was one in 1956 and 1969, but the worst I ever remember was in 1977. Most of the downtown never rebuilt at all.

The most pungent smells, like I was writing about earlier, were the creosote smells of the railroad ties. The railroad

company used creosote to preserve the wood
in the ties and the bridge supports, and
it had an unforgettable smell. The coal
tipples in Caretta and in War had the coal
dust smell that settles on everything.
The worst was the smoldering slate dump
outside of Yukon. It burned from as long
as I can remember until the 1970s when
the government sent in some people to
extinguish it.

This concluded the sheets that Pug had brought her, and she was disappointed not to move forward. She felt a kinship and affinity with the woman who'd written it and spent time re-reading the sheets she had before the light again went out.

+ + + + +

Pug made his next visit to the mine around 3:00 a.m. carrying more things than usual, going to Meredith's area first.

Pug took some more sheets from his knapsack. "Here, I found some more of my mother's stories." He extended his hand so she could take them. When he did, she put her hands around his again. In his hands, hers were cool, colder than before. They seemed frail, beyond his expectation for a woman he assumed was in her mid-fifties, near his own age. She held on for a few moments. He looked her in the eye again, seeing her as not his prisoner but as a cold, vulnerable, frightened woman. She seemed even prettier than the last time he'd looked at her.

"Thanks for bringing this," she said. "It has helped having something to do. Your mother's writing is clear and fascinating. She lived an incredible life."

"Yes, ma'am. She died in the flood."

"I'm sorry. I really am. Pug?"

"Yes?"

"Call me Meredith," she insisted, squeezing his hand tighter.

"Yes. Meredith. You're welcome."

Pulling his hand from hers, Pug left her to attend to the others. When he returned, she asked him, "How's it going with the ransom?"

"We're not sure."

She was silent for a few minutes. "Listen," she said, "I've been thinking about your situation. I'm sympathetic to the plight of your town and to your concerns. But you need another plan."

"Why's that? I've got Youngblood's note to his lawyer right here in my pocket. He'll pay up."

"Ransom isn't going to work. You've asked for hundreds of millions of dollars. They aren't going to pay it. If they did, where would they send it?"

"I don't know. I hadn't thought about it."

She said, "If they were to pay in cash, where would they get it? It takes 100 bundles of $100 bills to make a million. You've demanded, what, $220-million? It would take up a good size room. If they were to pay it in some type of wire transfer, it could be easily tracked and confiscated. If you sent it to an offshore bank, the Feds would know."

"I guess you're right," He concluded. "And if the money did become available offshore, most of the local people would never be savvy enough to get their hands on it. Most don't even have a computer. This area is too poor for much of any Internet services. Lots of people, even before the flood, struggled to get enough to eat."

She looked at him, searching for his next thought. She thought about it twice and then said, "You didn't give this too much thought beforehand, did you?"

He buried his head in his hands and waves of despair

swept over him. "Meredith, justice needs to be done."

"I understand that. But like I said, you might need another plan."

"Yeah." On his egress from the mine, he crumpled Youngblood's typewritten note and pitched it into a puddle of water on the mine floor.

+ + + + +

At 10:00 a.m. Pug made his next visit, again alone. He left food with the male prisoners, but other than some grumbling, they had nothing to say.

Around the corner, Meredith Goldschmidt said, "Any more thoughts about our situation?"

"I'm not sure yet what our next steps are. I'll tell you one thing, though. I'm in War because my brother is missing. He ran the mining company that my dad founded fifty years ago. There was good money in mining in those days and a little owner could support himself and a dozen workers. Now everything is corporate.

"West Virginia is the most corrupt state in the country. For sixty years, McDowell County has been declining, shriveling away. There's more people working for $10.00 an hour for Walmart in West Virginia today than are working underground in coal, but you wouldn't know it by our legislature, 'cause they're all in the pocket of big coal.

"Youngblood in there, that man is pond scum. His company has the worst safety record in the business. Hundreds of men have died in his mines in the last ten years. Black lung is on the rise. We have miners in their thirties who are already in advanced stages of black lung. Where you come from, Ms. Goldschmidt, do people work in jobs that kill them prematurely?"

"No, I don't suppose they do."

"Well, they do here. Where you come from, do people

have their wells permanently laced with carcinogens without the corporation that caused it punished?"

"No, I suppose not."

"Lawton, the inspector, he's crooked as a snake. Youngblood's company owned the dam that destroyed my hometown and took the life of almost every child in it. Lawton was responsible for the inspection of that dam. All I'm looking for is some justice. Right now, I'm just not sure what that justice looks like."

"Lucas, I am the Secretary of the Interior of the United States of America."

"Yes, ma'am."

"It is my job to oversee the actions of mining companies and to protect the air and water of the country. I have failed as well."

"Ma'am."

"Lucas, I am the sacrificial lamb of this administration. I'm the token. This administration is science-hostile, misogynistic, arrogant, smug, and domineering. The Vice President is a horse's ass. And the President is his puppet."

"So why were you picked?"

"Like I said, I'm the token. They need to show some sign of diversity. There's one black and I'm the one woman on the cabinet. But we've been marginalized. At cabinet meetings, I'm never asked to contribute and when I do, I'm ignored on good days, berated on bad ones."

Pug raised his left eyebrow. "And so they sent you here..."

"Yeah, 'Go to West Virginia and tell everybody how much we care about them in Washington.'"

"How much do they care about us in Washington?"

"You know the answer to that as well as I do."

"Yeah. They don't give a rat's ass about us here in West Virginia."

"That's putting it nicely," she admitted, sheepishly. Moments later she broke the silence and said, "What are you going to do?"

"I'm still not sure."

"Please," she begged, "make something happen soon. There are times I'd rather be dead than to be shivering in here for another hour."

Part 5

JAN 10, Friday

AT 11:30 THAT SAME NIGHT, Pug alone joined his captives, fed them, gave the men clean shirts, and changed their chamber pots. He didn't bring his male captives clean pants because he had no way to protect himself while unchaining them, and they had no way to change unless they were freed from their shackles.

He brought Goldschmidt together with the others. Still confusing them purposefully with regards to time, he said, "Tomorrow morning, when I return, Lacey, Zola, and Donnie will be with me. The manslaughter trial of Merritt Lee Lawton will begin. Then we'll try you, Youngblood."

"What the hell?" Lawton screamed.

Pug screamed back, "Shut up. Nobody is coming for you; no ransom is going to be paid. Justice will be extracted here. Now then. Here are our assignments. Youngblood, you will be the defense attorney for Lawton. When we finish Lawton's trial, you can defend yourself. Goldschmidt, you will be the judge. I will be the prosecuting attorney. Zola will be the jury. Donnie and Lacey will be jurors, too, if they want to. Lacey will do court reporting."

"What a sham!" Youngblood stammered. "Goldschmidt, what are you going to do about this?"

She looked at him disdainfully and pursed her lips. "I have a law degree from Georgetown University. There are a lot of dead people outside of this mine. I think I'd like to know why. I think we all deserve to know why. With regards to our illegal detention, I have no more cards than you do. But it seems like the best I can do is help you and Mr. Lawton get a fair trial."

"Goddamn," said Lawton. "God. Damn."

"Very good," Pug said smugly. "Lawton, you've been charged with 228 counts of manslaughter. I suggest you speak with your lawyer and have a plea for us by the time we return in twelve hours."

+ + + + +

As Pug re-chained Meredith in her cell area, she said to him, "Sounds like you have a new plan."

"I think you're right about the ransom; we're not going to get anything. If we do somehow, it will be a bonus. In the meantime, if nothing else comes of this, we need to know what really happened."

"Good for you," she smiled.

JAN 11 Saturday

Eight hours later, Pug, Lacey, Zola, and Donnie approached their prisoners. Pug unshackled Meredith Goldschmidt. They brought extra folding chairs, a low-slung folding table, and a battery powered lantern. Lacey sat in front of the table with the Smith-Corona typewriter on it. He rolled in a sheet of paper. Pug turned to Meredith and said, "Judge Goldschmidt, shall we begin?"

Before she could answer, Donnie yelled, "Hear ye, hear ye, all rise for Judge Goldschmidt." Several hard-hats clanged against the ceiling and Webber hit his head again, drawing blood from an already wounded forehead. Zola pitched him a dirty rag.

"Reporter," Meredith said to Lacey, "What day is this?"

Pug answered in a lie, "January 15th."

"January 15th," Lacey repeated, and then typed.

"In US Federal Court, makeshift, in the city of War, McDowell County, West Virginia, we are now in session,"

Goldschmidt asserted professorially. "Who is the accused?"

"Your honor," Pug began, "Mr. Merritt Lee Lawton is accused of negligent manslaughter in the second degree of 220 people, mostly children."

"Mr. Lawton, how do you plead?"

"We're not pleading anything with you clowns," Youngblood screamed.

"Mr. Lawton," Goldschmidt continued, "It looks as if you have a hostile legal representative. Would you prefer to defend yourself?"

Lawton looked at Youngblood. Then he looked back at Goldschmidt. Before he could answer, Youngblood shouted, "Not guilty. Lawton is not guilty of nothing."

Ignoring the double-negative, Goldschmidt said, "Very well. Mr. Court Reporter Lacey, would you please indicate that Mr. Lawton has accepted his legal representation and has pled not guilty."

Lacey nodded solely with his two index fingers and continued typing, the noise of the keystrokes rattling around the mine.

"Mr. Pug, would you please present your opening statement?"

"Yes, your honor. On January 3, an impoundment dam broke at the head of the valley here above War. In turn, it swept away a second dam. The wall of water came through town and within fifteen minutes, approximately 233 people were dead. That includes the names of the unaccounted for. There are 220 bodies.

"The federal government assigns inspectors to enforce regulations on all mining activity here in the Appalachians. Mr. Lawton, the accused, is the inspector for this area. It was his job to make sure the dam was in the proper condition to withstand any amount of rainfall and accumulated water behind the dam, and to enforce corrective action if that didn't happen. His failure to do so was contributory manslaughter and we ask that he be found guilty.

"The defense will argue that the dam break was an 'Act of God,' but your honor, God didn't put that dam up there. Man did. God put all this coal in the ground, but it is man's job to mine it safely. If Mr. Lawton had done his job, the dam would have been reinforced to withstand any force nature could put behind it. So we ask that the jury finds him guilty."

"Thank you Mr. Graham. Now then, Mr. Youngblood, would you like to present your opening defense?"

Youngblood shifted in his chair to rise, struck his hardhat against the ceiling, and promptly fell back into his chair. Donnie laughed convulsively.

"Order, please, Mr. Donnie. Mr. Youngblood, please proceed."

Not rising this time, Youngblood said, "I am Alvin Youngblood, President of Bessie Energy, speaking in defense of the accused, Mr. Merritt Lee Lawton."

Lacey typed.

"Mr. Lawton is an employee of the federal government. His job is to inspect the operations of the surface and subsurface mines in this area. This is not an exact science. The rains started coming pretty hard four or five days before the goddamn dam broke. There were floods happening in all the valleys around here. Mr. Lawton is innocent as he couldn't anticipate all this rain. God caused this flood, not Mr. Lawton."

"Thank you Mr. Youngblood," Goldschmidt said. "Now then, Mr. Pug, would you please present your first witness?"

"Yes, ma'am, your honor. I call Mr. Donnie Getgood."

Donnie smiled at Goldschmidt who said to him, "Mr. Getgood, please state your name."

"Donnie Getgood."

"Is it 'Donald'?"

"No ma'am, it's 'Donnie'."

"Very well. Do you promise to tell the truth, the whole

truth, and nothing but the truth, so help you God?"

"Yes, your honor, ma'am. I sure as hell do."

"Mr. Graham, please proceed."

Pug rose gently and bumped his hard-hat against the ceiling of stone. Then thought the better of it and sat down again.

"Donnie, you already stated your name. Where do you live?"

"I'm from over near Bradshaw. I don't live anywhere right now. My house, mine and Ronnie's, Ronnie is my dead brother – he died the other night apprehending all y'all – was swept away in the flood. Our houses were up the hollow, above the elementary school."

"Where do you work?"

"I work for you, Pug, in your family's mine."

"Please tell us your story."

"Six weeks ago, I had a family, Jennifer Thompson Getgood, my wife, and Roscoe, my son. My twin brother, Ronnie, lived next to me, too. He had a family, too. My wife, Jennifer is gone. My child Roscoe is gone. They was killed last month when a rock this big," he held his hands apart, palms facing one another, "flew through the air from blasting at Mr. Youngblood's mine and killed 'em. That was before the flood. Now that the flood has happened, my home is gone. Ronnie is gone, shot dead. His family is gone, swept away by the flood. His home is gone. I have nothing any more, except the clothes on my back." He sniffled and wiped his eyes on the dirty sleeve of his coverall.

"Donnie, what do you think about coal mining?" Pug asked.

"My father was a coal miner. His father and his father before him, they was all coal miners. I had an uncle who moved to Charleston and taught school, but all the other men I can think of in my family was coal miners. I love coal mining. Ronnie did, too. It's all we ever wanted to do. We was both in the military, but only because we thought it was the patriotic thing to do and nobody was hirin' miners then. But we always wanted to come back and be miners."

"Donnie," Pug said, "Please tell us what you know about Mr. Lawton."

"Mr. Lawton is a mine safety inspector. I am a miner, so I don't know entirely what that entails, but I have a pretty good idea. But really, it's pure horse sense; if you're inspecting a gob dam and you certify it, and then it breaks, I'd figure you are responsible."

The room was quiet for a moment as only the beep of the methane detector and the sound of dripping water could be heard.

A flash of a small flame lit the room as Zola flicked her disposable lighter and lit a cigarette. Pug winced, knowing the incredible flammability danger. Nobody moved to have her extinguish it.

"Will there be anything else," the judge asked.

Pug turned to Donnie, "Would you like to say more?"

"Not right now."

Goldschmidt then turned to Youngblood. "Mr. Youngblood, would you like to question the witness?"

He sat motionless for a moment, seemingly contemplating his options. "Yes. Mr. Donnie, or whoever the hell you are, please state your occupation again."

"I'm a coal miner."

"Surface or underground?"

"Underground."

"Have you ever worked on a surface mine?"

Goldschmidt interrupted, asking, "Is a 'surface mine' the same thing as a 'mountaintop removal mine?'"

Pug answered, "Yes, ma'am. It is."

"Please continue."

"Again, have you ever worked on a surface mine?" Youngblood echoed himself.

"No."

"Have you ever worked on the construction or maintenance of a gob dam?" Youngblood grilled, louder.

"No."

Turning to Goldschmidt, Youngblood said, "The testimony of this witness is irrelevant. He has no expertise in this matter."

Pug exclaimed, "His testimony is of a victim. If a man's car catches fire and kills his family, he doesn't need to be an expert on how the fire started to know what he's lost."

Goldschmidt seemed to be contemplating. "I suspect much of what we hear won't be totally relevant, but in my court, we'll hear it anyway. A victim deserves his chance to be heard."

Youngblood then turned to Donnie and said, "I have no further questions."

"Mr. Pug," Goldschmidt said, "Please present your next witness."

"I call Lacey Reedy."

Reedy backed away from his typewriter. Goldschmidt asked Zola to step in his place as court reporter. Goldschmidt swore Lacey in and Pug began questioning, obtaining Lacey's full name and occupation. Lacey stated his age as 69 and his part-time job as a preacher at Holy Mission Methodist Church. He told of his long employment with Pug's father and brother. Then he spoke of his father and grandfather.

Lacey said, "They was Union men. They fought a constant battle to maintain their rights from the coal companies. I remember sitting on my grandfather's knee. He worked in coal mining during World War II. The miners almost never got sent to war, because the country needed the coal production as much as it needed soldiers. He was proud of his service. He felt that he contributed to our winning the war as much as anybody. Men were being marched to death by the Japs in the jungles at Bataan while great-grandpa was marching into the cold earth every day to pick at a wall of black rock.

"He went into the mines when he was fourteen. There was boys, children really, goin' into the mines at nine or ten years old as helpers. Papa was a good student in school, but he had only two pairs of pants, and when the patches started covering the patches, he knew he needed to drop out and make some money. And coal mining was the only way to make money in those days. I remember him telling me that he and his siblings never got gifts on Christmas or birthdays, and they wondered what they did wrong.

"West Virginia has always given a disproportionate number of its young people to the military. We are a patriotic people and we don't mind serving; in fact we're proud to serve. But another thing that has made that happen is that there are frightful few opportunities otherwise. People here see the military as a way out. The military is a stable job with benefits, and the opportunity to learn a trade and to see more of the world than people here would otherwise. Yeah, it might get you killed, but so might mining. You remember Lynndie England, the former soldier who was convicted of abusing prisoners at Abu Ghraib? She was from West Virginia. So was Jessica Lynch, the soldier who was injured and captured earlier in the Iraq war. Nowadays, we're not just sending our men to war; we're sending our women, too.

"Anyways, as I was saying, coal miners have always been patriotic people, but we ain't dumb. We know who butters our bread. Or at least we used to."

Pug said, "Please explain what you mean."

"Coal miners have bound together to get their slice of the pie. The largest insurrection in the United States since the Civil War was in 1921 when 10,000 miners fought company men at Blair Mountain. Your honor, did you know that the battle of Blair Mountain was the first and only time the US government ever dropped bombs on its own citizens, and these were the miners from West Virginia?" He looked towards Goldschmidt, and then continued.

"The miners lost the battle and continued to lose ground until more and more coal was needed in World War II. Then, miners started to get an upper hand in negotiations for better pay and working conditions. But it wasn't for long. When the mines mechanized, starting in the 1950s, fewer and fewer miners were employed. The mining companies started winning the propaganda wars, dominating peoples' heads." He banged his knuckles against his hard hat. "Families who for years fought and died to gain basic rights started backing the coal companies, begging for work of any kind and at any cost. We were the founders of the labor movement and now our workers by the thousands have surrendered and are foot soldiers for the oppressors."

Pug looked at Meredith who seemed genuinely impressed by the old man's astuteness.

Lacey continued, "After the end of World War II, people started flocking out of McDowell County in droves. The good ones left first, the smartest and most able. In 1950, there were close to 100,000 people in this county. Grandma said it was the best place in America to be. Now there are about 22,000. Now after Mr. Lawton's flood, there's 233 fewer."

"Objection!" screamed Youngblood.

"Sustained," Judge Goldschmidt concurred. "Please, Mr. Reedy, don't go there."

"Yes, your honor. Anyway, I think there are only about 1500 miners now in this county, down from 40,000."

"Relevancy!" screamed Youngblood again.

"Madam your honor," Pug said, "I think Mr. Reedy's story about his mining past is relevant to our case against Mr. Lawton."

"Yes, I do too," the makeshift judge agreed. "And it is more interesting than anything happening here in this hell-hole for some time. Please proceed. Mr. Reedy?"

"Yes, ma'am. Anyway, I'm a coal miner. It's who I am. It's part of my identity. So many of my classmates and friends have gone elsewhere, to Charlotte, Detroit, or Washington. I hate those places. They're hot, crowded, miserable places. People hate each other.

"My people are molded by hardship. Turmoil. Adversity. McDowell County has given this nation and now the world more coal than any county east of the Mississippi, but we're by far the poorest county in West Virginia, which last time I looked was only behind Mississippi as the poorest state in the nation. Somebody tell me why if coal is such a blessing, why are the counties that have the most of it the poorest. But even so, nobody goes hungry here. People won't let a neighbor starve.

"I love these mountains. I have pride in this land. I have pride in my heritage. I love being a West Virginian. We're the butt of a million jokes, but you won't find a prouder, friendlier people anywhere. You won't believe this, but even though I take coal from these mountains, I love nature. I read somewhere that right in our state, we have more species of birds than in the whole continent of Europe. I have always hated what coal mining has done to these mountains. But it was always limited, the impact, until recently. In just this most recent decade of my life, and I'm 69, I've seen strip mining come in and destroy these mountains.

"Underground mining was always hard on the land, but it's nothing like strip mining. Strip mining destroys everything: the birds, the wildlife, the streams, the waterfalls, the underground water, the air, everything.

"We've always known that there is a fixed amount of coal in these mountains, although it's an awful lot. There's still an awful lot. But there's less now than in my father's time, my grandfather's time, or my great-grandfather's time. My great-grandfather mined seams seven, eight, and ten feet thick. All the best stuff is gone. We're mining increasingly thin seams with poorer burn content. They took the good stuff first.

"Anyway, when the coal is gone, what then? If we take care of the land, replant the impacted areas, and preserve the streams, our children and their children have a future. When we destroy the mountains and poison the groundwater and the streams, we kill the heritage and we have nothing. Our fate in poverty is sealed, forever. That's what Mr. Youngblood's company is doing to West Virginia today, permanently impoverishing my state. Someday he'll burn in hell for it."

Lacey took a dirty handkerchief from his pocket and wiped his eyes. Then he continued, "Ma'am, I don't think most people understand heritage. To me, it is as real as food and water. Heritage makes me and my people strong and proud and able to deal with living in one of the poorest places in America where our neighbors die prematurely from cancers and other pollution-related diseases that wouldn't be tolerated anywhere else. Appalachia's only remaining strength is its heritage, and that's being blown to fuckin' smithereens – pardon me Lord!

"As I was sayin', in recent years, the miners' allegiances have shifted. When I was new in the mines, the miners supported each other and the union. As companies needed fewer and fewer miners to mine more and more coal, our politics has shifted. Our area was once Democratic, because Democrats supported working people. Now, we've turned to the right, and people beg for any politician who supports the continued mining of coal, whoever is doing it and whatever damage they're causing. Do you know why so many of my neighbors are willing to pulverize these mountains and destroy their wells and creeks and poison themselves?" He looked at Goldschmidt first, begging for an answer. Then he looked at the others. Zola looked up from her typewriter and nodded in agreement. When nobody spoke, he said, "Because they are totally desperate; they have no other choice to feed their families.

"Your honor, they say the environmentalists is shutting us down. They say the mining companies give us good jobs and without them we'd be destroyed. But the truth is far more complicated. The coal companies own everything around here.

"My house was swept away by the flood, with my wife of 44 years in it. We'd done finally paid it off. But even then, we didn't own but eight inches of soil underneath it; the rest was owned by the coal company. They own the workers, because they actively discourage any other businesses from coming here. They own the air above us, because they're basically free to pollute all they want. Same with the water. They own the wildlife, because once you strip a mountain, there is no more wildlife. Bears are territorial; so are bobcats. When you destroy a bear's territory, the bears around don't simply make room for another. They fight to the death. How can anybody own the water or the wildlife? How can a company use them in a way that will diminish or injure their use by others?

"You know what else? We have some of the worst roadside trash in the country. You know why?"

He stopped and looked around with futility, as if fishing vainly for still another answer.

"I'll tell you why. Because nobody owns anything. If a man and a woman own a house, they'll take care of it. If they own their town, they care what it looks like. Around here, nobody owns anything. Everybody is apathetic.

"These impoundment dams, and there are over a hundred just in West Virginia alone, are like Swords of Damocles, hanging over the heads of thousands of people including the schools where most kids in Southern West Virginia go.

"When those dams broke, my community lost 230 people and has made over a thousand people homeless. All those houses that used to be here, they're all now scrap lumber and rubbish, laying all over the valley. Do you know who is going to pick it up? Nobody! That's 'cause nobody owns it."

"Lacey," Pug said, "Please talk about the issue at hand, the guilt of Mr. Lawton."

Judge Goldschmidt snapped, "Cut it out, Mr. Graham. Nobody's been found guilty yet. Lacey, please go on."

Lacey closed his eyes hard, wrinkling his face. "Mr. Lawton has been inspecting the mines around here for years. He's a power-hungry sonofabitch. He issues fines when he wants and uses his power to enhance himself."

Pug asked, "What do you think he saw when he inspected the two dams on Upper Horsepen?"

"Speculation!" yelled Youngblood.

"I retract the question," Pug said. "Lacey, that's all for now. Youngblood, your turn."

Alvin Youngblood turned to Lacey and said, "Have you ever personally witnessed Mr. Lawton doing anything illegal at the mine where you work?"

"No, sir."

Have you ever personally seen the two dams that broke at upper Horsepen?"

"No."

"That's all, your honor."

Goldschmidt turned to Pug and said, "Do you have another witness?"

"Yes, your honor. I'd like to question Zola."

"Okay, fine."

Goldschmidt read Zola her oath which she repeated, turning over the typewriter back to Lacey. She stated her name as "Zola Elswick Wilkerson."

Pug's questioning was about her upbringing and her experience at the Buffalo Creek disaster. Her story was repeated from what she'd told Pug on their trip home a mere two weeks before. Under further questioning, she indicated that the current flood seemed eerily similar to the prior one.

Then he asked, "In your estimation, who was responsible for what happened here?"

"Everybody. Everybody who touched this situation is responsible. Mr. Lawton is the inspector. It's his fault if the dam breaks when he certifies that it won't. Let's think about a dam for a minute. I'm no engineer, but I've seen dams before. We all have. They have a spillway that lets the water through. Spillways are concrete or some other material that won't erode, because water is designed to flow freely over them. Under normal conditions, the top level of the dam is always above the spillway. If the water level gets too great, it can come over the top of the dam, and of course it can still flood the valley below it. But even with water sweeping over it, a dam should never break, should it?"

She became quiet for a moment, as if waiting like Lacey before her, for an answer that never came. She took off her hard-hat and swept her hand over her bald head, now just growing a delicate fuzz of hair. Then she continued, "Mr. Youngblood is responsible because his company owns the mine and the dam. Madam Secretary Goldschmidt, if your agency is over mine safety, then you're responsible, too. But I think we should be asking as well who is not responsible. The people of War are not responsible for their own deaths. This is the United States of America. We are the richest, most prosperous nation the world has ever known. Nobody in our country should have to live under the dark threat of instant death because the corporation that dominates their community economically doesn't take the steps, and the government doesn't force them to take the steps, to protect those communities.

"Two hundred and thirty-three innocent people, most of them children, are dead. I'd say there's enough blame to go around."

In his cross examination of her, Youngblood asked the same question of her that he'd asked of Lacey, whether she'd ever seen the dams that broke, and she admitted that she hadn't.

At that point, Pug asked if he could ask another question of Zola, permission for which was given by Goldschmidt. "You said earlier that nobody should have to live under the threat of death from a corporation's activities. I suspect you have more on your mind about that."

"I sure do. Even before that dam broke, Mr. Youngblood's corporation has inflicted damage on the people of this and countless other communities in the central Appalachians that would never be tolerated in other parts of the country or by other corporations."

"Such as?" Goldschmidt asked.

"When a mountain is decapitated, the first step is destroying all living things, the trees, plants, and animals. The trees are dumped into the valleys and burned. Then the blasting begins. Every afternoon throughout West Virginia, formerly quiet hollow towns are shattered with the violence of hundreds of blasts of thousands of tons of ammonium nitrate, the same explosive that was used in 1995 to destroy the Federal Building in Oklahoma City. For hours, clouds of dust and debris rain from the sky, including the rock that killed Ronnie's wife and son. Imagine how damaging this is to somebody's nerves!

"The dust is filled with fine particulate that can contain lead, mercury, silica, selenium, and all kinds of other toxic shit. This stuff gets into the lungs of everybody who lives downwind. Incidentally, the demolition people never check which way the wind is blowing before they start blasting. We hear stories all the time of seemingly healthy people dying of heart attacks from the shock. An elderly man I knew died of a heart attack in his shower when a blast went off after hours one evening. Asthma, cancer and tumor rates downwind of mountaintop removal mines are dramatically higher than other places.

"The shock waves eventually wreck the houses nearby, as foundations and chimneys crack. Windows don't fit moldings any more. Roofs develop leaks. Houses lose all their value and the owners' equity is destroyed.

"Then the wells start drying up or yielding pollutants. Every commode and every bathtub in southern West Virginia is stained orange-red from the polluted water. Everybody has to drink and cook with bottled water, assuming they can afford it. They bathe in carcinogens. They wash their clothes and dishes in carcinogens. People stay and fight as long as they can, because they love these hollows. But eventually most people give up and move away. They get nothing from selling their homes because nobody else would ever move into them. And do you know what the company compensates them for this? Jack-shit. Typically nothing at all. And if it is anything at all, it isn't enough to live anywhere else. A friend of mine bought a house two years ago for less money than he paid the year before for his pickup truck. Banks won't lend money to anybody who wants to build a house because the day it is finished, it is worth less than the materials they put into it. I bet there haven't been a dozen new houses built in south McDowell County in the last ten years.

"The result is the de-population of the coalfields, which is exactly what they want. Fewer people means fewer complaints and fewer obstructions to Mr. Youngblood's company's operations.

"I'd ask you to imagine any other corporation doing this kind of damage. If Apple Computers or General Motors or Raytheon or Hewlet-Packard came to any town in America and did this kind of damage, there would be widespread outrage. Mr. Youngblood's company does this all the time.

"And why does it happen here? Why is the coal industry allowed to destroy the ancient mountains and clear, flowing streams of Kentucky, Virginia, and West Virginia? Can you imagine this level of destruction in the Catskills, the Smokies, or the Sierra Nevadas? The Boston brainiacs would go crazy if somebody proposed strip mining the White Mountains in New Hampshire. But it happens here in the central Appalachians because we've always been totally dependent and powerless.

"How about Mr. Youngblood's workers? What would make a man deliberately destroy his own children and their friends and their communities? The coal companies so effectively keep any employment diversification from occurring that workers are desperate for any job. None of today's modern companies would ever open a facility or put new jobs in the coal fields. What kind of Faustian bargain is this?"

The room became silent. The lantern flickered. Goldschmidt said, "Thank you, Zola. Any further questions, Pug?"

Pug decided that they'd all heard enough for the day and he asked Meredith to put the court at recess until the next visit. He told the prisoners that it would be 12 hours later, but he planned it for actually only seven in the continuing escalation of time.

Pug returned Meredith to her cell area and again replenished the battery in her lantern, thanking her for her service. She dove right in again on Pug's mother's memoirs.

```
I went to Big Creek High School in
War. I got a job at the Yukon Company
store in 1956. This was the beginning
of an era of diminishment. Coal mining
was being mechanized then and fewer and
fewer people were needed. People started
migrating away. It's really sad. People
leave. Friends leave. They've been leaving
ever since. Almost 4000 people lived in
War then. We're under 1000 now. Sometimes
people come back to visit, but there's a
distance between us that we didn't feel
```

before they left. Some are successful and
they vacation in California and Florida.
Some used to send post cards, but nobody
does that any more.

Only people who have experienced this
loss can understand it. Those of us
left behind weep for the loss of these
precious friendships. We weep for the
abandoned, decaying, collapsing buildings,
the houses where we played with our
neighbors, the schools where we frolicked
in the playgrounds, the tipples where our
husbands worked. We watch as the windows
break, the bricks fall, and the foliage
engulfs.

The economy would come and go, cycles of
good and bad. When the markets were good,
everybody had jobs and money. People would
have fun and spend it, some recklessly.
Others knew bad times were coming just
around the corner and they prepared for
it. But each valley was deeper than the
one before and each peak was lower. People
would talk about coal coming back because
there was always a lot of it. But it never
came back as strong as before.

Still, there were good times. We didn't
need much to stay entertained.

Social life revolved around the school,
with sports and dances. There was swimming
at Berwind Lake and a dance hall. There
was a Teen Town community center for
teenagers for music and dancing and
hanging out. The boys played football,

basketball, and baseball at the schoolyard and marbles in the streets. My earliest prized possession was my bicycle and I rode it around just like the boys. We played badminton and shuffleboard. I was in a church group and I loved to read. I visited the church library and I read all the Hardy Boys and Nancy Drew books.

We were poor, but some of the kids were even poorer. One girl almost always came to school in a dress made from a grain sack. Flip-flops were a fad and she had to make her own with twine and some rubber cut from a discarded car tire. People made fun of her.

The store smelled of denim, leather, and cornmeal flour from big bins. I loved opening the incoming boxes and stocking the shelves with new merchandise, smelling the shoes and the belts and all the leather.

I loved the store, seeing all my neighbors all the time. Each aisle smelled different, with skin creams and shaving lotions on one, glycerin and rosewater lotions on the next, and packaged coffees and teas on the next. The store had a wooden floor and floor wax was applied regularly, giving it a freshly waxed smell. The floor creaked when people walked on it and you could hear it from below when working in the stock room in the basement.

The light flickered in Meredith's lantern and then went out.

JAN 12 Sunday

The next time court was in session, Judge Goldschmidt asked if Pug had any other witnesses. Pug asked if he could put himself on the stand, answering his own questions. Over Youngblood's objection, Goldschmidt gave Pug her permission to proceed. She swore him in and had him identify himself. Then he began, telling his life story until his return to War. He explained how he'd recently lost his father to black lung disease and his mother to the flood.

"I am trying to run the mining company that my father started and my brother ran until his disappearance. Our mine is heavily regulated. If we're doing something wrong, something that is damaging to our workers or our environment, we'll get called on it, and usually fined.

"I know Mr. Lawton is responsible for the two dams that burst. I'm not an expert on dams, but I know they all should be engineered to absorb or release any amount of water nature can ever throw at them. That's all I have to say."

"Mr. Youngblood, would you like to question Mr. Pug?"

"Yeah, why not," the big man bellowed. "Do you know what an impoundment dam is, Pug?"

"Of course I do. Whenever coal is mined, there are other materials that are removed from the ground that aren't coal. So the coal must be cleaned and separated from it. I'm not intimately sure how the process works, but I know that you have thousands, no millions, of gallons of water filled with gunk, er, gob, to deal with. So it is put behind dams in impoundments where the bad stuff settles out and the water can be returned to the streams."

"Have you ever been to the Horsepen where this dam break occurred?"

"No."

"So you've never seen the dams?"

"No."

"Have you ever seen any impoundment dam?"

"Only from below them," Pug admitted. "They look like a giant embankment."

"Then you don't know shit."

"Stop it!" Goldschmidt screamed. "In my court, we will treat each other with respect."

"This is a fuckkin' sham," Youngblood countered, angrily.

A pall of silence set over the low-roofed room. Then Pug spoke. "Mr. Youngblood, my hometown is now nothing more than a pile of rubble. Over two hundred people are dead, most of them children. The worst thing that can ever happen to someone in life is losing a child. When you lose your parents, you're called an orphan. When you lose a child, we don't even have a word in the English language to describe it, 'cause it's so awful. This happened because people who needed to care enough to prevent it didn't. You can think whatever you want about these proceedings, but I want you to look around. Nobody you see is going to be alive in another week if we don't learn the truth."

The room got quiet again. Finally Goldschmidt spoke, suggesting that the court recess until the next time the captors came. Pug returned Goldschmidt to her separate room, and while re-shackling her said quietly to her, "Thanks." She smiled softly.

+ + + + +

Seven hours later, the kidnappers rejoined their captives and after the requisite replenishment of supplies and emptying of chamber pots, everyone gathered again to resume the trial. Secretary Meredith Goldschmidt brought her courtroom again into session. Pug had the defendant,

Merritt Lee Lawton, sworn in.

Goldschmidt spoke first, "Mr. Lawton, do you understand that you are being charged with the crime of manslaughter in the deaths of 233 people?"

"Yes, I do."

"Very well then. Mr. Graham, please proceed."

Pug began, "Mr. Lawton, would you please tell the court your occupation?"

"I am a mine safety engineer for the state of West Virginia."

"Where were you educated?"

"I went to Clinch Valley College; it's the University of Virginia at Wise now."

"And what is your degree in?"

"I never finished."

"So you dropped out?"

"Yes," Lawton admitted.

"By what credentials did you get your current job?"

"My brother was in the agency. He helped me."

"Fine. Nepotism. So how were you trained for your job?"

"I worked in a mine when I was in high school. My family is all coal miners."

"Is that it?"

"I had training in the agency."

"In what areas?"

"Mine ventilation. Mine electricity. Mine injury prevention."

"What do you know about surface mining and mine tailings?"

"Only common sense," Lawton shrugged. "I was never supposed to be inspecting strip jobs and dams. My agency never has enough money. When the last guy retired, they assigned me to this area's strip jobs, tipples, and dams."

"Mr. Lawton," Goldschmidt interrupted, "What is a tipple?"

"It's a coal preparation facility, ma'am. It is the factory,

I guess you'd call it, where the coal is cleaned for shipment."

"Thank you. Please continue your questioning, Mr. Pug."

"Mr. Lawton, when did you last inspect this dam, the dam that broke?"

"In early December, two or three weeks before it broke."

"And what did you find."

"I certified it. It was fine."

"Obviously it wasn't fine. In your estimation, why did it fail?"

"An act of God."

"Yes, that's what I understand. I'd like you to be more specific, please."

"It rained, all right? It kept raining. The water overwhelmed it."

Becoming impatient, Pug said, "Isn't it appropriate to believe that a properly engineered dam would withstand any level of water behind it, otherwise the overall level of the dam could be lowered to allow less water before it all ran over the top?"

"I suppose so."

"You SUPPOSE so! Aren't you supposed to know?"

"I was never really trained. I don't know that much about dams."

"What does your common sense tell you?"

"I guess the same as yours. A dam should hold as much water as its height allows to collect behind it."

"What is this dam made of? Is it concrete?"

"No. It is an earthen dam."

"What does that mean?" Judge Goldschmidt interjected.

"It is made from the rock and soil material around the area."

Pug, "So it is just a long, shaped embankment of rock and dirt?"

"Yes."

"Was it ever reinforced with anything, like concrete or

steel beams?"

"Not to my knowledge."

"Any timbers?"

"No."

Pug let this information sit for a few moments. Then Zola tapped him on the shoulder and motioned him away. Pug said to Goldschmidt, "May I have a moment of recess, please?" She nodded her acknowledgement.

Zola marched ahead of Pug to an adjacent corridor, marked only by their headlights. "What's up?" he asked her.

"This is the same argument the officials used at Buffalo Creek. But I seem to remember something from that situation that you should ask about."

Pug and Zola returned to the courtroom area and Pug said to Meredith, "If it pleases the court, I would like to adjourn for now."

"Why is that?" Meredith asked.

"I have some things to sort through and some research to do. May we re-convene tonight?"

"Do you have any objection, Youngblood?"

The big man scowled, but said nothing.

Goldschmidt continued, "Then court is adjourned."

+ + + + +

On their way back to War, Zola invited Pug to walk her to Mill's house that she was now occupying. Inside, she said, "I probably shouldn't be doing this, but I've been shuffling through some of Mill's private stuff. I found his passport and a diary."

"You've been reading my brother's diary?"

"Yes." She explained that in recent months, he had been writing about increasing fines levied by the mine inspector, Lawton, on his company's mine. Mill had confronted Lawton several times, the last few angrily. Zola was convinced that

Lawton was responsible for Mill's disappearance.

"How do you think I can convince Lawton to implicate himself?" Pug asked.

"Hell, you're the prosecuting attorney. I think the arrogant bastard will hang himself if you give him enough rope," she said.

+ + + + +

That afternoon, Pug found a copy of the day's Bluefield Star Sentinel with Red's lengthiest article yet about the disaster.

War flood disaster investigation continues

Ten days ago, following several days of torrential rain produced by tropical Hurricane Thad, the Upper Horsepen Impoundment Dam three miles north of Bishop, West Virginia, collapsed, producing a flood that devastated the War Hollow area.

Much is still unknown about the cause of the dam break, but engineers and investigators have provided this information.

Coal has been actively mined throughout Southern West Virginia since a rail line was extended into the area in 1899 by the Norfolk and Western Railroad.

An inevitable by-product of coal mining is waste material comprised of slate, low-grade coal, or other rock. In the separation process, immense quantities of water are required. The solid waste material has traditionally been dumped wherever convenient. The liquid material is compounded to enable the solids to settle from it behind impoundment dams, often earthen and in many cases comprised largely of the same solid waste materials.

Two impoundment dams were built near the headwater streams of Upper Horsepen Creek by the Bishop Coal Company, in 1942, specifically to mine the area's coal in support of the military buildup to provide steel for the Army and Navy during World War II.

Bishop Coal and all its holdings and operations, through a series of mergers and acquisitions, were eventually acquired by Bessie Energy. By the time of the catastrophe, the upper Horsepen Impoundment was approximately one mile long, 83 feet deep and 600 feet across at the dam and contained 180 million gallons of sludge. The lower Horsepen Impoundment was one-half mile long, 67 feet deep, and 450 feet across at the dam and contained 98 million gallons of sludge.

Operations diminished during the economic crisis of the early 1980s, but by 1999, a vast mountaintop removal mine was opened on the border of West Virginia and Virginia, and a coal preparation tipple was built to process the coal for shipment. The impoundment dams were raised and widened, allowing for a total of 272 million gallons of particulate-laden water. As the particulate matter settled, clearer water was recycled through the tipple on an ongoing basis.

Neither of the dams was built to any engineering plan, but were merely slapdash pilings of waste material, expanded several times over the years to accommodate growing capacities. In 2003, the dams' spillways were reinforced with concrete at the insistence of Federal Inspectors, but the dams themselves had no engineering analyses nor reinforcement performed or applied. Newspaper articles from 2003 indicate resistance from the company to making the mandated improvements with vice president of Operations Alvin Youngblood quoted as saying, "If the spillway overtops, the spillage will kill all the fish. People need to decide whether they want fish or not." Youngblood is now president of Bessie Energy.

Investigators have been unable to locate anyone who was in proximity of the upper dam the morning of its collapse. However one witness saw a red, late-model pickup truck driving at a high rate of speed northward on SR-16 moments before the flood ensued. It has not been identified.

Angus Wilson, 57, a resident of Jacobs Fork, is the closest surviving witness. Wilson is a retired miner with advanced black lung, who walks with a cane. He told reporters and a state investigator this account of his experience. "I was walking back down the hill to my trailer from the outhouse. I felt the ground a-shakin' and I looked to the east. The ground went a-shakin' again and I heared (sic) two explosions, maybe 20 seconds apart. I seen a mushroom cloud risin' over the hilltop. Next thing I knowed this wall of black muck swept the trailer away with my Carol in it. My dog was on the porch and I yelled at her and she a'ran up to me. She's all I got now."

Investigators have speculated that the sounds Wilson heard were steam explosions. Coal will spontaneously combust if not routinely dampened. Small concentrations of coal can smolder under piles of dirt and slate for years or even decades. When the wall of water smashed into smoldering slate piles, it uncovered the burning coal, causing it to react with water in steam explosions, throwing mud and rocks 400 feet high and produced a volcano-like cloud of steam.

The rushing tsunami of water was estimated at over 50-feet high and traveling at 55 miles per hour as it leveled Jacobs Fork, Johnstown, Squire, Newhall, Cucumber, and Rift before smashing through War itself. The wave diminished in speed, height, and energy as it continued downstream through Yukon, English, Bradshaw, and Iaeger where it joined the larger Tug Fork River.

Approximately 38 miles by the course of the creek separates Bishop and Iaeger. Between 3500 and 4000 people lived along the watercourse. There were between 1750 and 1850 occupied homes. By the time the flood had subsided, there were 228 dead, 12 missing, 390 injured, and 3054 homeless people. Personal property damage is estimated at $17.2 million, with 1120 homes and 72 commercial establishments destroyed, with another $122 million of infrastructure in roads, schools, and railroads destroyed.

In the days since the flood, disaster relief stations have been staffed near the former sites of War, Bradshaw, and Iaeger. A main relief center has been established at River View High School in Bradshaw, which is currently housing 276 homeless survivors. Grief counselors are staffing each center.

The West Virginia National Guard, assisted by troops from the U.S. Army stationed at Fort Lee, Virginia, is attending to the rebuilding effort. Mud and coal waste continue to permeate the entire hollow. The railroad anticipates a 60-90 day rebuild period for the damaged tracks, which has shut down all coal operations in the area. WVDOT anticipates a 120-day rebuild effort to restore the highway along the corridor. State police have forbidden any travel to or from the area other than official vehicles and movement of the immediate families of the victims. FEMA officials have delivered 84 trailers to the area with another 52 anticipated within days.

Materials from many of the homes that were destroyed have been set ablaze, and the valley is often choked with smoke from burning wreckage.

Coincident with the flood, several dignitaries including the United States Secretary of the Interior Meredith Goldschmidt and Bessie Energy president Alvin Youngblood were kidnapped. Ransom has been demanded by the kidnappers, who are as yet unidentified and no group has claimed responsibility.

Federal mine inspectors are scouring the former dam sites seeking clues as to the upper dam's collapse. A preliminary report is due on January 28.

Yesterday, a protest rally was held at the state capital in Charleston, demanding the cessation of operations and eventual removal of the 319 slurry impoundment dams in West Virginia. Similar rallies were held at the state capitols of Virginia and Kentucky, where dozens of similar impoundments exist. The President of the United States has yet to make a proclamation. Cessation of operations would effectively shut down operations of the coal industry in the central Appalachians.

Presenting 28,000 online petition signatures from 45 states and 11 foreign countries to the Governor, historian Bremer Alexander of Bluefield said, "Floods like this have happened before many times. Now it has happened again, our worst ever. There will be more to happen in the future. Now is the time to decommission them." Alexander explained that Bessie's proclamation that the flood was "an act of God" as was heard decades earlier at Buffalo Creek further inflamed hatred. He said the overwhelming sentiment among the signers was the pervasive sense of the inability of governmental agencies or the mining companies to adequately regulate their activities, ensuring the inevitability of future disasters.

JAN 13 Monday

The next day, Lawton was sworn in again. Pug renewed his interrogation.

"Mr. Lawton, was there any type of drainage system to draw off water if it got too high?"

"No."

"Was it built to any engineered plan?"

"I don't know. If it was, I never saw the plan."

"How do earthen dams break?"

"Well," Lawton removed his hard hat and scratched his short hair, and then replaced it, "As far as I know, there are a few ways. If they're overtopped, the soil can erode quickly."

"Wait," Pug interrupted. "What do you mean by overtopped?"

"Just like it sounds. The water level raises so high it sweeps over the top of the dam. A properly engineered dam will have a spillway so the water can go there without eroding the top."

"Was this dam overtopped?"

"I don't know. When I inspected it, water was flowing smoothly over the spillway. I do know that by the time the top dam failed, the other one was doomed."

"What else?"

"They can fail through seepage. All earthen dams are permeable, meaning the water will seep all the way through them. This is normal and planned for. But it must be controlled in quantity. If the dam is too permeable, too much water makes its way through the interstices of the dam and it widens them. This is called 'piping'. Once a whirlpool is observed on the water's surface on the reservoir side, the dam is doomed and likely to collapse within minutes."

"Is this what happened?"

"Again, I don't know what happened. I wasn't there. When I last checked the dams, they were fine. With all the water God rained on them, the top one failed and the other one had no chance for survivability. But I wasn't there when it happened. My office was to begin an investigation right away, but as you can see, I've been waylaid," he said, sarcastically.

"Are there other ways?" Pug persisted.

"A million of them. An earthquake can shake things loose."

"Blasting nearby?"

"Yeah, I suppose so."

"What else?"

"The lake drain may have a structural problem. Freezing and thawing of the rocks may loosen something."

"Mr. Lawton," Goldschmidt interrupted, "Are you saying that this type of dam is permeable enough to allow for the water inside of it to freeze, thus widening the cracks?"

"Yes, ma'am. Coarse refuse is used, meaning all kinds of rock, coal and slate. It has to be properly compacted to maintain integrity, and it will not stay compacted except within a narrow moisture content range. It's a weak material and it is even weaker when it's wet. And it was really wet!"

Pug resumed his interrogation, "Mr. Lawton, you have testified that there were multiple potential problems with these dams in the way they were engineered, constructed, and maintained. What fines did you charge Mr. Youngblood's company with, say in the last twelve months?"

"I don't recall ever fining him."

A hush fell over the room as each person processed this admission. The silence was interrupted several moments later by Zola, who said to Goldschmidt, "May I ask a question, please, your Honor?"

"Yes, go ahead."

"Mr. Lawton, what has the coal industry learned in the 40 years since Buffalo Creek that has been applied to newer dams?"

"I don't know the answer to that question," he admitted.

"I sure as hell do," Zola shrugged. "Not a damn thing."

Goldschmidt looked at Zola condescendingly. Then she turned to Pug, "Do you have any further questioning or witnesses?"

"No, your honor."

"Then will that be all for Mr. Lawton's trial, Mr. Graham?"

"Yes, your honor."

"Very well. We are adjourned. I think it is best that Mr. Youngblood's trial happens next before we reach a verdict on Mr. Lawton. So we'll begin there at our next session. Please be ready, Mr. Youngblood."

Youngblood sniffed loudly, then spit on the West Virginia University carpet.

Lacey's pitter-pattering on the typewriter's keyboard continued to catch up.

+ + + + +

By the light of Pug's headlamp, Meredith walked back to her place of confinement ahead of him, scraping her hard-hat on the ceiling of stone. She said, "How do you think things are going thus far?"

Pug wiped his face with a dirty hand. "Okay, I guess. I think we're getting some answers."

"I think you're leaving too much on the table," the tall woman said, succinctly.

"What do you mean," Pug asked, incredulous that Goldschmidt seemed so eager to help him.

"I hear some things in here. I look at body language. Don't let these guys get off so easy."

"What do you think I should do?" he asked.

"Think about it," she said. "Remember Watergate and Deep Throat? 'Follow the money'."

Part 6

𝕿HE MAKESHIFT COURTROOM was assembled again, this time at 4:00 a.m. local time, but with the captives convinced it was early evening. Judge Goldschmidt said, "It is now time to proceed with the murder trial of Alvin Youngblood."

Pug said, "If it pleases the court, I would like to ask Mr. Lawton a few more questions."

"Mr. Youngblood, do you have any objections?"

"What the hell?. Go ahead."

Goldschmidt swore Lawton to the truth again.

Pug said, "Mr. Lawton, are you aware that my older brother Millard Graham ran our family mine after the retirement of my father and before my return?"

"Yes."

"Did you have any dealings with him?"

"Yeah. I inspected his mine." Lawton hockered and spit on the West Virginia University carpet.

"When did you see him last? And where?"

"I inspected his mine in November. I'm not sure of the date. Somebody told me he disappeared and I never saw him again."

"Did this mine appear qualitatively different from the others you inspected regularly?" Pug grilled.

"They're all about the same."

"You have stated that it is your job to inspect his mine, along with several others. You levy fines when mines are not in compliance. Is that correct?"

"Yes."

"If Mill's mine is just about the same as all the others, then why did it have four to five times the number of infractions as similar mines in the county?"

"I wasn't aware..."

"Are you not aware of the fines you levy?"

"Your brother's mine had..."

"My brother's mine received five times as much as the Hatcher mine in Caretta and over four times as many fines as the Wilkenson mine in Coalwood. Why?"

"Well, your brother's quality control..."

"My brother's quality control was exceptional!" Pug screamed. "There was not a single hour missed due to injury in over seven years. And the fines you levied were eight times your predecessor. Why?"

"I... I" Lawton stammered.

"Shut up, Lawton," Youngblood screamed.

"We'd like an answer," Goldschmidt said. "Now."

Lawton wavered for a moment, and then he said clearly and unapologetically, "Corporate mining is our future. Private underground mining is too inefficient. Your brother was an impediment. You'll find his body 50 yards from the entrance of the Shop Hollow mine #2."

A pall of silence fell over the room. Pug felt his heart racing and goosebumps forming on his arms. Seemingly, nobody knew what to say. The methane detector rang out and water dripped from somewhere in the dark. Finally Pug said, "Your honor, I would like to request a recess. I need to find my brother's body."

Goldschmidt recessed the court. Pug, Lacey, Donnie, and Zola made sure the prisoners were properly secured, and then they departed, with Pug leaving Meredith another battery for her lantern.

Pug dropped off Lacey and Zola, taking Donnie with him. They found Mill's body exactly where Lawton had said. Due to the coolness of the abandoned mine, the body was in good condition overall. Donnie emitted a string of angry expletives as Pug examined his dead brother's body. He could clearly see that Mill had received a blunt force wound to his left forehead, as if struck by a baseball bat. Pug decided to leave the body alone, at least for now, taking only his dead brother's wallet.

+ + + + +

Back in her prison, Goldschmidt switched on her lantern and began reading the memoirs again.

Every day I thought about Grammammy and her experience in the store and was glad those days were over.

We never let ourselves believe that good times weren't coming again. We had dances and movies. We had roller skating rinks. I always thought McDowell County was the best place in the country to live. Coal made lots of people rich, but we all knew we were paying the price.

I met my Emmett in 1956 and married him the year later. We met at the roller rink in town. He'd come over from his home in Iaeger to visit with his cousins here. When we met, I convinced him that we'd need to stay in War to help take care of mammy and Alice in their later years.

Emmett was working his way up in the mines and he formed his own company in 1967, Graham Mines. After the company store closed, I got a job starting as a floor clerk and eventually managing the Piggly Wiggly department store downtown.

Within a few years, all the company stores
were shutting down and regular commercial
stores were opening in the towns and
cities. I decided to return to school and
I got a degree in English at Bluefield
College. Then I got a job as librarian at
the High School.

My area of West Virginia is the butt
of everybody's jokes. I live in one of
the poorest areas in America. But what
we don't have in money, we have in other
things. There's a strength, endurance, and
perseverance that comes from our history
and culture. People become hardened
with adversity, and they are able to
absorb difficulties and disasters and the
tribulations that life throws us better
than other people.

Our difficulties have brought us bonds
of friendship that are deeper than other
places. Some of my friends have left over
the years and they live in places where
neighbors don't know each other or ever
socialize with them. They tell me when
they come home, they feel a peacefulness,
a comfortable familiarity and fierce pride
come over them. When I look at the old
photos, even though I see the poverty, my
heart wells up with memories and love that
money cannot buy or replace. The trees on
the mountains wave to me and the birds
call my name. Our mountain streams sing
peaceful songs to us.

We have a concern here for our

neighbors. People have a common decency,
uncommon now I suppose, and do favors
never asking for anything in return.
People leave their homes and garages
unlocked and people come by to borrow
things and bring them back without asking.
People are honest, most of them, and
they respect somebody who does a good
job without bragging about it. We don't
brag on ourselves, but we brag about each
other. Our work and our deeds speak for
themselves. You will never leave a home in
West Virginia hungry and nobody in need is
ever left alone. We always cook a little
extra, just in case somebody stops by,
just like we were taught.

We can tease each other, but don't let
an outsider do it, because we protect our
own like siblings. We are loyal to each
other, not afraid to get our hands dirty
and to earn our living. We instill in our
children the things that our parents and
grandparents instilled in us.

We love God and this land and its
fruits that he so graciously gave us. We
are singularly blessed. We're country
hillbillies and people in New York and Los
Angeles and Dallas look down on us, but
we have nothing to be ashamed of. We have
bonds with each other in these coal towns
that outsiders can't understand and that
time can't diminish. When I travel these
winding roads, they seemed unchanged as if
time has no power over them. We know and

understand our land and how it protects
and nurtures us. Appalachia is like no
other land.

Sorry, how did I get on that tangent?
Our boys, Millard and Lucas came in
1958 and 1960. They were bright boys.
Mill always seemed to want to follow his
daddy's footsteps. Lucas needed more space
for himself. He went to college and then
he moved to Virginia. He was manager of a
textile mill until it shut down recently.

Mill took over our mines, Graham Mines,
when Emmett couldn't work any more. He ran
it for years, keeping lots of the same
employees. I think they like him like they
liked Emmett. There have been good and bad
times in the mines, just like always. Mill
bought a trailer just above our house. He
lives there now, or did. A few weeks ago,
Mill didn't come home from work. We all
suspect he's dead.

Just since I've been writing, Pug, well
that's what we call Lucas now, has come
home to help take care of Emmett and me
and run Mill's mine until we learn what's
happened to him. We're happy to have Pug
home, but we know he hates coal mining.

Christmas is behind us and the New Year
is nigh. Emmett's breathing is more and
more labored. I'm sure he'll be gone soon.
I'm old now myself and I'm sure I don't
have too many more years. But I'm always
excited when the New Year arrives. The
opening of a new calendar gives me hope.

The makeshift federal court of Her Honor Meredith W. Goldschmidt re-convened 16 hours later, with the court reporter indicating that a full 23 hours had elapsed. By agreement between Pug and Meredith, all testimony would be heard before any verdicts would be reached or any sentencing would be made.

Lacey took his seat in front of his Smith-Corona.

"In U.S. Federal Court, makeshift, in the city of War, McDowell County, West Virginia, we are now in session," Goldschmidt proclaimed again. "Who is the accused today?"

"Your honor, if it please the court, today Mr. Alvin Youngblood, president of Bessie Energy, will be found guilty of the deaths of 233 people here in the area around War."

"Mr. Youngblood, how do you plead?"

"I'm not pleading a goddamn thing," Youngblood screamed.

"Mr. Youngblood," Goldschmidt continued, "Don't put us through your histrionics again. You're chained up in shackles. The people who you face this moment are armed with weapons and they have your life in their hands. We're going to ask you some questions about your involvement."

"Well, you can ask all you want but I'm not saying a damn thing. This is a sham, a charade, a farce. It was a mistake to go through the deal with Lawton. I ain't tellin' you people anything else. Charade, nothing more."

The room grew quiet, save the constantly dripping water.

"Charade," Donnie echoed. "It's a fuckin' charade," he said, in mocking agreement. He squirmed in his folding chair. He looked around at the others. Then pulled a Ruger pistol from its holster and gave it a long, pensive look. He pointed it at Youngblood. He cocked the gun. "A man has confessed to the murder of another man, yet the murderer is still alive. Ain't murder punishable by death? Ain't it a charade, a sham, if the murderer is alive?" he asked rhetorically. "We still have capital punishment here in West By God Virginia, don't we?"

As Pug watched incredulously, powerless to act, Donnie shifted the aim of his gun to the face of Merritt Lee Lawton, and then unhesitatingly pulled the trigger. The room exploded in percussion and blood spattered around the room. Lawton slumped in his chair, exposing the gaping, bloody hole in the back of his skull, then fell to the floor, dead.

Nobody moved.

Donnie re-holstered his gun.

"Charade," Donnie echoed again. "Fuckin' right."

Nobody moved.

Drip, drip, drip.

Finally Meredith broke the silence, removing her hand from her face where she wiped away some of Lawton's blood. "I suggest we adjourn for now."

Pug returned Meredith to her lair while Donnie and Lacey unshackled Merritt's ankle from his chains and dragged his body deeper into the mine. They tidied up as best they could, but the massive bloodstain on the carpet was indelible.

Leaving the captives again in the dark, Pug, Donnie, Lacey, and Zola took the long, familiar trek outside, where the temperature was thirty degrees colder than inside the chilly mine. Pug thought again and again to question Donnie and his motives, but felt he had a good idea of his employee's intentions; no explanation would be necessary or provide any insight or satisfaction. Pug knew Donnie did what Donnie felt needed to be done, and Pug knew the execution was justified.

+ + + + +

Court reconvened 8 hours later, a point Lacey indicated was 15 hours later. Donnie failed to arrive at the appointed time. Pug assumed he was assisting in continuing recovery efforts, but Pug told Goldschmidt that he wished to continue the trial regardless.

Once they'd gathered again Goldschmidt said to Youngblood, "I'm guessing our incident of yesterday will add a new dynamic to today's proceedings. Mr. Youngblood, yesterday you indicated your unwillingness to cooperate. Have you reconsidered?

Youngblood wavered for a moment.

"Yeah."

"We appreciate your cooperation. Do you promise to tell the truth, the whole truth, and nothing but the truth, so help you God?"

"Yeah, I'll tell you piss-ants the truth."

"Are you represented by counsel?"

With Lawton dead, Youngblood looked at Webber, condescendingly. "Nope, I'm on my own."

"Please proceed, Pug."

"If it pleases the court, today we will prove beyond doubt that Mr. Youngblood is guilty in the second degree of the conspiratory deaths of 233 people in this valley. Mr. Youngblood owned the dams that collapsed. Therefore, he is responsible."

Pug looked towards Youngblood and said, "State your name please."

"Alvin Youngblood."

"And where are you from, Mr. Youngblood?"

"I'm from Uneeda, West Virginia."

Interspersed with Pug's questioning, Youngblood laid out his life history.

"I was raised by a single mother. My parents divorced when I was three. My mother was the strongest woman I ever met. She was a Hatfield, you know, from the feud. I was tops in my class at Madison High School and I went to Fairmont State College where I got a degree in mining engineering. I got a masters degree in finance from the Darden School of Business at the University of Virginia. It was the most arrogant place I've ever been. Fukkin' snobs! Nothing but a kindergarten of privilege.

"Anyway, coal is essential to our modern world and maintaining the wealth and power our nation deserves. God shed his grace on thee, as the song goes. Our nation isn't like all the others – we're exceptionally blessed. We have resources that are unmatched anywhere in the world and God has put them here for us to use.

"Coal is responsible for over half the electricity we use in this country. No energy source is foolproof or without environmental impacts. Nuclear energy has massive radiation and waste problems. Wind turbines are an eyesore, they are bird Cuisinarts, and they only work when the wind blows. Solar panels chew up massive amounts of rare materials and don't work on cloudy days or overnight. You think the people who run those massive computer banks at Google or Microsoft are gonna only want to run during the day? Me neither.

"The coal my company extracts is inexpensive, allowing unparalleled prosperity. It is reliable electricity.

"Here in West Virginia and in the rest of the central Appalachians, coal mining is the dominant industry. I pay people $60,000, $70,000, sometimes $80,000 a year or more, way more than what any other occupation around here pays. People like coal mining. It's hard work but it is satisfying work for those few people left in our lazy-ass society who think honest work is good work.

"And the trickle-down effect throughout the communities around here means that even those who don't directly work on coal still depend upon it. Without coal, this area and most of West Virginia would shrivel up and die.

"The strip jobs we do leave behind flat land that is suitable for industrial applications and even residential development. You may have noticed that there isn't much flat land around here and so all the development needs to be in these tight valleys where everybody is at risk for flooding. When we level a mountain, you can put all kinds of things on it. There's a golf course on one north of Welch. There's an airport on one west of here in Grundy, Virginia. If all those people in War had been living on a mountain instead of in the hollow, they'd be alive today.

"It really pisses me off to hear from all the well-intentioned tree-huggers and liberals who decry what we're doing out here yet can't live 15 minutes without their cell phones, their GPSs, or their air-conditioning. You tell me how long these people could continue to live in Atlanta or Orlando or even Washington without A/C. It burns me when celebrities take their cross-country airplane flights wearing designer clothes to attend rallies to convince people we're the enemy.

"I'm president of Bessie Energy. We're the fifth largest coal mining company in the country. We rule this part of the world."

Pug said, "Please tell the court what you mean by that."

"Like I said, we rule this part of the world. In West Virginia, coal is king. We provide the only jobs around here that anybody can get that'll keep them off welfare. We are the largest landowner south of Charleston and west of Beckley, all the way to the banks of the Tug Fork River where my momma's family battled the McCoys. My grandfather was a barber and my great uncle was an undertaker, but all the rest of the men in my family were miners. Thousands of families throughout the coal fields owe their livelihoods to me. This state is nothing but a pile of crap without coal, and my company delivers it.

"Cheap coal means cheap energy. That improves the quality of life. You go places in this world where energy is expensive and you'll find terrible living conditions. We like to say we keep the lights on for America."

Interim judge Goldschmidt suspended testimony for the session when Pug asked for a recess. The trial was to continue six hours later.

JAN 15 Wednesday

The court began on schedule as testimony continued.

"And what part do Federal Regulators play?" Pug asked.

"They mostly get in the way. We live in a free market economy. I've been to communist countries. People lose their initiative. They give up their car and start walking or riding bicycles just like they did 80 years ago. They sit in putrid apartments wearing coats in the winter, wondering how they'll get warm. They stink because they never bathe, wondering if they'll ever take a shower.

"Washington politicians can't get out of their own way, much less run our nation. It is up to industrialists like myself to run the country."

Pug said accusingly, "Your mines have some of the worst safety records in the country."

"Listen, coal mining is dangerous. People have always gotten hurt. That's why it's such a brave and noble industry. We're also converting to mountaintop removal mining, because it is much safer per ton of coal mined. But we take care of the families when miners are hurt or killed. I love children. I give gifts every year at Christmas to thousands of them. I glorify God by helping people."

"Let's get to the matter at hand," Meredith admonished Pug.

"Yes, your honor." Then to Youngblood, "Is it true that until a few weeks ago, you owned a dam at Horsepen that held back thousands of gallons of mine tailings?"

"That's what I'm told. That's why I came to War, to express my sympathies."

"How do you think the dam failed?"

"How the hell do you think I know?" Youngblood retorted angrily. "It rained too much. It failed. I have hundreds of these ponds near my mines in the Appalachians. Do you expect me to monitor the condition of all of them personally? I follow the rules. When the rules aren't worth following, we get them changed."

"I beg your pardon," Goldschmidt pleaded, incredulously.

"You heard me right, lady. The government of the state of West Virginia is in our pocket. Most of your administration in Washington is, too. We didn't bother buying you out, lady, because you're powerless. You're impotent. So go fuck yourself."

The low-ceilinged room fell into absolute silence, save the distant dripping of water. Pug was astounded by the big man's arrogance and temerity, especially given the actions Donnie had taken at their prior session. Yet Youngblood seemed petulant and unapologetic. Nobody seemed to know how to speak or what to say. Nobody knew who had authority, who had power, and who would make the next move.

Youngblood's venom was clearly rising as he shouted, "It's over, or it's going to be over soon. I ain't stupid. You and your playmates, Pug, bit off more than you can chew. You're out of your league. You have no idea what to do with me and you're too much of a coward to kill us yourself, although all bets are off with your buck-wild partner Donnie. So let us go before you die a miserable death."

"You're not going anywhere until you tell this court the truth, you motherfucker!" Pug screamed.

"I don't care what you know, because the gig is up. The FBI is closing in. You're going to be as dead as your brother soon. Here you go; chew on this for awhile.

"Lawton killed your son-of-a-bitch brother because I paid him to. We were closing down your brother's mine because he wouldn't sell me the mineral rights. I can't have people turning down my fair offers now, can I?

"And Lawton put plugs of ammonium nitrate under that Horsepen dam and blew it up 'cause I paid him for that, too.

We're planning the largest mountaintop removal mine east of the Mississippi above the city of War, and we couldn't very well have everybody suing us. So we destroyed the town and enough of the people in it that nobody'll be left.

"And if it's truth you're after, I recently paid the Vice President of the United States of America $7.2 million in cash for a favorable ruling on a challenge to SMCRA that would have prevented this mine from being permitted. Are you happy now? You wanted the truth; now you've got it. Now let me loose, you little pieces of excrement."

Drip. Drip. Drip.

"Pug?" Meredith asked.

Drip. Drip.

"Pug, is there anything further?"

Drip. Drip. Drip.

"You're a sack of shit, Youngblood," Pug shouted.

"That's what I'm told."

"Is there anything further?" Meredith asked again. "Mr. Youngblood?"

"If it pleases the court," Pug said, gasping. "I think we know what we need to know."

Meredith said, "In our next session, our last before I call for verdicts, I would like to say some things about my observations. We are adjourned."

As Lacey finished typing to catch up, the other kidnappers returned their prisoners to their places.

JAN 16 Thursday

Meredith Goldschmidt brought her court into session for the penultimate time, with Pug, Lacey, Donnie, Zola, Alvin, and Doug attending.

She said, "I would like to say some things about my experience as judge here, if I may." Nobody said anything. "It is clear that a terrible wrong has been committed outside this mine to the people of War. Never in my wildest dream did I expect to get a confession that the deaths of 233 people were deliberate. But prior to that, I had reached a personal conclusion that generations of terrible wrongs have been perpetrated upon the people of the coal fields. Everyone is to blame. Mr. Youngblood, you and everyone in your company who has made these tragic decisions deserve a special place in hell. I'm assuming Mr. Lawton is well on his way there now. As a high-ranking federal official, I accept all the blame I'm due for allowing the ongoing rape of the coal fields. I, like most Americans, have turned a blind eye to the abuses. But it is inexcusable for me, as I have real power over what goes on, and I failed. Laws are only as good as the people who enforce them. At least I'm willing to express my remorse.

"Now then, does anybody else have anything they want to say before we adjourn?"

"Yeah, I do," Youngblood bolted. He snorted and began, "Y'all know about Darwin and his assertion of Survival of the Fittest? What you don't know is that Darwin never used the term. It was coined by a British economist, Herbert Spenser, in 1864. People think survival depends upon being the strongest. But strength is measured lots of ways. General Motors was once the strongest car company in the world, but they failed to take advantage of opportunities to the point where the government needed to bail them out.

"In business, it isn't the strongest that wins but the one most ready to take advantage of opportunities. My company has been there for those advantages. We have even created our own advantages and opportunities.

"It's a dog-eat-dog world. If I don't dominate you, you'll dominate me. You people somehow expect me to apologize for that, but facts are facts. Over a million people die every year worldwide, some of natural deaths after long lives and some not. But every action we take has consequences. Actions I take have huge consequences. Some collateral damage is inevitable. So y'all deal with it."

Meredith said, "Just so I'm clear on this, Mr. Youngblood, to you the 233 people you had killed in War are nothing more than collateral damage."

"Deal with it, Madam Secretary, your goddamn Honor."

"When we reconvene tomorrow," Goldschmidt said, "I will ask the jurors to render their verdict. Zola, Donnie, and Lacey, I will expect verdicts from you tomorrow on Youngblood here. I'll ask for a verdict on Lawton, too, but with him admitting to murder and being dead already, it won't much matter. You are welcome to discuss the trial amongst yourselves as you attempt to reach a decision. However, you may not discuss this with anyone else, including Pug. Do you understand?" The three of them nodded. "At that point, my services as a judge will be surrendered. Very well. I think we'll recess and let the jury deliberate overnight."

"Yes, your honor," Zola, Donnie, and Lacey said in unison. Lacey continued to type, properly recording Youngblood's admission of guilt.

JAN 17 Friday

That night, Pug, Lacey, Donnie, and Zola returned to War. Zola, Donnie and Lacey departed for Mill's old house to discuss the trial. The men came back to Pug's house near midnight, and all found some sleep.

Pounding at the door at 3:25 a.m. roused Pug from his bed. He opened the door to find Zola, shivering in the cold, clear night. An inch of snow had fallen and vapor rose from her mouth as she said, "We need to move them. Now."

Pug let her in and they woke Donnie and Lacey. "I've had a premonition," Zola said. "We need to move the prisoners right away. They're closing in."

"Who's closing in?" Donnie asked.

"I don't know. The Army. The FBI. We just need to

move them." Feeling their skepticism, she said, "Please, guys. I can feel it."

"Where can we take them?" Lacey asked.

"There's another abandoned mine across the hollow. We can take them there," Donnie said.

"Let's go," Pug said.

The team of kidnappers grabbed their hard hats and lights and made their way to the Sienna, with Zola handing Pug his rifle on the way out. The moon was 3/4 full and was bright enough to cast their shadows on the snow. They drove the first mile without headlights, past the piles of wreckage from their destroyed town.

In the mine, they found the captives awake and animated, as if waiting for them. Pug said succinctly, "Hold out your hands. We're moving."

"Where are we going?" Youngblood insisted.

"We have new digs for you," Donnie sneered, while zip-tying the hands and feet of his prisoners together. Following Pug's instructions on the way over, each prisoner's legs were allowed roughly 18" of movement so they could all easily walk but not run. Webber, the officer, bumped his head painfully again on the roof of the mine, drawing blood still again.

"Let's go," Pug insisted.

The procession made their way to the mine entrance, following the circuitous route the kidnappers had always used coming in. Within minutes, Meredith announced, "We left behind the court transcripts!"

Pug said, "Lacey, you, Zola and Donnie keep going to the van. Meredith and I are going back to get the papers. We'll meet you there shortly."

Pug and Meredith hobbled back to the hideout and retrieved the papers. Meredith said, "We forgot your mother's memoirs, too." Pug scampered to Meredith's area and picked up that folder, tucking the transcripts inside and the whole lot into his coveralls. With his rifle in one hand

and Meredith's sleeve in the other, they retraced their steps to follow the others.

Meredith looked at Pug and he smiled at her, as if thanking her for remembering the vital documents.

Meredith and Pug reached the entrance area of the mine with the others already outside. The outside air was forty degrees cooler than underground. As the light of the moon illuminated their exit, two gunshots rang out. In an instant, Lacey and Donnie fell back hard on the ground, Lacey's neck taking a direct hit and Donnie hit in the chest. Zola turned towards Pug, immobilized, with a look of absolute terror before another bullet found its mark in her back, and she crumpled to the snow herself.

The prisoners they'd held for so many days were now free. Without hesitation, Pug took aim with his rifle and blasted Doug Webber in the back of the rib cage, felling him. Pug cocked another round and aimed it for Youngblood, but Youngblood tripped on the slippery ground and fell away from Pug's aim. Pug shot again, but the bullet zinged over Youngblood's head.

Pow!, another shot rang out towards Pug. A spark flew from above Pug's head where the bullet fired from an unseen gun ricocheted off the wall and struck him in the right shoulder. Pug dropped to his knee and his rifle flew from his hands onto the ground.

Meredith looked at her captor, now wincing in pain, and retreated a step out of harm's way. She looked towards the frozen outside world, into the cold clear night where she would run, turning herself over to the protection of the FBI.

A lifetime of thoughts and fears reverberated through her mind's eye. She saw Arnie, her cheating husband, lying atop a nubile graduate student, impregnating her. She saw the Vice President, berating her. She saw her own terror in the hands of kidnappers, and the bone-chilling cold she'd experienced.

She looked up and saw the blood of her erstwhile captors

and fellow captives, spurting bright red onto the pristine moonlit snow. "Don't shoot, I'm Secretary Goldschmidt," she envisioned yelling to her liberators. Yet no movement came from her legs, and no voice from her lungs. She stood immobilized, paralyzed in indecision.

"There's a back way," Pug said, standing up and clasping his shoulder. "Come on."

Reflexively, she followed him back into the mine. He stopped abruptly, drawing a switchblade from his pants pocket. He popped opened the blade, which reflected brightly in his headlamp. Then he bent to the floor and sliced the zip-ties from her ankles and then from her hands. "Let's go."

They scampered directly back to the place where Meredith had endured so many painfully cold nights, as her legs ached in the sudden activity after weeks of immobility. Pug found the dynamite Donnie had left and set the timer for three minutes. "This way."

Pug led Meredith through several more passageways. Finally, they emerged again on the other side of the mountain again into the frozen air. They scurried fifty feet down the mountainside when a blast reverberated through the mountain and set a tongue of flames shooting out the entrance of the mine.

Pug doused the light on his headlamp, in case there were more FBI agents in the area. They reached the creek at the bottom of the hollow, waded through the ice-cold water, and continued to the railroad track on the other side. They followed it a half mile west, then turned and walked up a steep gravel road, water from their soaked socks squeezing from their shoes. After 20 minutes of difficult climbing, Pug turned to a smaller road and continued uphill, less steeply. They walked another few hundred yards past some old mining machinery. Meredith's quads and calves screamed in pain, after her days of inactivity. But she was elated to be standing tall and walking again.

They reached what Meredith thought was the most rustic cabin she'd ever seen. Pug used the barrel of his gun to pry the locked latch from the door and they let themselves inside.

Pug turned on his headlight and flashed it across the room. There were many boxes of provisions, an oil lantern, and a small propane heater and stove. Pug handed Meredith a plastic lighter and she used it to light the lantern. He doused his headlamp. While he heated some bottled water, Meredith removed her shoes and then Pug's so they could dry.

The bullet fragment had penetrated the skin and muscle at Pug's shoulder, but it had lost most of its velocity from the impact of the mine wall. Meredith was able to extract it with Pug's knife. She found a first-aid kit and applied some antiseptic. She was worried about infection but could do little to prevent it.

They heated soup from a can. As they sat down to eat, Pug's strength gave out and he slumped over. She assisted him as he walked to the nearby cot and covered him with an Army surplus blanket. She unfolded another and fell asleep herself.

Part 7

THE NEXT MORNING DAWNED bright and clear, still cold but with the sun sending warming rays through the window. Meredith was dazzled by the intensity of the light, as blindingly brilliant as her underutilized retinas could process. Pug continued to sleep nearby. She looked outside the window upon a scene of amazing tranquility and peacefulness. A crimson cardinal pranced on a nearby pine branch. Her heart sang with the perception of color, so long absent from her being.

She donned a pair of boots she found by the door, hobbled outside, and found an outhouse with a moon cut-out on the door. Inside were bawdry posters, mostly of big-breasted women and big-wheeled pickup trucks.

Back inside, she re-lit the propane space heater and rubbed her fingers in the fleeting warmth. She sat beside Pug on his cot and rested the back of her hand on his cheek. She said, "I need to check your wound."

She removed the bandage and the wound was warm and swollen, with some pus coming from it. She said, "We need to get you to a doctor."

"No. We can't. Please do the best you can."

She took a sterile razor from the kit and sliced away some darkened skin. As he winced in pain, she applied more antiseptic and replaced the bandage. She heated some water and had him sit upright to drink.

"You could have gone to them. You could have run from me," Pug whispered.

"I know. Don't think it didn't cross my mind."

"Why didn't you?"

"I don't know. I just knew I didn't belong wherever it was they were going to take me. I felt I needed to stay with you."

He reached up with his good arm and cupped his hand behind her head. She drew it to his and he rested her cheek on his. She closed her eyes and felt human warmth, human kindness, and human life energy. It felt good. He removed his hand, but she held her cheek in place alongside his. Then she kissed him softly on his lips. "This is where I need to be."

"What happened last night?" he asked.

They chatted for an hour, recounting the experiences of the past few days, sipping tea and eating powdered eggs. Finally he said, "What's next for us?"

"I don't know. I know you are a wanted man."

"Yes, it would seem so."

"Let's just camp out here for a few days and get you well. Then we'll figure out our next steps."

That night, they slept side-by-side, wrapped under the same blanket atop separate cots.

JAN 19 Sunday

The next day was quiet at the cabin, both survivors resting and rebuilding their strength. Meredith continued to act as nursemaid, helping Pug to and from the outhouse and preparing his meals. She continued to tend to his wound, changing his bandage and re-applying antiseptic.

That afternoon, after lunch, they talked for hours. Meredith told Pug about her husband's car accident, sparing no details about the graduate student and her subsequent death. She talked about her own experiences with the President and the Vice President, and her antipathy towards them. The talked with ongoing astonishment about Alvin Youngblood's breathtaking admission of his part in the destruction of War and of his collusion with the Vice. They were unsure whether Youngblood had survived his attempted escape and what they would do if they ever saw him again.

They reaffirmed their conclusion from the day before that technically, Pug was a wanted man, and would be tried and likely executed for treason for his kidnapping of her, a high-ranking government official. Her status, vis-à-vis the outside world was unknown to them. Decisions about their future would need to wait until Pug's wound had healed better.

JAN 20 Monday

The next morning, there was a foot of freshly fallen snow, covering all their tracks from the day they arrived. It was a scene of primordial, crystalline beauty. Meredith made her morning trek to the outhouse. On her way back, she spotted a man walking gently through the woods. He had long, flowing hair, as red as the cardinal, was dressed in camouflage gear and was carrying a rifle with a scope. She sprinted to the cabin where she awoke Pug. "There's a man outside with a gun."

Pug got up from the bed and grabbed his rifle. A broad grin came over his face as he looked out a window, and he sprinted to the door where the man was approaching. "Mousie! What the hell?!"

"P-P-Pug, you're d-d-dead, aren't you?" he shouted, ambling over to the cabin. "Wh-wh-what are you do-do-doing here?"

Pug let his former employee inside.

"You can see I'm not dead," Pug said cheerfully. "This is Meredith Goldschmidt. She's from DC."

Mousie's eyes widened to saucers. "You're the w-w-woman that was killed! You're w-w-with the g-g-government, aren't you? I s-s-saw you... you weeks ago at the ch-ch-church downtown, t-t-talking about how the g-g-government was go-go-going to make everything al-al-all right a-a-again."

"Hi, Mousie, pleased to meet you. Has the government

made everything all right again yet?"

They talked for an hour, Pug and Meredith telling the story of the kidnapping, the trial, and their escape. Mousie said there was a brief story in the Bluefield newspaper about the tragic end of the kidnapping ordeal. Mousie assured them that from his perception, the government wasn't making everything all right at all, mirroring Pug's thoughts. Nobody in official circles cared about Southern West Virginia before the flood and nobody cared afterward.

As Mousie was preparing to leave, Pug said, "Would you do me a favor? Would you get in touch with Red Hazelwood from the Bluefield newspaper and bring him to see us tomorrow?"

"Sure, boss."

"Oh, and please don't tell anybody else that we're alive and up here."

Mousie assured his former boss that he would act as requested.

That night was blisteringly cold. Meredith turned the small propane heater on high to warm the small cabin. By the light of the propane lantern, she read to him from his mother's memoir. They smiled and laughed at the funny parts and cringed in vicarious agony at the horrible parts. Pug was impressed by his mother's work and he missed her.

Before they slept, Meredith again dressed Pug's wound. Her touch on his shoulder brought his other arm to her breast, where he rubbed gently through her jacket. She unzipped it to give him better access, and they made love, her atop so as not to disturb his wound.

JAN 21 Tuesday

Meredith slept as deeply as she had in months, rousing only when the extreme cold of the cabin shook her awake. She found a fresh propane tank in a small shed and carried it back into the cabin. Around late morning, Mousie returned with Red, who embraced Pug deeply. "Gosh, man, I'm so glad you're alive!"

Red brought a copy of that day's newspaper and a lengthy article he'd written about the tragic conclusion of the kidnapping before Mousie had told him about Pug and Meredith's escape. Red read it aloud to Pug and Meredith:

War kidnapping ends in tragedy

According to FBI Supervisory Special Agent Tom Fleck, the January 5 kidnapping of United States Department of the Interior Secretary Meredith W. Goldschmidt, Federal Mining Inspector Merritt L. Lawton, and McDowell County Deputy Doug H. Webber ended in tragedy early Wednesday morning, with only Bessie Energy president Alvin B. Youngblood surviving the ordeal.

Fleck released this statement to the media. "Early on the morning of Wednesday, January 15, FBI agents from the Beckley office, assisted by agents from Charleston and Quantico, Virginia, acted on an anonymous tip and entered the abandoned Over Bay Hollow 7 coal mine between Excelsior and Yukon. The agents were able to locate and secure the release of Youngblood, who suffered three cracked ribs during his escape. However, the kidnappers were able to set off an explosive charge that killed the remaining hostages, all the kidnappers, and six FBI agents. Youngblood, being released early in the raid, was able to escape before the explosion."

One kidnapping victim, Jennifer Wilson Wilkins, an aide to Secretary Meredith Goldschmidt, was released the night of the kidnapping and has returned to Washington, DC.

The deceased FBI agents are:

Bremer Alexander, Oak Hill, WV

Carson Berry, Beaver, WV

Kelly Cain, Quantico, VA

Byron Fulce, Glen Jean, WV

Horace Lynch, Cromwell, VA

Terry Schneider, Beckley, WV

The kidnapping received widespread media coverage following the tragic flood that swept through the War area on January 3. Many rallies were held in major cities across the country, expressing sympathy for the tragic loss of life and in support of the kidnapping and ransom. A rally at the state capital in Charleston on January 11 drew 10,000 people.

The kidnappers were believed to have been:

Donnie B. Getgood, War, WV

Lucas T. Graham, War, WV

Lacey S. Reedy, Yukon, WV

Zola E. Wilkerson, War, WV

The explosion in the mine ignited the coal seam and rescue personnel have not been able to enter the mine to retrieve corpses or establish definitive identities, however Youngblood was able to make preliminary identifications in collaboration with local law enforcement agencies.

Lucas Graham, known by his nickname "Pug" was believed to be the ringleader. His father died on December 31 and his mother, Delores Graham, was killed in the flood. The Graham family owns a working mine in the Yukon area. Ownership of the mine is now uncertain with no surviving family members.

Zola Wilkerson was believed to have been Graham's second-cousin. She is a survivor of the Buffalo Creek flood in 1972 which killed the rest of her immediate family. She has been active in efforts to repeal and discontinue new mountaintop removal mine permits. She was featured prominently in a protest at the state capitol last October and was easily distinguished throughout War in recent months prior to the flood due to her bald head, her hair shorn at the protest.

Donnie Getgood worked in the Graham mine. He lost his wife and two children in the War flood. It is believed that his twin brother Ronnie was part of the kidnapping plot, but was killed by gunshot the night of the capture, along with West Virginia State Trooper Vernon Dale Coles, Jr. Coles' body was recovered, however Ronnie Getgood's body has never been found.

Lacey Reedy also worked in the Graham mine. He was minister of the Holy Mission Methodist Church in Atwell.

A memorial ceremony is being conducted at 7:00 p.m. on Monday evening at the Living Waters Full Gospel Church of War to celebrate the lives of those lost in the tragic kidnapping.

According to survivor Alvin Youngblood, he and the other victims were repeatedly tortured, with sleep deprivation, psychological abuse, and food and water withdrawal, and in fact Merritt Lee Lawton was murdered by a close-range gunshot wound prior to the deaths of the others. "It was hell, what those bastards put us through. Particularly Ms. Goldschmidt suffered terribly under their physical, sexual, and emotional abuse. Oh, that poor woman; she sobbed to herself continually throughout the ordeal. It's hard to imagine the type of people who would perpetuate such mindless cruelty. It's a good thing they're all dead. I'm damned lucky to be alive myself."

Because of the explosion in the mine, it will be weeks or perhaps even months before investigators can enter and fully investigate. However, Youngblood has provided a detailed description of the area of his imprisonment. The bodies of the deceased captors, kidnap victims, and FBI agents may never be recovered.

As Red finished reading, he turned to Pug and asked with incredulity how Pug and Meredith had been able to escape. Pug recounted the story in detail, concluding by showing Red and Mousie his mildly infected wound. He also told them about the confessions they'd obtained from Lawton and Youngblood and his discovery of Mill's body. Meredith could see that Red was actively processing the information, trying to determine the newsworthiness of it.

Red asked Meredith her plans. "You're a well-known public figure. Surely your survival will become known."

"I, mean we, don't really have a plan," she said, winking at Pug.

"Well, there's something you should know about. Next Saturday, there is a scheduled event where Youngblood is to appear for the first time in public. The Vice President of the United States is flying down by helicopter. The two of them are going to announce a new economic development initiative. There will be a new federal prison built on a reclaimed mountaintop removal mine two miles from the Virginia line, not far from where the dam broke that caused the flood. The new name for the prison will be the Meredith W. Goldschmidt Federal Prison."

"What?" she screamed.

"That's right," Red reaffirmed. "They're naming it after you, the tortured and martyred late Secretary of the Interior."

"Holy shit," Pug laughed sardonically, pinching his nose.

"Wow," Meredith echoed. "So Vice is coming to West Virginia! Imagine that."

Mousie and Red were on their way out the door, promising another visit in the next few days with further news, when Red turned to Pug and said, "I can't believe you're alive."

"Me neither. I'm a wanted man, so it's gonna take some maneuvering to keep me that way."

JAN 22 Wednesday

Pug's recuperation continued as Meredith busied herself cleaning up the cabin. They talked for hours about the Stockholm syndrome, and she told him about her visit to the Stockholm bank where that kidnapping had happened only a year after the Buffalo Creek disaster. The story captivated the world in much the same way as Buffalo Creek. She told him about it crossing her mind as he was holding her captive.

Hours later, he said he'd been thinking about how there was a similar position the residents of the coal fields had taken relative to the coal industry. The industry for decades had held them captive, but they tended now to sympathize with their enslavers. Since the labor strife and coal mine wars of the early 20th Century, it had taken decades of dependency and propaganda for the industry to turn its workers from being wary foes into being foot-soldiers in their own destruction. The behavior of Merritt Lawton couldn't have been atypical, with the people entrusted with mine safety hovering in the pit of the pockets of Youngblood and his privileged ilk.

Mousie came over for a visit in late afternoon on a clear, mild day. Meredith had been thinking, and she said to Mousie and Pug, "With Vice and Youngblood speaking here on Saturday, it might make for an opportunity for us. I suspect if I'm the guest of honor, I wouldn't want to miss it," hinting at an idea she'd been thinking about.

"Mousie," she said, turning to the redhead, "Would you mind being my date and giving me a lift there?"

"I'd be hon-hon-honored, ma'am."

JAN 23 Thursday

The next morning, Meredith could see that Pug's wound was beginning to heal and his energy was returning. When Mousie arrived again, she said, "Let me tell you about my plan."

They knew that the fact of Pug's death could never be disproven. Meredith asked Mousie to go to Mill's house in War and bring his passport back to them. Pug made a deal with him. In exchange for some taxiing for Pug and Meredith, he would sign a transfer deed to Mousie for the houses where his parents and Mill had lived, forged in Mill's name. He told Mousie how to execute the property transfer such that it would be completed before Mousie would lead authorities to Mill's body. Details were ironed out and memorized, and then Mousie departed.

Meredith took a look at Pug's wristwatch and was to her surprised to see the date was January 22. She said, "Your watch must be wrong. It is February 1st or 2nd. I've kept track of time since our kidnapping."

Pug laughed so hard it hurt his gut. He explained their time torture system, concluding with, "By the final days, we were elapsing a 24-hour day in about 14 hours."

"You jerk!"

"Hey, don't be so angry. You've got four or five days you can live all over again."

She laughed and gave him a peck on the cheek.

"Listen," he said, "Thanks for taking care of me. You certainly didn't owe me anything."

"You're welcome. And I know that. Somehow I just felt that both of us could use some tender, loving care for a change. The night of the kidnapping when your guy shot that officer, I was scared and angry. But it didn't take too long to understand who the real enemy was. After Youngblood made his confession, you could have knocked me over with a feather. How did you know he would do that?"

"I was as surprised as you were. He admitted to crimes I had no idea even that evil bastard was capable of. I just gambled that he'd be as cocky as that Marine commander, 'You can't handle the truth!'."

Around 5:00 p.m. as darkness was falling, Mousie visited again, bringing Mill's passport, $260 in cash, and his credit cards. He also brought the wallets Pug had taken from Youngblood, Lawton, and Webber. Meredith said, "From now on, Pug, you will be Mill."

They again swore Mousie to secrecy and arranged for Pug's conveyance the following day.

JAN 24 Friday

Mousie arrived promptly at 4:00 a.m. Pug was waiting for him, ready to depart. Pug gave Meredith a huge kiss and said, "You go girl. I'll see you on Sunday. Knock 'em dead!"

"Maybe you'll see me on CNN on Saturday afternoon."

Mousie held Pug's good arm and escorted him down the slick gravel road to Mousie's waiting Jeep. They were beyond Princeton, crossing the New River, when the sun rose in the eastern sky ahead of them. Leaving West Virginia gave Pug the courage to remove his hood and sunglasses, and have his face seen again, even if by his friend.

"I'd say y-y-you're h-h-home fr-fr-free," Mousie crowed.

Seven-and-a-half hours later, after a lunch stop in Charlottesville, Mousie dropped off Pug at Reagan International Airport. "Good l-l-luck to y-y-you," Mousie said.

"And to you my friend. Take care of Meredith for me."

"I w-w-will."

Pug quickly found Meredith's Lexus, found the spare key hidden under the left rear wheel well. He let himself inside, paid the $294.00 fee with Meredith's credit card, and used the GPS to direct him to Meredith's house, thirty minutes away in DC. He used the automatic garage door opener to drive inside to park. He went first to the kitchen where he threw away all the rotted food from the counter and the refrigerator into the disposal. Then he went to work in the office. He made 12 sets of photocopies of the trial transcripts. Then he prepared envelopes to mail them to the Washington Post, the New York Times, the Los Angeles Times, and all the major national newspapers, plus CNN, the Huffington Post, Fox News, Time, and Newsweek.

+ + + + +

Pug got a good night's sleep in Meredith's bed. He left the note for Meredith's housekeeper that she gave him, explaining that she would be away for several weeks, and packed two suitcases of Meredith's clothing. Then he drove himself to the Days Inn in Saluda, Virginia, not far from the Rappahannock River. Pug entered the nearly deserted 8-room motel and paid for three nights with Meredith's cash.

+ + + + +

About the same time, Mousie drove all the way back to War and returned to the cabin where Meredith was busily working on her short speech to give her an update. They made arrangements for their date the next afternoon, with the ceremony set to begin at 3:00 p.m.

JAN 25 Saturday

Around noon, Mousie returned to the cabin. Meredith fixed him lunch with some of the dwindling supplies and prepared the cabin for his ongoing use. They made final preparation for her departure and re-confirmed their plans. They walked down the gravel hill to his awaiting car.

By arrangement, she let him off 1/2 mile from the site of the ceremony and she drove his car to the destination where 50 or so other cars were parked on the near edge of the vast former mountaintop removal mine site. It was a partly-cloudy, cool day, with a light wind. The helicopter of the Vice President of the United States was parked in the distance away from a ceremonial stage, which was draped with bunting. There was a podium in the center. At a distance of a mile or more were two higher mountains, both sculpted into cliffs where mining had been done.

There were Secret Service agents all around, checking people for weapons as they entered. Meredith wore a heavy camouflage jacket formerly belonging to Ronnie that she found in the cabin. She was patted down by a female agent and then allowed to move into the gathering crowd. She kept as low a profile as possible and avoided eye contact with anyone in the audience.

Bleachers were set up alongside the stage, where a local high school band began playing "America the Beautiful" to begin the ceremony.

West Virginia's governor, Matthew Underhill, began, "Welcome ladies and gentlemen to this historic event, the groundbreaking to a new economic development initiative that will bring 120 temporary construction jobs, and ultimately 60 permanent jobs, to your ravaged community. We have suffered enormously through the recent devastation in War, but this new project will get us back on track. We are honored and delighted to have the Vice President of the United States, Dennis James Hughes with us today, the first time in 64 years when a sitting Vice President has come to our state."

There was a smattering of applause.

"Before we begin, I ask the reverend Randall Wolfork, to lead us in prayer."

An older man limped to the podium. "Let us pray. Dear gracious and heavenly Father, we are gathered here today to celebrate a new beginning in McDowell County. We bear witness to your immortal wisdom and ask not why so many of our fellow citizens, especially children, have been taken from us, as your will and grace are not ours to question. Let us be brave and move forward from the wreckage in the hollow below here and consecrate this landscape to a new beginning. Amen."

"Amen," everyone echoed.

Underhill returned to the podium and said, "Since I became governor, my Number 1 priority is creating stable, good-paying jobs for West Virginians. I have worked closely with the state legislature to make tough financial decisions. Our foresight and discipline have put our state in a position to grow.

"Our state has always faced challenges; none greater than today. We have always relied on extractive industries like coal, timber, and natural gas. Those resources are still abundant and we will always exploit them. But diversification will help us survive the vicissitudes of the market. This new federal prison will help make that happen.

"Many of you personally know Alvin Youngblood, president of Bessie Energy which is donating this land. Alvin has recently survived a horrible kidnapping when he came to help the people of War. Alvin, would you please say some words to the audience?"

As Youngblood walked to the podium to shake Underhill's hand, Meredith pulled the string of her hood tighter around her face.

"Ladies and gentlemen, it is an honor to be here to donate this land to the federal government so they can build this prison for y'all. I've just been through an awful trial, being held for so long by those kidnappers, may their souls burn in hell. With me was Meredith Goldschmidt, our national Secretary of the Interior. She was a brave woman who suffered through their torture and acted lady-like to the end. I mourn for her and curse those who put her through such misery.

"But ladies and gentlemen, this isn't about me, it's about you, and your future. My company has always provided jobs, some of the best jobs, to be had around here. We've taken some of these mountains down so there would be spaces for wonderful facilities like I know this one will be. I have always felt parental about my duties to the people of West Virginia, and I'm blessed to be able to give this land to the people.

"Mountaintop removal mining has kept our coal competitive with the coal of Wyoming and around the world, where otherwise we'd have long fallen behind. It does a lot less damage than highway construction or city construction, because when mining is over, we can reclaim it and put it to good use, like we're doing here. Big cities were once forests, too, but they'll always be covered with concrete and asphalt while most of this mountain, the part the prison isn't using, can go back to nature. I suspect every one of you, your lives are dependent upon coal. I bless the Lord that I am in a position to provide the jobs that pull that resource from the ground and provide for all of you."

Spatters of applause rose from the audience.

Youngblood concluded with, "Thank you Governor Underhill," and returned to his chair.

Underhill approached the podium again and said, "Now then, it is one of the distinct privileges of my life to now introduce the Vice President of the United States, Dennis James Hughes."

Again, applause rose gently from the crowd as Hughes rose from his chair and approached the podium. At that moment, two Air Force fighter jets streaked across the sky overhead, prompting more applause from the crowd.

"Thank you Governor Underwood, and thanks to the fly-boys over at Langley for the introduction. This community suffered a terrible tragedy a few weeks ago in that awful flood. Then there was that brutal kidnapping where good people like Trooper Webber and the Secretary of the Interior Meredith Goldschmidt were lost. It's a wonder and a blessing that Alvin Youngblood survived. He is being considered for a National Medal of Freedom for his heroism."

The Vice President rambled on for some time, echoing many of the same themes as Youngblood, the paternalism he felt, and the need to continue the exploitation of West Virginia's abundant resources to create more jobs. He also did a disingenuous, seemingly heart-felt tribute to Goldschmidt, recounting her history and her tenure on President Cooper's cabinet, thanking her for her contribution to the people of the United States. "Ladies and gentlemen, President Andrew Cooper and I are always thinking of you. We haven't forgotten you. We will always be there for the people of Southern West Virginia and Southwest Virginia. Thank you, and God Bless the United States of America!"

As Hughes wrapped up his comments, Governor Underhill shook his hand briskly and approached the podium. "That concludes our remarks today. We're going to hear from this great band from Bluefield again, playing the Star Spangled Banner. Then we're going to step from the podium and use these fancy gold-plated shovels to turn some dirt from the soil. Please keep your distance from the Vice President, folks, as his Secret Service men get antsy when people crowd him," he chuckled.

The bandleader waved his baton and the band began to play the national anthem. As the audience's and the speakers' attention was diverted that way, Meredith worked her way through the crowd and towards the steps leading to the stage. At the bottom step, a Secret Service man, the one who appeared to be in charge, put his hand out to block her way.

She opened the hood to her heavy jacket and said, "It's me, Russell."

"Oh, my gosh, ma'am," Secret Serviceman Russell Eisley said. "You're supposed to be dead."

"Well, as you can see, I'm not. Since this gathering is in my honor, would it be okay if I spoke for a moment to the audience?"

"Well, yes ma'am, I suppose so. Please," and he took her arm and escorted her up the six steps. She walked directly to the podium where fortunately nobody else reached out to impede her. At that moment, the fighter jets screamed over once again. As their sound trailed into the heaven, she spoke into the microphone.

"Governor Underhill, ladies and gentlemen, distinguished guests, I am Meredith Goldschmidt, and I am delighted to tell you that reports of my demise have been greatly exaggerated. Unless I've been replaced already, I am honored to serve the people of West Virginia as the Secretary of the Interior of the United States of America."

Several in the audience applauded heartily, while everyone eagerly anticipated what this presumed dead woman might say. She looked behind her where Youngblood wore a scowl of terror on his face.

"I am only here before you by the grace of the Almighty and the benefit of blind luck. As you may know, I have suffered through a tremendous ordeal at the hands of brazen, ruthless criminals and scofflaws. I have also faced kidnappers."

The audience, initially tense, laughed at her reference.

"You see, the criminals and scofflaws of whom I speak are sitting behind me." She turned and waved her arm at Youngblood and Vice President Hughes. Both were seething in anger. "What I learned while in captivity was that Alvin Youngblood engineered the blowout of the dam that killed 233 innocent people in your community and has conspired with the Vice President of the United States to overturn decades of environmental and health protections."

"Stop her right now," Hughes screamed, standing from his chair.

Governor Underhill and Secret Service agent Eisley stood between Hughes and Goldschmidt. Underhill said, "We're dedicating this prison to her. She should have her say about it."

Meredith knew her time was short, so she continued succinctly, "I have sworn testimony obtained in a court of law where Mr. Youngblood has confessed to these crimes and has implicated the Vice President of the United States in his. Copies of this have been distributed to the media this morning. If there is to be a federal prison here in my name, my hope is that these two men will be its first residents. Thank..."

The microphone cut out on her last syllable, but the damage she intended to inflict was already done. She heard someone yell, "Arrest her!" At that moment, Youngblood rushed to pull her away from the microphone and the Vice

President stood, with an astonished look.

Then, gunshots rang out! Sssss! Pow! The bunting behind the stage was shredded by bullets. People from the distant ridges were firing at them! Sssss! Pow! Sssss! Pow!

Panic overcame the dignitaries, as Vice President Dennis Hughes scampered to the safety of his Secret Servicemen. Meredith was able to run behind the speakers' chairs and she hopped to the ground and sprinted to the woods behind the stage. Red was waiting for her there, saying, "Good going! That should do the job!"

"Let's get out of here!" she screamed.

JAN 26 Sunday

At 2:30 a.m. the next morning, Mousie, arrived at the home of Red's mother-in-law in Bluefield where Meredith had spent the night. Mousie was almost giddy over the prior day's events. "My b-b-boys sure got the Vi-Vi-Vice President j-jumping!"

"You did a great job," Meredith assured him. "We'll talk more later. But let's get on our way, shall we?"

"Yes, m-m-ma'am!"

Highway US-460 was dreamlike in its dark quiet solitude, with an utter lack of traffic at that wee hour of the cold winter morning. Mousie drove at exactly the speed limit through Giles and Montgomery Counties in Virginia before reaching Interstate 81. Along the way, he bragged about his friends taking their high-powered rifles to the hilltops a mile from the ceremony and at his signal by mirror, they fired at the stage. "Oh, n-n-nobody needed to w-w-worry. My g-g-guys can shoot the eye-eye out of a mosquito at-at a m-m-mile away. If they wanted to k-k-kill anybody, they would have. B-B-But j-just like I asked 'em to, they-they only f-f-fired above the crowd."

Meredith reached over and pecked him on the cheek. He

smiled broadly, his face turning as red as his hair.

They left I-81 south of Staunton and as they crested the Blue Ridge at Afton Mountain on I-64, they were greeted by a magnificent sunrise to the east.

It was just before noon as they pulled into the parking lot of the Days Inn in Saluda, where they rejoined Pug, he and Meredith exchanging a warm hug.

"Mousie, thanks for everything you've done," Pug said as Meredith nodded in agreement.

"Y-Y-You're welcome, P-P-Pug. Thanks f-f-for all... all you've d-d-done, too."

Mousie returned to his car and did a burn-out, leaving the empty parking lot in a smoky-rubber blaze of glory.

Pug had already emptied the motel room of his few belongings. Before they locked up, Meredith used the toilet. Her mind did a flashback to the fateful cabinet meeting where her tears streaked down her cheeks and fell onto her thigh. This time, there were no tears, but her eyes moistened nonetheless in hopeful anticipation. Pug handed her the keys and she drove her Lexus to the marina where she and Pug walked past and said hello to Morris, the manager.

Pug and Meredith worked together to free Hopeful from its slip. They backed it gracefully into the waters of the Rappahannock and within moments were sailing briskly southeasterly to the Chesapeake Bay.

Hours later, they sought shelter by anchoring overnight in the quiet waters of a cove not far from Wolf Trap Light, at the tip of the Middle Peninsula. It was only at that point he asked, "Where are we going?"

"I've got a friend in Barbados. Let's stay there for a couple of weeks. It is the perfect place to recuperate and shed our trauma. And warm up! Then I'm thinking Thailand."

"Wow!" he said. "Just wow."

JAN 27 Monday

They sailed across the Chesapeake to a small harbor near the southern end of the Delmarva Peninsula. They walked from the pier into town and bought some provisions at a gormet grocery. They paid with cash Pug had taken from Meredith's house, still reluctant to show charge cards from either Meredith or Mill.

While at anchor in the harbor, Pug fixed Meredith dinner of fresh cod and rice, and he uncorked a bottle of West Virginia white wine. He said, "I found something at the store."

"What is it?"

"Here you go," he said, handing her a newspaper. The headline said, "Vice President resigns!" with a sub-head, "Amidst emerging allegations of fraud and collusion, VP Hughes has tendered his resignation."

Meredith's eyes widened. "Oh, my god!"

Her eyes continued to scan the article, forcing the words into her head as fast as she could. "Look at this," she screamed, "It says Youngblood is under investigation for treason for buying Hughes' vote. An arraignment is scheduled for February 4th. Can you believe this?"

"It's amazing, isn't it?" Pug agreed. He walked to her and kissed her warmly on the cheek.

They congratulated themselves on their survival, affection, the success of their newly-formulated plans, and the expectation of their lives together, clinking their wine glasses together frequently.

"Listen, I know we had planned to stay anchored here overnight. But the wind is light and the skies are serene. This boat is capable of steering itself, isn't it?"

"Absolutely!" she crowed. "Let's move on, shall we?"

"That's what I'm thinking. I'll rest much easier when we leave US waters."

"Me, too."

They finished dinner and tidied up the boat, then pulled anchor, hoisted the sails, and were underway. Once they cleared the Chesapeake Bay Bridge Tunnel and the shipping lanes, well out of sight of shore, they went below and consummated their freedom together again.

JAN 28 Tuesday

Cape Hatteras sits on a thin ribbon of barrier islands off the coast of North Carolina. Off shore is the famed Graveyard of the Atlantic, but mid-winter days are often cool and peaceful, where overhead the sun makes its foreshortened trip across the vast sky. This late January day was no exception, with the morning sun rising gently from the horizon of the cosmic Atlantic Ocean. As Pug Graham and Meredith Goldschmidt sailed her Island Packet 42-foot sailboat close enough to see "The Big Barber Pole" lighthouse, ungainly brown pelicans soared gracefully a foot or so above the small waves. A metal clip clanged lightly against the main mast. Black-faced gulls soared overhead.

Pug sat peacefully on deck of the Hopeful sipping a cup of coffee as his new lover slept peacefully below. He felt a sense of optimism and security long forgotten as he scanned the ocean in a scene that had played out since time began. He noticed a small strand of Christmas lights at the boat's bow that he envisioned Meredith placing there before their acquaintance and shared ordeal.

Meredith emerged from the cabin and brushed her grey hair that, along with her pink blouse, fluttered in the light breeze. He admired her beauty and her resiliency. Saying nothing, he approached her with a hug. She put her cheek against his and held it there for the longest time.

About the Author

Photo by Bob Abraham

MICHAEL ABRAHAM

I was born, raised and educated in Southwest Virginia. I am a businessman and writer. I have an adult daughter and I live in Blacksburg with his wife, two dogs, and four motorcycles.

For information on my books, excerpts, sample chapters, and upcoming presentations, visit my website at: http://www.bikemike.name/

Write to me via email at <bikemike@nuvunwired.net>

I welcome your feedback!

Also by Michael Abraham:

The Spine of the Virginias
Journeys along the border of Virginia and West
Virginia

Harmonic Highways
Exploring Virginia's Crooked Road

Union, WV
A novel of loss, healing, and redemption in
contemporary Appalachia

Providence, VA
A novel of inner strength through adversity